John Keifman

¶ *Frontlist*, 2009

First Paperback Edition January 2009

ISBN: 9780779502646

Frontlist
PUBLISHING

Published by:
1, 1235 64 Avenue SE
Calgary, AB, Canada T2H 2J7
www.frontlist.com

For information on bulk orders contact orders@frontlist.com or fax 403-253-5642

Distributed to the trade by Ingram Books ∞

AWAKE

PROLOGUE

Omar Has'sir's people crawled through the hot unbearable desert for six days now. The humans in the clan were dying of thirst. They were in desperate need of water. The vampires in the group needed their sustenance—they needed blood. Many people around the region heard of Omar's transpirations. He was becoming well known and led the largest group of assassins ever assembled. Having been turned into a vampire a few years before, he was the first recorded vampire to ever have walked the earth.

The human ally's in the group joined, not in hopes of being turned to vampirism, but because they had nowhere else to go. Their lives were forfeit according to the rulers of the neighboring cities. They simply followed Omar, because he gave them answers. He also gave the vampires the answers; they sought for their unique abilities and characteristics. The vampires lived in peace with the humans of the group. They were brothers and sisters all per Omar's teachings. They knew their need for blood, but would not dare attack any human in the group for fear of what Omar Has'sir would do to them.

Omar was beginning to regret taking his clan of assassins through this particular desert, the hottest desert in India. Each man and vampire in his clan had specific characteristics to grant them entrance into the clan, but none could fight the beating pressure of the hot sun. The vampires skin, showed red from burns of the scorching heat. They shielded themselves with cloaks. They had to push on more at night, although temperatures dropped well below the freezing mark. The humans were the ones to suffer then. The vampires welcomed the chill.

CHAPTER 1

He shoots from the three, two, one, and swish. That is game my friend." Derik did a victory dance that involved the running man.

Ty stood, mouth agape, staring at the hoop. "I don't believe it," he said. "You beat me at the last second and I was creaming you the whole game."

"That's the name of the game bro. This is my turf," Derik laughed as he playfully punched Ty in the arm.

The sun was soon setting in the neighborhood basketball park. The boys grew up in the same neighborhood for about as long as they could remember. Ty was adopted by two very loving parents, and Derik's dad left him when he was a baby, but his mom loved him very much. The two seventeen year old boys were inseparable. In growing up and going to the same school; they shared everything, even girlfriends. When the girl became bored or tired with the one boy, she would move onto the other. Some thought they were brothers, but they weren't.

"Come on dude, I should get going. It's going to be dark soon, and my mom doesn't like it when I cut it too close to dark," Derik said, as he ran over to grab the ball.

"Oh yeah," Ty noticed as he looked up. "Let's get goin' then."

"Dude did you see Miss Charlotte, the new Homec teacher?" Derik mentioned, as he came running back with the basketball.

"Oh yeah, I actually changed my extracurricular course so I could be in her class," Ty laughed.

"You dog," Derik burst, and dribbled the ball twice as they walked. Suddenly Derik grew serious. He looked at the setting sun going behind one of the taller buildings in the neighborhood and made mention, "It's crazy what kind of neighborhood this is huh?"

Ty looked at all the people rushing home to their personal houses. "Yeah," he breathed to a whisper.

They were coming up on Derik's apartment building, and walked inside. Up the steps they went, but something seemed amiss to Ty. The walls were covered in graffiti, gang symbols of every kind. The lights flickered on and off, and those were the ones that even worked at all. There were holes in the walls, and Ty heard babies crying and people screaming at each other from behind the various doors. Ty heard loud televisions in other apartments, no doubt to blot out the incessant noise screaming and banging coming from the other rooms.

Ty looked around confused and Derik took notice. "What's up man?" he asked.

"This place. . ." Ty's voice trailed off. "It's different somehow."

"How?" Derik insisted. "What do you mean different?"

"It wasn't like this before. Yesterday even. It was nicer. What happened to the doorman, Gene?" Ty asked.

Derik laughed. "Doorman? Bro have you seen this place? Would it look like we would have a doorman?"

"No you did," Ty persisted. His name was Gene. Every day he would hold the door for us, and ask us how our day at school went. You would even give him a few bucks. He wore a nice suit, and had some kind of English accent or something."

"Dude what are you smoking? I don't even know a homeless guy named Gene. There never was a doorman, bro."

"There was, and the place didn't look like this. It was nicer. There was a huge chandelier hanging in the lobby, and the lobby was bigger. Dude I'm not kidding. I am dead serious that's how it was on Tuesday."

Derik stopped and stared at Ty; his eyes just wide as can be. He rubbed his forehead, and looked around his apartment hallway. They had two more flights of stairs to climb before they reached his floor, but he couldn't believe what he was hearing. "Bro are you sure; you're not jerkin' my chain?"

"D. If I was I would have told you by now," Ty earnestly said, looking Derik in the eyes. "I can't be any more serious bro. I swear that is what I saw."

Derik rubbed his head and looked around again. "Well I tell you what; why don't you head home and we'll check each other at school tomorrow. See if some good rest won't do something for you."

The two boys tapped fists, and Ty started down the two flights of stairs that they already climbed and left out the door. He then rubbed his head looked back at the apartment complex, just thoroughly confused, before continuing on. As he walked he could slowly see the sounds of night seeping into the city, although the sun wouldn't fully be down for another hour. The vehicles on the streets thinned out, even more, as any last minute people, who didn't want involved with the nightly gangs, rushed home to be with their families. He was only a few blocks from his house, so he assumed he would be alright, considering it was later than usual.

Ty stepped across a cross walk and a car; he didn't see, slammed on its brakes. It awoke Ty from his day dream about the apartment building so fast that he noticed the driver giving him a hand gesture. Ty, not wanting to get involved with any disputes, merely lifted his hand in a surrendering sign to the driver. He looked up at the driver, a man fairly muscular from what Ty could see, with a really nasty look on his face. Ty shrugged it off and continued on, but he did notice before leaving, an indentation on the cars right bumper right where his leg was. He was sure the car didn't touch him, but there about six inches from his leg was a perfect dent that his leg would have fit into. He shrugged it off, thinking that the driver must be hitting other pedestrians or signs.

Ty walked off and noticed the car driving very slowly behind him. Ty took off running and quickly made it to his adopted parents' town house. He looked out the peephole and the vehicle was directly outside, the driver looking at him. That is when he noticed also, for the first time, the passenger.

"Honey is that you?" Ty's mom called from the kitchen.

He peeled himself away from the door and called back, "Yeah mom."

"Oh good. You boys played late tonight. Go up and wash up. As soon as your father gets home, we'll eat."

"Alright mom," Ty yelled, as he ran up the steps. He figured he'd have a few moments before his dad got home, so he decided to check his laptop for any incoming messages he might have gotten. He didn't get anything special and really couldn't stop thinking about Derik's apartment. He turned on some music to clear his head. The music wasn't loud, but the normal volume and Ty was bobbing his head to the beat when his door burst open.

His father stood in the door way, a fairly large man in his mid 40s. His tie was dismantled and his suit was wrinkled. There looked like blood on his shirt, but what surprised Ty the most, was the half full whiskey bottle he was holding. His adopted father never drank, even at social events.

"I thought your mother told you to get down stairs. MOVE IT!" his father screamed.

Ty never saw this side of his father before. He thought maybe something happened at work.

The pause, just instigated Ty's father all the more, and he threw the bottle at him. Ty dodged is and the whiskey spilled all over his computer knocking it backwards off the desk. Ty got up and quickly moved down stairs. His mother was crying, and wouldn't lift her face from the table.

His father came down soon afterwards, and sat in his chair. "EAT!" he bellowed. "NOW!"

Ty looked at his mother.

"Do you need permission from her?" his father asked dryly.

Ty looked at the dishes in front of him, and quickly started spooning them onto his plate. His mother looked up to dry her eyes with her napkin and Ty noticed a huge gash on her head, and a cut on her cheek. That must have been the blood on his father's shirt.

Another screaming "EAT!" made Ty and his mother jump and move faster at spooning the contents of corn and chicken onto his plate. This time, however his father was looking at his mother. Ty's heart started racing. He didn't know what to do or what to say. He had never seen his father like this. He couldn't breathe all of a sudden. His vision began to blur, and he started to see images of something else. It began to focus in and out a different world, a much happier world.

Ty focused back to his current state, and saw his father getting ready to strike his mother again. His eyes blurred again and again. He looked down and saw his fork. His breathing became worse; his heart felt like it was about ready to jump out of his chest. His eyes; his cursed eyes would not focus. Suddenly everything went black. A moment then another went by. An image came into view. It was the image he saw before. Yes. He was sitting at the same table, with his parents. No they were different parents. He cocked his head at the site. The sun was shining in the rather large picture window of the dining room. He knew he was moved from foster care to foster care until he was adopted from his parents now, but these people he never saw before.

The vision was so vivid. It could have been real for all Ty knew.

"You know your son, Ty got an 'A' on his Algebra test," Ty's new mother spoke to his father.

"Did you son?" his brand new father asked, looking right at Ty. "That's great. You know if you keep your grades like that, getting into Williamson University shouldn't be a problem. You may get a full ride."

Ty blinked a few times, and then rubbed his eyes. "Are you okay sweetheart?" his mom said sincerely concerned.

There was no fighting. This was better than his original adopted parents before. He thought he was dreaming, but it just seemed so real, like one of those lucid dreams.

"Uh…yes…I'm fine," Ty stuttered.

"Good," his father spoke, "because after dinner, after we help your mother clean up, of course, let's say you and me go out and throw the old pigskin."

"Daniel," Ty's mother said. "No one says pigskin any more. It's a football. Goodness."

Ty looked back to his father who was laughing. "Oh excuse me, my mistake." He put a hand on his heart for surrender. "Go out and throw the old football, then."

"Uh…yeah, that'd be great if you want," Ty muttered again.

"You know what; you don't need to help me clean up. It's getting dark here in the next few hours so why don't you go out now and teach him some of your college moves honey." The couple held hands and kissed.

Ty was mesmerized. He got up from the table, and his vision started blurring again. He heard someone's voice in the back of his head. It wasn't anyone at the table, or anyone he ever heard. The voice got louder and louder. It stung at his ears causing an insistent ringing.

"What happened kid? You tell me right now!"

Ty was lying in a hospital bed. An officer was a few inches from his face, yelling way too loud for comfort. A heart monitor was beside him beeping.

"Is he awake?" He heard a voice from behind the cop.

The cop turned and said that he was.

"Then you get out and leave my patient a lone for a while. I want to see if there is any permanent damage." The voice was a firm female's voice.

He wondered if the cop would actually comply and was astonished when he saw him turn to leave. He turned back toward Ty however and said, "Don't think you got off the hook that easy. I'm onto you." With that he walked out the door.

A grandmotherly nurse closed the door behind him and spoke very softly to Ty, "I don't know what happened in that house, but I am not about to let that detective yell at you, especially when we thought we lost you."

Ty was confused. His eyes must have showed it, because the nurse asked, "Oh you don't really know do you? Well I'll tell you when you get better." She turned to leave, but Ty grabbed her wrist.

The nurse jumped and turned, and Ty said as softly as he could, "Please tell me now. What happened?"

The nurse looked at the door, and back at Ty. He sat up a bit. "I didn't see, but I've been hearing the police talk outside. Apparently both your parents are dead."

Ty gasped.

The nurse eyed him curiously. "Apparently there was a fork lodged in your father's eye. Your mother had a steak knife in her throat."

Ty couldn't believe what he was hearing. His mouth, he was sure, was as low as it could go. He blinked a few times. This had to be a dream. He remembered eating with his makeshift, and his father yelling, but nothing after that, except waking up in the hospital.

"For the record, I do not pass judgment. You have obviously been through a lot tonight, and it is my job to take care of you. Also on the record, the detective outside is waiting, until you are the least a bit coherent to talk to you," she paused. "He wants to take you in."

This sparked interest in Ty. He couldn't believe everything that had happened in the last twelve hours, let alone what was happening now.

"I'm going to give you a few minutes until the detective comes back in to collect your thoughts." She looked toward the window.

"You know," she began, "it's a very nice night tonight. It's a nice night to take a walk, clear your head. I'll give you a few minutes with your thoughts."

The nurse walked over toward the door. "Oh before I forget," she whispered, "your street clothes are washed and waiting for you right over there beside your bed." She smiled and closed the door softly.

Ty wasted no time, catching her hint. He quickly sat up, his head racing with thoughts. He pushed them all aside and concentrated on the work he had to perform at this moment. He threw the gown off, and shoved his legs into his pants. While he was slipping his feet into his shoes, he was putting on his shirt. He took a brief look toward the door, and ran to the window and slid it open. To his luck a beautiful iron fire escape awaited him. He slipped outside and rushed down it. Fortunately he was on the third floor of the hospital, so he hit ground running, past the entrance out onto the sidewalk. He was going to run, when he noticed something in his pocket. It was twenty dollars and a note. He read it quick, it was an address. He hailed a cab, and told it to take him home to his address. He had to get the rest of his clothes and leave town as soon as possible. The cab pulled up to the address that he gave the driver, and there was caution tape blocking the front door.

"Oh did I say 740, I meant 640 a few houses down. I just moved to the neighborhood," he lied. The cabby shrugged and took him to the address 640, and let him out. Ty paid the driver, and he drove off.

Ty ran through back yards to get to the backdoor of his house. He snuck in an old basement window that he used to break into all the time when he forgot his keys. The investigation must have been over for tonight. It was coming up on midnight and no one was there.

Ty didn't bother to turn on any lights because he knew that the cops were outside watching. Ty silently moved up stairs and slipped in his room as quiet as any burglar could. He grabbed his book bag, and dumped out all his books from it. He began to fill it with whatever clothes he could find, shoving them in tight.

Ty then went into his parent's room and grabbed some cash he knew they stored in there for rainy days. It was about two hundred dollars. That would have to get him out of this town.

Ty slipped back down stairs, and into the driveway where the family van was parked. He opened the door, and slipped into the driver seat. His head started throbbing with pain, but he quickly pushed that aside. He had to focus. Ty couldn't black out now. He dropped the keys twice before finding the right one, and started the van. Half a tank of gas had to be enough. He didn't bother turning on the lights, until he was safely a few hundred feet away from the house. He checked his rear view mirror a few times, but didn't see any vehicles behind him. With relief he sped up a bit, to the normal speed, not wanting to draw attention to himself either way. The tank took him out of the neighborhood, and out of the city. Until he had to get gas at an old hole in the wall station about thirty miles out. He pulled in not long after the gas light came on, and got out. "Please pay inside," was what the sticker said on the pump.

Ty walked inside small mini mart. The clerk didn't even bother to look up. He was watching some show on a thirteen inch screen TV. Ty grabbed some chips and handed the guy forty bucks. The rustic looking clerk took the money and scanned the chips. Ty looked at the television. A commercial. No not a commercial, but a news broadcast. The news caster was urgent in her message, about a boy at the age of seventeen escaping from a hospital in Williamson Heights City Limits. "He is to be considered armed and dangerous," she had said. "He had been convicted of the slaying of his two parents just earlier that evening."

The clerk looked up at Ty, and noticed his eyes wide. The same clerk then turned to face the TV just when Ty's picture came up.

"And here is the most recent picture the police have of the suspect." Ty heard them say. He gasped for air, but none came. His heart felt like it stopped, but he knew it didn't. His eyes begin to blur; he tried to shake it but couldn't. The fear over took him. He barely noticed the clerk going for the phone, barely noticed the clerk reaching for an under the counter gun with the other hand. Ty barely noticed the clerk dialing the number nine, when everything went black.

Ty didn't go anywhere on this blacked out trip, but he did remember waking. He was running out of the store. His legs felt like jelly. He was holding a hand gun, and the chips and his 40 bucks. He just kept running. He got in his van, and drove off as fast as he could.

Ty looked down at his hands while he was driving, and noticed they were bloody. He looked in the rear view mirror at his face, and it had splatters of blood. He remembered hearing a loud noise in the blackness, but that was all. He could only have guessed what happened. He drove a little over thirty miles, when the van began to sputter. He suddenly remembered the gas. He never got any. He couldn't believe it. It was rounding two hours after midnight, and he was stuck in the middle of nowhere, when the van finally stopped. He sat there staring straight ahead. He sat staring at the endless rows of trees on both sides of him. Shaking. He looked at the chips, blood all over the bag. He looked at his gun which was obviously recently shot. He couldn't believe what was happening. His mind was racing. His mind was so filled up with what just happened to him that it froze into nothingness. All his thoughts dissipated into thin air.

He knew he had to do something, so he got out of the van and started walking. There was no going back to the van; they were already looking for it anyways. It would be only a matter of time before someone realized the clerk was dead. Ty begin to run. He ran and ran for what seemed like hours until he couldn't run any more.

The coolness of the night helped calm his nerves a bit. It did cool him down and hold the sweat at bay from running.

He walked for what seemed like hours, but judging that it was still dark; he knew that that wasn't the case. Suddenly out of nowhere, amongst the trees, a chopper appeared. In the dead of night, bright lights filled the area. Ty didn't know what to do; he didn't know where to go. He took off running down the road, but the chopper flew low, a few feet from the ground. The chopper was chasing him; he couldn't believe it. He turned twice to see it. Ty ran and ran until he felt a sharp pain in the back of his neck. He reached back but felt nothing but the pain. His running slowed; not because he was tired, but because his legs refused to move. His brain refused to tell them to move any more. He fell to his knees. So this is it? He thought.

His head hit the road a lot harder than he wanted it to, but he didn't feel any pain other than the slight tingling in his neck. He thought he was going to black out for a second. He didn't. There were no dreams. There were no visions, but the blackness did finally consume him.

The last thing Ty remembered thinking was, so this is what death feels like; so peaceful, as the darkness over took him.

CHAPTER 2

It was a rough blowing steady sheet of icy rain. The kind that made a person pull whatever articles of clothing tighter about them, the kind that left sheets of ice in a matter of minutes on any kind of surface, the kind that no one wanted to be out in.

The two men in the herse pulled up to the desolate hospital in the middle of the night. There weren't many people in the nearby town since the war. The battle that swept through this town left most of the buildings in ruin. Rumors had it that since a few of the biological weapons were used over fifty years ago, people haven't been the same. This rumor alone kept people from wondering too close to the ghost town, other than the handful of people that refused to leave in the first place.

The generator out back was all that gave this small hospital any significant power at all. The flickering-dimming lights gave anyone entering the impression that it was going to stop working at any moment. The windows were boarded up to keep the hard wintering winds of Siberia out, considering the lack of heat filling this three story monstrosity.

The two men got out of the car and flinched once their faces hit the cold blowing rain. "I'll open the back hatch!" the driver yelled over the whistling wind to his passenger. The two men walked to the back of the car and grabbed a heavy body wrapped in a medical body bag.

"Be careful with this one, don't drop his head like you dropped the last patient we brought the Doctor," the driver yelled smirking.

The other man ignored the comment as they walked as fast as they could, considering, the eight steps to the hospital and the freezing winds pushing them backwards. The small porch gave some relief from the weather, as the driver tried knocking on the door, while holding the feet. They were bringing the body to a man called the Good Doctor. They only worked with him a few times, but he seemed very urgent that he get this particular body. They didn't care; the money was good, and that's all they were interested in anyways.

The door opened abruptly, and a rugged looking nurse motioned the two inside.

Inside wasn't much better as far temperature was concerned, but at least there was no ice rain. Some dripping from the ceilings above was amended by buckets placed strategically throughout the flickering foyer, overflowing in puddles on the floor. The men weren't sure if it was from the rain leaking through the floor boards or from whatever fluids were leaking through from the floors above. Lights to the foyer flickered on and off. The men still tried to take solace in the eerie hospital, but couldn't.

"Come with me," the nurse said to the two straining men.

Shaking off the wetness they followed the woman down a dark hallway. Some of the rooms were boarded up, supposedly not in use. There were holes in the walls exposing sliced flickering electrical wires, and steaming pipes. That with the water on the floor could not be a great mix. The whole area smelled like something or someone died a very long time ago. The two men never got used to the smell no matter how many times they visited this smuck of a town or this creepy psychotic place. They followed the tattered nurse to a ghastly looking elevator.

"You can't tell me this thing works," the passenger holding the head said.

The woman said nothing just pushed the button and the doors opened. Upon entering the third floor; the doors opened to the creaking elevator, and they journeyed on.

"Do keep up gentleman," she called not turning around. She rather sung the words, as if she was quite at home in this cold, dark-dingy hospital.

"That's easy for her to say," the driver mumbled to the passenger who was practically about ready to drop the body.

As they followed the nurse down a short hallway, scurrying rats hurried to get out of the way of the walking trio. The nurse took them through a non-existent door; where a frail looking man was standing in the corner of a dark dismal room.

The years had definitely not been good to this man. Hunched over; he wheezed as he hobbled over to the two men. His cane doing most of the work; creaked with each step he took, or that could have been his back, for all the two men knew. His eyes were sharp however, full of more life than the two realized, as he came closer to them.

"Excellent gentleman." The Good Doctor's voice was the sound of someone who had years of built up phlegm. "Just put the body over on the table over there." His smile was most unsettling.

"Finally," the two men sighed and slammed the body down on the metal operating table.

"Careful you idiots; this is prized property. I take it you were not rough with the body to get him here." The Doctor's whole persona changed. He was only less than five and a half feet tall, but the two men backed up a bit.

"Uh ... no trouble," the driver of the horst stated. He wasn't about to tell the Good Doctor of the slight chase that had occurred when they were found, loading the body into the herse, and the flipping around of the body, as they screeched around turns to lose the pursuers.

"Yeah … no trouble at all," the passenger finally reaffirmed.

"Good," the Doctor said at last. "You may go. I will call you at the same number if ever I need your services again."

The driver cleared his throat, obviously to indicate their payment.

"Oh yes, Olga, I almost forgot. Would you pay the men and see them out," the Doctor instructed.

"Actually we can see ourselves out; just the money will be fine." The two had no indication to watch the nurses rather large backside for any more then they had to, although that was much more attractive than her plump distorted face.

"Very well," the Doctor said. He turned around as if to grab what the driver's thought was their money, but instead grabbed a gun. He shot them both in the knees before they could react. They hit the ground hard before they even felt the pain.

"Do not resist, this won't hurt a bit. At least it shouldn't," the Doctor laughed a wheezing coughing laugh. He hobbled over to the two moaning men who were holding their legs. The Doctor grabbed their necks from the back to give him a better view and hit them with a syringe. The men hit the floor and were out like the lights in this place.

The Doctor looked at Olga and said, "Well I guess that will do. We'll move the bodies later. I want to make sure this specimen is working properly."

The Doctor motioned for Olga to join him near the table, and he unzipped the body bag to see a young man, perhaps mid twenties in great physical condition. It was hard to believe that this patient was still alive, but the pale steady breathing let the Doctor know everything was going as planned. The young man was just heavily sedated.

Olga smiled at the Doctor and the two shared in a passionate kiss. After the placement of each other's tongues; she handed him a syringe filled with some sort of liquid. The Doctor quickly and brutally plunged the syringe into the patient's neck.

Olga took the cloth covering off a large metal tray. The Doctor turned to cough an awful pleghming cough. When he was done spewing blood into a handkerchief; he picked up an old rusted hand drill.

"Shall we begin," the Doctor pronounced, as he placed the drill up side the man's head.

Derik couldn't believe what he was seeing. Derik and his mother were both gathered around the twenty inch screen television set on the edge of their seats.

His mom looked at Derik and said, "Isn't that-?"

"Yep," Derik answer finishing her thought.

They watched the ongoing man-hunt for Ty as live coverage brought them to the parent's home, the hospital, the gas station, and the abandoned van site. It was on every channel; no News station wanted to miss this captivating story. Ty was top three of America's most wanted. Various helicopters showed a bird's eye view of the ground in and around the surrounding woods where the van was parked.

Derik Fisher and his mother didn't understand. They both knew Ty wonderfully. He spent many days over at their apartment playing games, and talking. Derik even just bought a gaming system, and they would sometimes be seen playing on it, quite a few times actually.

Ms. Fisher loved Ty as she did her own son. He was always so sweet. She just couldn't believe that he was capable of doing this.

Just then they heard a pound at the door. The two looked at each other, as the pound came again even more urgent and resonant than the first one. Ms. Fisher slowly got up take a look out the view hole. She saw two rather large men in brown trench coats and sunglasses standing on the other side of the door. She made sure the chain was in place, and slowly opened it.

"Yes ... may I help you?" she asked through the small crack.

"Are you Ms. Fisher?" the one man asked.

"Um … yes," the woman replied. "What is this regarding?"

The men took out two shiny badges, and asked to be let in.

She quickly complied, not sure what exactly was going on, but the last thing she wanted was to put her son or herself in any type of danger with the law, concerning Ty or anything.

The men walked in and looked around. The one man looked at Derik, and asked, "Does anyone else lived at this address."

"Um … no. My son and I are the only ones." Derik's mom answered in place of her son. "What is this concerning again?"

The one man started checking rooms. The other asked Derik if he had any siblings.

Derik politely and quickly answered, "No, with a confused look on his face.

"Maam, you do not have a husband?"

"Uh … no, tell me what is this concerning. I will not answer any more of your questions." Derik's mom raised her voice a bit.

With that the men looked at each other, and quickly drew two silenced weapons. They put a bullet in both skulls of Derik and his mother. They were both dead before they hit the floor, Derik slouching in the chair before he fluddered to the floor. The men simply left the apartment without saying another word.

Detective Miller, we found some trace evidence over here in front of the van about twenty-five feet or so."

The detective was awoken out of his trance. He turned to regard the forensic scientist. "Be right there," he said.

The Detective was baffled. He was sure the nurse had to of helped the boy escape from the hospital, but why. She was in questioning, not giving them a dime for their time. They couldn't prove she helped Ty anyways; so as soon as she got up to leave, she was technically free to go. It was only a matter of time before she realized that. He had the dead clerk about thirty miles back. He could believe that. The boy obviously snuck back to his house, stole the van, and drove it as far as he could go. For some reason got spooked in the gas station and never gotten gas. Drove thirty miles, and then left on foot.

Detective Miller had forty good police officers searching the woods in a five mile radius, but the boy could be even further than that by now. The body was over six hours old, and this boy named Ty could be miles away. He didn't have much to go on.

He finally decided to go check what the scientist had found. "What do we got here?" he asked walking over to the man who was knelt down by the road.

"We have a piece of paper. It must have fallen out of the boy's pocket. It looks like it is written in a females handwriting, but I have a handwriting expert making sure. Looking closer at the piece of paper, though there is an address on it. Could be where the boy was headed."

The detective looked closer to the paper. "Forty-one Roanoke Road, Feelsburg, WV," he said aloud to himself. He then looked at the scientist and pronounced, "Yeah, could be an address someone had given him to run to. I don't know. I want to head up to this address and see what we find, but I also want to know who wrote this note. First I'll head back to the city, and question the nurse before she heads out. Tell Bill Manley to get a team together. The boy isn't hiding in the woods nearby; I can be sure of that."

The scientist nodded and the detective walked away. He was about to get into his truck, when he got a call on his cell. "This is Detective Miller, what is it?" he said, picking his phone out of his breast pocket of his unbuttoned blazer suit coat, and flicking it open.

Sir we found something a few miles from your location came the voice on the other end.

"Something between us and the store?" the detective asked.

"No sir. It's a few miles south of your location. Just follow the road and it'll take you right to us."

"Be right there."

Detective Miller drove his vehicle another four miles, until he came upon a few parked police cruisers on the side of the road. He put his truck in park and got out, walking over to an excited officer.

"Sir we found something here, it looks to be blood," the officer said.

The detective looked at his sown on name tag, that read 'Philmore.'

"Philmore we are in the middle of nowhere. You do understand that it could be a dear or some other wooded animal's blood."

"Not true sir. The blood was coagulated enough to tell that it was indeed human blood. See after a few hours the blood becomes-"

"Spare me the Science lesson, son. Where's the blood?"

"It's right over here," Philmore answered as they both walked a few feet to other crouching scientists. "The thing is, we have to test it for DNA to find out whose blood it is, but that's not all we found."

"What else did you find, son, spit it out?" Detective Miller was growing impatient.

"Well we found windblown trees that stretched about fifteen feet. We also found, a small cartridge, which had some kind of residue on it a few feet from the blood. We are also testing that. And we also found a witness."

This sparked an emotion from the Detective Miller. "A witness?" he asked.

"Sure he's right over here." Philmore led the detective over to a rustic looking man sitting on the hood of a police cruiser. "His name is Gerald Funk."

Miller nodded and approached the man. "Mr. Funk?" The man nodded. They shook hands. "Detective Philmore here said that you saw a little bit of what happened."

"I did," was the reply from Gerald.

The detective looked at Philmore and then back at Funk. "Would you mind telling me what happened Mr. Funk?" he asked.

"Well I was setting some traps for coon huntin' and"...the man stopped to spit a wad of tobacco juice on the road.

"Sir please continue. What did you see?" Miller pressed.

"Well I was close to the road. Sometimes the passing vehicles will scare the coons right into my traps, and I heard this heavy breathing. It was steady breathing like a human. I move real silent, see, through the woods. My grand pappy was born on this land, and three generations of Funk's lived here. I remember going hunting with my old man when I was three. He taught me—."

"Sir what else did you see," Miller interrupted. He rolled his eyes when Mr. Funk wasn't looking.

"Right," Funk said. Realizing he got off track. He spit another huge wad of tobacco juice on the road. "See I moved real silent toward the road, and I saw this boy running full blast as if the devil himself was on his tail. He didn't run more than a few steps until he stopped. He kept looking behind him, the whole time. Then out of nowhere, and I mean out of nowhere, I thought the rapture or an alien invasion was happening. This big ol' chopper comes out of nowhere shining big lights on the boy." He spit again.

"Big chopper?" the detective asked. He looked at Philmore, who looked back and smiled knowingly. "Tell me more Mr. Funk."

"Well this big bird shines its light real bright like, and of course, I have to duck behind a tree more so; then I was before in order to not be seen, that is. The boy starts running, full sprint down the road, like a dirty terrorist was in that there chopper see. He takes off like a bandit. The chopper swoops down and starts chasing him ground level like. Not more than ten or so feet, did the boy run until he fell straight to his knees. Then the chopper touched down on the road. These men with masks on—."

"Like burglar masks, like full face masks?" Miller interrupted again.

"No like one of them space suit type masks. The kind you see in those sci-fi movies. I couldn't believe it myself. The masks were all black as well as the body suits. Almost couldn't see them even with the chopper lights right on them. They looked like robots at first. I thought we were being invaded by aliens or it was a terrorist vendetta." Funk then whispered looking around, "I've been watching on the TV about those sneaky terrorists. I have an armament of weapons and an underground tunnel ready for 'em if 'in they try to invade my land, I do." He spat again on his pretty healthy looking puddle of brown juice on the road.

"So then what did the men do when they got out of the chopper?" Miller asked.

"The space men terrorists then picked up the boy who was lying on his face. They took him back to the chopper, and it took off. They were gone as soon as they appeared. Which I still don't know where they came from; you'd figure you'd hear a chopper if 'in it was blowing down trees. You know?"

"Yeah, I do," the old Vietnam veteran, detective said.

The man was escorted away; he had been enough help already. As confused as the detective was just then; he did actually have more insight as to what has just perspired than he had before. He looked at his watch; it was nearing noon. He had to get back to the city to interrogate that nurse. He climbed in his truck and drove off toward the city.

CHAPTER 3

"Doctor, are you there? Doctor!?"

The Good Doctor looked at the intercom's light beeping on the wall. "Oh it's the buyers. Probably wondering how the body is doing," the Doctor remarked. "Olga, be a gem and go down and fetch them. I'll prep the body so it looks good."

"Yes Doctor," Olga the nurse answered. She smiled, and quickly left.

At the door, stood three rather large men, and a much shorter man in front of them. Their boss Mr. Jonas, as he was known by many, may have been just less than five feet tall, but he was not a man to be tussled with. He built a rather large private organization in Siberia, and with that, a very fearing reputation. Not one to scare away from a fight; his forms of "persuasion" as he liked to call it was a bit unorthodox to the normal God fearing man. He wore a rather large scar slashed vertically on his eye, where he had it out in his prime against a man with a hatchet. He wore it with pride. His face was readjusted in many other areas, from street fights, with his climb to the top of his completely replicable organization. Growing up on the streets was not easy on the man, but he did a little of this, a little of that, until he started running guns. Later he put his talents and muscle into real-estate, and then moved onto bio-chemicals. His private scientists created a drug that could change the memories and thought processes of an individual. Unfortunately for them, they asked too many questions upon finishing the experiment, and were no longer needed by Mr. Jonas. Rumor has it, they are all over the world—their many different body parts at least.

Mr. Jonas' new talent, which his investor wants, is a bio-weapon. He was quick to exercise his expertise in the matter, and four years later, it looks like they are ready to test it in the material plain. The man upstairs has been in a comatose state of mind for the last four years, practically a vegetable. His memories have been observed, and even altered to adhere, to now, the next phase of experimentation.

Mr. Jonas needed no reasons to justify his actions. He was merely a business man now. The subject in the hospital room upstairs was a young man, a nobody from what Mr. Jonas knew. He had no family; no one that loved him. The Good Doctor had said that his mind was the most perfect for the experiment, more than all the other subjects they had experimented on. All the other subjects seemed to be rejecting all the experiments, except for this one particular young man upstairs. His mind was susceptible to the experimentation, almost fully.

A French scientist, by the name Pierre Tralboam, took over the research from the Americans. His research alone made great stands in the experimentation. Pierre found out by inserting particular memories into the man's head; he may be able to change what he was, making him into whatever they needed him to be. In this case, Mr. Jonas needed him to be a weapon for a particular enemy, a very complex and powerful enemy that many people didn't even know existed. The experiment had to work; it had to be a success. It had to make him into what Mr. Jonas needed him to be for his investor. He didn't know why this particular man was taken, but as the Good Doctor said, 'his mind was perfect.'

Mr. Jonas got wind of Pierre's success on the subject, and hired him to complete the experiment, under his watchful eye. It didn't end the way Mr. Jonas thought it should, and the subject apparently rejected the memories. There was a DNA strand that could not be hacked into. There was no way for Pierre to break into this last strand and finish the long awaited project; so Mr. Jonas merely killed Pierre and his team, and hired on the Good Doctor, as he was known, to complete the experiment.

Mr. Jonas smiled at the thought of the publicity he would gain from this. If he was to complete this experiment, there was no organization in the world that could top him. He would not only sell the subject to his investor, but he would make hundreds of them. He could open up a whole new deal on the black-market, making billions of dollars. Suddenly his face grew very serious, "What is taking them so long, to open this cursed door?" he growled.

With that the door opened. "Aha, Mr. Jonas," the nurse sung. "What a joy to see you. Please come in out of the cold."

"Yes, where is the Doctor?" Jonas demanded.

"Right this way. Please follow me," Olga instructed.

The four men followed the nurse on the same path she took the two men just a few hours before. Upon entering the room, the first thing Mr. Jonas saw were the bodies lying on the floor. "What happened to them?" he asked flatly.

"Oh them, just some baggage, I had to dispose of. Not to worry; they are not dead, rather sleeping."

"With all the blood, it's a wonder they're still breathing," Jonas remarked, as he noticed the two very large puddles of blood on the floor.

"I injected them with a neuro-toxin. Their wounds will heal posthaste. They however, will be in a vegetable state until I say otherwise. Think of it as a side experiment." The Good Doctor smile was most unsettling.

"Using whose money?" Jonas asked.

"Do not worry, my dear Jonas. It's my money. They just an insurance experiment to see what this one is capable of in case . . ."

"In case what?" Jonas demanded. "There had better not be any mistakes."

"Not to worry . . ." The Doctor started.

Mr. Jonas slammed his hand down on a nearby counter. "You know you keep telling me 'not to worry'," he repeated. "Do you know what I will do to you, if there are any discrepancies with the subject? I already know I was taking a chance getting your own private guys to fetch him from the hospital, where he was under too much surveillance to the experiments, but what is this place?" Jonas made a face looking around the dark room. Mr. Jonas continued, "The lights don't even work half the time. How can I trust that the subject is being well cared for? What have you done with the money I've given you?"

"Do not . . ." but the Doctor cut his own voice short this time. "Mr. Jonas," he paused, his persona taking on a more respectful tone. "I do not need high powered machines in order to complete these experiments. Do you realize in the war, I brought three men back to life with my so called 'old school methods'. It baffled my current associates, no doubt. Let me show you the subject."

Jonas motioned for his guys to stay put, as he followed the hobbling Doctor over to the body. He saw an ancient heart monitor hooked up to the body with the normal readings. He saw a small machine measuring the amounts of a chemical memory drug being inserted into the subject's brain every couple of seconds. Mr. Jonas even saw a rather old looking dialysis machine. The man on the bed's chest rose and fell in solid deep breaths. He was perfectly healthy.

"You said you wanted a weapon, Mr. Jonas. You will have one." The Doctor turned and coughed into his rather solid red colored rag. "Excuse me."

Jonas made a face, and then moved into a stern look at the Doctor.

"I am about to insert the new chip, you have given me."

Jonas started, "There have already been complications. His mind has been changing advancing. My old scientist and doctors told me they've never seen anything like it. What safeguards have you put up in order to change all that? I trust you because of your experience with such subjects. You know the money. Now can you do this?"

"Mr. Jonas, the chip you gave me needed adjustments," the Doctor started. "I and my assistant." Jonas looked at Olga, who smiled and waved. Obviously Jonas made another disgusted face. "Excuse me—lovely assistant, have made some changes to the chip."

Jonas looked back at the Doctor. "What kind of changes?"

"Simply, changes to make it work faster; changes to make the subject ready within the month. Perhaps by the end of this month," he finished.

Jonas paced around the room. He thought that if he could have the subject done for his investor earlier than expected that would really upgrade his organization. He afforded the best scientist; too bad he kept killing them off, when they asked too many questions; then had to find better ones.

Jonas stopped pacing and looked back at the Doctor who was smiling effortlessly. That would really put him on the map. He would be the one to come to when the need for a bio-logical human weapon was needed. No one had a human weapon like this. This new form of training was brilliant; he just hoped the Doctor and his quote, lovely assistant, would be up for the task. Well if he wasn't; Jonas would just dispose of them anyways.

Mr. Jonas turned back to the Doctor. "You have by the end of the month then. I'll be back then. For the mean time, I will to bring in some guys to rework the power in this place."

"That won't be necessary; we have a generator in the basement," The Doctor put in.

Jonas looked at his boys, and back at the Doctor. He rubbed his face, his hand sliding back to his balding head. "Very well. The end of the month I'll be back. Have him done by then."

With that Jonas and the boys, backed out of the room, and headed back the way they came to get to their vehicle.

"Pleasant man is he not?" the Good Doctor told Olga once the men had gone. "Now that their gone, shall we do the drilling. We must insert that chip." He placed the drill bit up to the young man's head, yet again.

Detective Miller got back to the precinct just before a little before seven o'clock. He had been up for about thirty hours now; pretty much shooting stale coffee through his veins. He got out of his truck, straightened his shirt and blazer, and walked inside.

Another detective walked up to him, "Goodness, man how long have you been up?" he asked.

"Well, I haven't caught up with our suspect yet, so apparently not long enough. Tell me; is the nurse from the hospital still here, Roanoke?"

"Yes. Round the clock interrogation, but we cannot legally keep her much longer before she will inevitably leave." The detective paused for a moment. "In other words, we still got squat."

"Alright, let me have a few rounds with her. I'm going to grab a cup of coffee, and head on in there," Detective Miller said to Detective Roanoke who was about fifteen years under him.

"Okay, she's in interrogation room two. She's all yours. I've had a couple cracks at her, and either she actually doesn't know anything, or she's a crafty old badger."

"Yeah, well let this crafty old badger go at it with her," Miller didn't smile, but the other detective did, perhaps to lighten the air a bit.

Detective Miller walked into the interrogation room. He sat down and slapped a file on the desk, took a sip of his black coffee, breathed a few deep breaths, and finally looked up and said, "Good evening. Ms. Darnell is it?"

"You read my name tag in the hospital," was the only reply he got.

"Indeed, I did." Miller smiled, trying to be polite although he wasn't the polite type when he even was awake. He had seen too many murders and too many people trying to cover them up in his time. He took out a tape recorder, and placed it on the table and hit record. "You don't mind if our little conversation is recorded do you? My memory doesn't seem to suit me well these years."

"Perhaps you should retire," Ms. Darnell said.

"Perhaps I should. Perhaps I will after this case is closed." Miller continued, "Tell me Ms. Darnell, you're getting a bit up there in age too. Do you mind me asking how old you are?"

"I have no idea what that has to do with this investigation," she replied.

Miller smiled. "Just trying to make nice. Tell me Ms. Darnell, did you know the suspect before you saw him in the hospital?"

"The suspect's name is Ty, and no I did not."

"Why did you help him run?"

"I did no such thing," she lied.

"Well, I suppose he just happened to look out the window, and see the fire escape. You distracted me a long time out in the hallway with idle talk, which really had nothing to do with the suspect," Miller paused then emphasized, "TY! You seemed to get very close to him before he escaped."

"Sir it is my job to care for all my patience. Everyone is still found innocent until proven guilty in my book, and in the Constitution, if I'm not mistaken."

"You're not mistaken, Ms. Darnell. Tell me Ms. Darnell, do you recognize this note?" Detective Miller pulled out the note in an evidence bag and slid it across the table so the nurse could see it.

Her face became flush, and Detective Miller surely saw it.

"No. I have never seen that paper before in my life," she was quick to say.

"Well, I am surely hoping that is the truth for your sake, see I have a handwriting expert comparing your handwriting with that of the letter. You of course, wrote on a lot of patient's files so it shouldn't take long," Miller claimed without skipping a beat.

He leaned back in his chair. "We'll have the results any minute now. Surely you wouldn't lie to the police, and impede an investigation, would you?"

Nurse Darnell, tried not to stumble over her words, but she fumbled for an answer. She knew what the detective wanted to hear, but didn't want to give him the satisfaction. She was held to a much higher code, higher than the code of a nurse. She would impede this investigation as long as she could.

"Ms. Darnell? Hello? Are you there?" Miller leaned forward again and placed his arms on the table.

She blinked a few times and quickly came to. "Yes, I am fine. What else do you have to ask?"

"Can I get you a coffee or water or anything? The coffee taste like mud but it helps the aliments, if you know what I mean."

"Um … water would be fine. Thank you," she said at last.

"Alright, I'll get you some," Miller grunted, as he hoisted himself out of his chair using the table.

After he was outside the interrogation room, Detective Roanoke approached him again. He saw the whole thing. "Well she's obviously lying."

Miller leaned against the glass of the interrogation room. He breathed out a long breath. "Yeah, and I don't know why. She's protecting him for some reason, and I have to go on more than her gut." He looked up. "Her rep sheet?"

"Come on, Miller. Did you actually think we would find something on it? She doesn't even picket abortion clinics. This lady is squeaky clean," Roanoke nearly laughed aloud.

"Yeah, that's what I figured. What about that handwriting expert or whatever; any word on that?" Miller asked.

"Yes. Actually it came back a perfect match for her hand writing. No question," Roanoke said.

"That's what I thought. Alright, do you have that—?"

But before he could finish Detective Roanoke handed him a faxed official statement signed by the expert. Also he handed him the two comparisons of her handwriting and what the expert used to distinguish the similarities, between the two. The golden spots were circled with a computer.

Detective Miller looked at the two papers for quite a while. Roanoke thought he had fallen asleep standing up. He moved suddenly which made Roanoke jerk. "Give me a glass of water. I'm going back in with these," he told Detective Roanoke.

"Where's Detective Miller?" He heard a voice say from behind him when he started walking toward the interrogation room. Miller turned and one of the receptionists was coming up with a package.

"Detective Miller," she said at last when she finally walked up to him. "There was a man that dropped off this package for you. He wouldn't give his name, just dropped it off and said that he wanted me to give this personally to Detective Miller."

Miller looked at Roanoke who hadn't gotten Nurse Darnell's water yet. He looked back at the receptionist and took the package. "Thank you," he said.

He walked over to a nearby desk and took out his pocket knife and cut the sealant tape on it. Inside he saw a lot of rapping, but when he sorted through it he found a typed note which read:

Dear Detective Miller:

I understand you are hot on my tail. I regret to inform you that I am ghost. Not in the literal sense of course, but in the sense that you will never find me. I understand fully that you are a veteran cop, but there are things beyond your control here. Please give up hope, in searching for me, or you will see more people die. The world is a horrible place indeed, and perhaps there are ways to make it better. No offense, but your ways are a little outdated, and well simply don't work anymore. I have ways of purging the earth from its evilness and brining a new light to this world. I have ways of making evil people good and good people evil. I have my eye on you dear Detective Miller. I would hate to have you slip up, and be chasing the wrong suspect. Perhaps you should turn your eyes to the many evil things that are going on in your "fine city". Perhaps you should focus the rest of your short life toward those things, because I want to make myself very clear. If you keep pursuing me, there will be no end to the destruction I will bring. There will be no end to your problems for the rest of your very short life. More and more people will die if you keep on this bogus mission of yours. I've beaten you. There is no stopping me. There is no going back. Please consider my offer, oh and to help with that decision I've given you a little gift.

Yours Truly,

Ty

Detective looked in under the wrapping a little further. There was a little box. He cut it open, and inside was an unmistakable human finger.

CHAPTER 4

The Good Doctor was singing while he was working. He had made quite the progress in the last few days. The subject was hooked up to all kinds of monitors, and computers. Cords and hoses went from this way to that, mostly hooked up to the young man's head. Olga was in and out of the Doctor's path, hooking things up and reading various other things. The chip implanted in the drilled out hole of the young man's head was in place and ready to be turned on.

"Oh everything is going as planned," he told Olga. "We should have the boy up and running in no time." In the brutality of his activities, anyone watching from the door would assume the Doctor mad; by the way he sung an old melody to himself and tapped on the young man's skull with a hammer.

"Everything's done Doctor," Olga said as she finished hooking up the last of the wires to the computers.

"Excellent my dreamy, piece of sugary substance," the Doctor replied. This, of course made Olga blushed and she grabbed his rear-end. The Doctor turned abruptly, and then a smile came to his face.

"And now we hit the switch." Olga smiled.

The Good Doctor shivered with excitement. He pushed a button on one of the computers, and it started to hum. The boy jerked, which made the Doctor and Olga also jerk, but then the subject settled back down in a relax state. The Doctor read the monitors, everything was going as planned. The heart rate was perfect, the breathing rate was normal, the subject was excellent. He turned to Olga, and pulled her close. They embraced in a feeling kiss of passion.

He realized his eyes were open because he squinted at the first few pieces of piercing light that shown through. Everything was blurry. He blinked a few times, and slowly things began to take shape around him. He sat up. He was in a room of some sort from what he could make out. The room was actually rather large. A very nice room too. He saw, through his blurry eyes, a wooden dresser and pictures on the walls. He saw a sitting area. Things began to take shape a little more slowly but surely. He could make out the one picture across from his bed. It was a beautiful sail boat off a coast with an eloquent lighthouse. It was a very relaxing picture. The room was also very relaxing. The wall was a sky blue with tan border. The floor was wooden, stained a deep oak brown. He listened and heard the sound of the sea crashing the shore. He shifted his weight onto his hands, and turned to stand. He noticed his left hand was bandaged—tight. The whole thing was wrapped, down to the wrist. He felt absolutely no pain however, which he thought was odd for how woven the wrap was. He didn't remember falling, he didn't remember much of anything, then again, with his head feeling the way it did, it was no wonder.

His legs weren't quite as stable as he would have preferred, but he could walk slowly. He moved across the floor to the room's one huge window. When he pulled back the curtain, the light flooded into the vastness of the room. This made his newly opened eyes squint all the more. When his eyes adjusted, he saw a beautiful ocean. The waves crashed the shore ever so lightly, and the sparkle they left behind was exasperating. It looked mid-summer outside. The sun was shining ever so brightly, gliding off the water like diamonds.

He moved away from the window, and noticed a monitor beside his bed, on the night stand. He walked over to it, and bent down to look at it. It was blank. As soon as he bent down; a voice came on making him almost trip in retreat from the sudden noise.

"Aha, good to see you are awake, Mr. Ty Livingston."

Ty didn't see anything on the blank monitor, but he heard the voice coming from it.

"Livingston?" Ty asked. "Who's this Livingston? My last name is …" He paused. He couldn't remember his last name. He barely remembered his first name had the monitor man not just said it.

"From now on, you will be known as Ty Livingston." The voice continued, "That is your new name to go along with your new identity."

"New identity, what?" Ty asked. "Look man, I don't even remember how I got here, why's my hand bandaged, who are you and—"

"Everything will be explained in due time," the voice cut him off. "For now, you are well, and that is the good thing. There are some clothes in your closet. Please meet me down in the dining hall for breakfast. The cooks are preparing an exquisite meal. I would say it should take you no more than ten minutes to get ready. See you then."

The voice stopped, and the static sound depleted. Ty looked around the room, then to his hand. He wanted to take the bandages off to see what the problem was, but decided against it. The people or person, who owned this place, obviously cared about his comfort. This was better than jail, he supposed. He felt something went wrong, in his past, but he just couldn't remember what. It was if all his memories were wiped clean.

This place did seem nice enough though.

Ty walked over to the closet and opened it up. There weren't a lot of clothes, but the clothes that were there, were in pristine condition. They were pressed to perfection and organized to the letter. All the clothes were actually the same style, just various colors. The pants were loose fitting slacks, with absolutely no pockets. The shirt was a pull over T-shirt that fit Ty exactly. There were four pairs of shoes, at the bottom of his closet completely identical. He slipped a pair on, and walked toward his door. He kept looking at his hand every so often.

Ty opened the door to a beautiful hallway. Pictures of various beautiful sceneries filled the corridor, which stretched about a hundred feet. There were doors every thirty feet or so crisscrossed in an orderly fashion. The hallway reminded him of a cruise ships hallway to the living quarters, or maybe a hotel. Ty looked both ways and didn't see anyone, so he figured a direction and started walking.

He made about four steps, when a voice came from behind him. "So hoping everything is to your liking, Mr. Livingston. Please follow me to the dining hall. Your presence is requested." A younger looking girl, maybe in her early twenties stood there, wearing a professional looking jumper uniform, perhaps from Middle Eastern descent.

Ty obviously followed having no idea where he was, or what there was to see. He followed the girl down the hallway to a large stair. "What is your name by the way?" Ty asked.

"My name is Noel," she replied. She held her hands in her pockets.

"Noel," Ty repeated looking at the ceiling, as if trying to place that name to his memory.

Noel took him down three flights of stairs to a wide area. She slid the door open with her right hand and stood by it. She motioned for Ty to go on in. He smiled and slid in the opening.

"Mr. Livingston, how wonderful to finally meet you." The same voice now put to a face, stood up from a large twenty-five person table. The man was tall, definitely well built. He wore a casual suit of the color blue. His white button down shirt was loose fitting with the two top buttons unbuttoned. With blue pants to match the suit;

he also wore brown loafer shoes. The man looked right in place on a cruise ship, Ty had thought. He was probably mid-forties, from Ty's estimate. He stood tall, almost opposing, with a fresh wavy hair that was combed back his head, blonde. His smile was not opposing, but very welcoming. The man didn't seem threatening in any way, but yet Ty feared the man even without knowing him. Perhaps it was the uncertainty of what was going on.

Ty shook the man's hand, "I'm afraid I didn't catch your name," Ty said, while still having hold of the man's hand. He didn't let his guard down one bit.

"How totally rude of me. You can call me Bones," the man said, his left arm behind his back.

"Bones," Ty repeated letting go of the new host's hand. "Is that because you break bones with your incredible grip?" Ty thought to see what this guy was made of. If he said a little sarcastic comment, he wanted to see if the man would bite back, or simply let it go.

The man didn't let the sarcasm bother him one bit. "Certainly not," Bones replied with a comforting smile. "I have had my fair share of broken bones also. Perhaps why most of them have been replaced by metal rods," the man said, grinning from ear to ear politely.

From the grip of the hand shake, to the way this gentleman carried himself; Ty could tell he was a fighter.

"Please, please have a seat." Bones motioned for Ty to sit at the one end of the table, as he took a place at the other.

Right as Ty was sitting, the door to the kitchen burst opened. A chef with all the attire, even the hat, brought out a large tray. On it was a delicious looking fruit salad, with fruits Ty hadn't even recognize, as well as some of the more common fruits.

The man wore a goofy smile on his face, and worked quickly. After placing the fruit bowls in front of the two at the table, he quickly grabbed a large cloth napkin from his front apron pocket, and fanned it to the laps of Ty and Bones. He wore oven mitts the whole time, which Ty thought was odd considering, he wasn't handling hot foods at the moment. With that, he returned to the kitchen without as much as a word.

Ty looked at the many forks, spoons, and knives before him. "Start from the outside, and always work your way in. Never go wrong with that schematic," Bones told him.

Ty didn't know whether to grab a fork or a spoon, so he grabbed a spoon guessing. Bones noticed his confusion, and chuckled. Ty dipped it in the bowl and scooped up a banana and a mystery fruit. Before eating it, however, he said, "So why is my hand bandaged?"

Mr. Bones, who was digging in, with manners of course, quickly looked up and smiled. He pretty much wore the same smile the whole meeting, but it somehow grew wider. "You're an inquisitive one, aren't you?" he asked.

Ty just shrugged.

"The Doctor said it will heal properly," Bones said at last.

"What was wrong with it?" Ty asked.

"That is assuredly not dinner conversation I will tell you. You feel no pain?"

Ty's eyebrows narrowed. "Should I?" he asked.

"Not with the medicine that was administered." Bones paused. "Just wondering. Tell you what. Finish your fruit, and we'll go through a little walk through the facility."

Ty nodded, and scarfed down his fruit bowl. The fruit was fresh, and cool. It tasted very good almost too good.

Not soon after the fruit breakfast, Mr. Bones stood. "Shall we take you on the grand tour now; perhaps answer some of those nagging questions you have?" he said, smiling.

Ty stood, but noticed, Mr. Bones quickly placing his hands in his suit pocket. Ty couldn't be sure, but he noticed something different about his left hand.

“How soon until we can get this tested?” Detective Miller, pretty much yelled the question to anyone that would, or could do the task. “I want to know what this person had for dinner the night before this finger made its way to our doorstep.”

“I’ll take it down to forensics,” one of the officers frantically said. He carefully picked up the finger, and placed it in an evidence bag and sealed it.

“I want to know what you know, within the hour,” Miller pointed at the officer very sternly.

“Will do,” the officer said before disappearing out the front entrance.

“Okay, I need you,” Miller instructed and pointed to Roanoke. He handed him the piece of paper, he had copied of the address, the nurse had written. “To go to this address. Take a team. Find out what you can and get any leads you can find.

“I’m on it,” Roanoke said. He got on the phone and was quickly out of the door, when about seven officers gathered around his desk.

People jumped, people got out of his way. Miller grabbed a cup of water from the water cooler and took it back into the interrogation room for Ms. Darnell.

“You were gone a while for just some water,” the nurse noticed.

The detective didn’t say anything for a brief moment. He stared straight forward as if in a trance, until jerking into his next few words. “Ms. Darnell,” he started. The nurse jumped at the lash out, but Miller wasn’t trying to be threatening, he just wanted some answers fast. “I just got a special package.” He showed her the note from the package, and kept talking. “It would seem as though your boy is cutting off fingers now. What do you make of that?” he said, looking at the note, then at the nurse.

“I don’t know,” she quickly answered. One he is not my boy. He is a troubled boy; I will say that.” She read the note quickly, frowning as she got to the bottom. "I just don't think he's entirely in the wrong. I think there is someone or something pulling the strings with him."

Miller leaned back in his chair taking a breath—a deep breath. "Yes," he said at last. "Troubled indeed," he reiterated.

"Ms. Darnell, you haven't known the boy before you saw him in the hospital?" he questioned again, from the first time, in this same room just moments before.

"I told you no. I do not have a reason to lie," she said, staring Miller in the eyes.

"That's funny," Miller quietly said.

"What is?" the nurse asked.

"The fact that you don't have a reason to lie." Detective Miller leaned forward picking up the file folder on the table. "The handwriting expert got back to me with the results." He reached in the file and passed her the two papers he had faxed over.

She looked at them, and her face flushed again.

"Yeah." Miller shook his head. "You lied about that, what else are you lying about, Nurse Darnell?"

"Nothing," she started.

Detective Miller slammed his hand down on the table in a fit of rage. Nurse Darnell jumped. He grew impatient. "Ms. Darnell, we have a human finger being sent over to our lab for analysis. This boy will kill again. I don't know why you are protecting him, giving your clean rep sheet. Do you want to go to jail?" Miller got louder as he finished. "Tell me, Ms. Darnell, Do…You…Want…To…Go…To…Jail." He leaned back in his chair again making sure he reiterated each and every word. "Because that is a huge possibility. You are an accomplice to murder if you do not start helping me right now. Going to jail is becoming a very huge possibility." His voice calmed toward the end.

The nurse's face grew red, and a tear started to fall. "I just don't think he's guilty," she said again. Through a good many tears, she repeated. "I just don't think he's guilty at all."

Detective Miller breathed a long breath out. He looked up to the ceiling, then to anyone that was looking through the glass, although it was just a mirror from his side. He was running out of options. "You're free to go," he finally said, barely audible.

The nurse looked up. "I'm what?" she asked.

"You're free to go," Miller said a little louder, not yelling, but a little more distinct.

"Right now?" she asked.

"Right now," he said, raising his shoulders, and pointing toward the door. "Go ahead it's not locked. Do you need a ride home?" he asked when the nurse had stood.

"No, I . . . I'll be fine I'm sure."

"It's no trouble. I'll be happy to give you a ride," he said again.

"No that will be fine," she said again. "I'll take a cab." This time lowering her brows to a furrow. Not wanting to press the point or get on the detective's bad side any more than usual, she let it go at that and left.

When she left, the detective stood up from the table and gathered the file. He walked over to the door and looked outside, and saw that Ms. Darnell was heading toward the door.

"What was that all about?" The captain came barreling up, having watched most of the ending part of the interrogation.

Miller held up his finger, for the chief to wait, while he dialed a number. "Philmore, where are you?" Miller paused for the answer. "Out front?" he asked making sure he heard correctly. Listen, I need you do me a favor. Do you see a short white haired lady walking out the front right now? Good, follow her. Let me know where she goes, and what she does. I want to know if she gets on the phone. I want you so close you know who she's talking to. Thanks Phil, I owe you one." Miller hung up the phone and looked at the captain. "Yes captain," he said calmly.

The captain just rolled his eyes and walked away back to his office.

Miller's phone rang, "this is Miller," he quickly said, barely opening the cell. "The finger is female? I'll be right down." He closed the phone and rushed toward the door.

CHAPTER 5

Mr. Jonas sat atop his twenty-nine story tower at his desk. His hands folded in front of him; he was thinking. He was thinking about his rise to power. The organization he had built, and the enterprise that was fast on its way to the top. This was a different world he lived in. The darkness of night seemed darker than ever. The sun, when it did shine wasn't very bright. It wasn't explained. Humanity, scientists, the space programs, could not explain what was going on. All around the earth, more crimes flooded in. It wasn't safe to walk the earth in the dark, unless you were predator. Even then, you couldn't guarantee your safety. More and more around the cities, there were wanna'bees. That's what the local news stations called them anyway. This infatuation with vampires was growing. Mr. Jonas couldn't even believe the word. What started out as a street gang in Southern Tokyo quickly grew, to become one of the world's largest crime syndicates. Everyone denied their existence of course, out of fear no doubt. People didn't venture out at night, so no one truly saw them. The ones who did venture out, usually never came back anyways. The amount of suicide's rose greatly due to the depression in the darkness of night. A new form of killing yourself it was said was to venture out in the deep darkness to give your life to the streets mercy.

The life that Mr. Jonas knew as a boy was quickly changing indeed. He didn't know much about these so called Vampires. He knew the urban legends. He knew the stories. They were a very discreet bunch of individuals, that he was certain. He had no idea what they were capable of doing, or what they represented. He was sure there was no such thing, there couldn't be. "Probably a bunch of kids pretending to be something they're not," he told himself.

Still the mystery of it all baffled Jonas. He used to be fully in control of his streets. He was fast rising to rule the world. Every time his boys had duties at night he would send them out in twos or threes. They saw nothing, heard nothing. Still the rumors knocked on his door, like a bad dream that he keeps having. He would hold on; he must hold on. He built too much to let it go to a bunch of street thugs pretending to drink blood, and claim superpowers. He built too much to let it all go to a so called group that called themselves vampires. Besides vampires didn't even exist; it was legend.

Suddenly his thoughts were broken by a knock at his door. "Come in," he ordered, grabbing his old-style revolver from the drawer. You never could be too careful, especially if you were Mr. Jonas.

"So sorry to disturb you boss, but the investor is here to see you," one of Jonas' men said.

"Right send him in," Jonas said. He was expecting Mr. Gobaleski this afternoon.

"Mr. Jonas," Gobaleski said in greeting to the man at the desk, who quickly stood when he saw who it was for sure. Mr. Gobaleski was a good head taller than Mr. Jonas, but a little thinner, and still no less to be feared. Mr. Jonas didn't know much about Mr. Gobaleski, only that he put up a rather large sum of money to build a weapon using bio-chemicals and chips, and that was about it.

"Mr. Gobaleski," Mr. Jonas greeted in return, as he put his hands out wide, and came around the desk to give Gobaleski a Russian embrace. "Please sit, sit," he then said.

Mr. Gobaleski's two men brigade stood on either side of his chair as he straightened his coat before sitting.

"Tell me what is on your mind?" Mr. Jonas asked his investor.

"I want to know, of course, how far along is my weapon." Mr. Gobaleski sat back in his chair and crossed his legs. He raised an eye brow, and placed his elbow on the chair leaning his chin on his hand.

Mr. Jonas had to make this look as good as he possibly could. "Well I just got done speaking with The Good Doctor on the phone." Mr. Jonas started. "The Doctor said that he altered the chip a bit, and that—"

"What do you mean altered?" Gobaleski cut in.

"He made it better, let me explain." Mr. Jonas was growing uneasy, and this was very unlikely in the protection of his own tower, with his guard men right outside the door.

"I'm not all into science myself, but apparently, he changed it in a way, that will make your weapon even more powerful than even you or I could imagine."

Mr. Gobaleski was intrigued. "Go on," he said.

"The test was failing before, I'll be honest." Mr. Jonas said nervously.

Gobaleski's eyes narrowed, but he said nothing.

Jonas continued, "The subject's mind was hard to work with, to put it lightly. I mean we are changing a random boy to an assassin." Jonas shifted in his chair nervously. "Pierre Tralboam was making great stands in making the weapon, and he took it so far. But he ran into a problem."

"What kind of problem?" Gobaleski shifted in his chair, but not nervously, but as if to get a better handle on a particular weapon.

"He couldn't hack into a certain strand of DNA. It was blocked somehow. It couldn't be explained."

Gobaleski eyes went down in a scow. "And the good news," he

demanded.

“That is why I had him taken care of, and I found this new Doctor; a genius in the sciences of bio-chemicals. He calls himself the Good Doctor. That is what he prefers, but his talents with this experiment do not go unheard. He set my mind at ease, and is even finding ways to make your weapon better, more effective if you will.”

“Okay, I understand, go on,” Gobaleski said, his demeanor changing to more relaxed. “Can he fix the previous doctor’s mistakes and move the experiment forward?”

“I believe he can. His mind is extraordinary at this sort of thing. He already has made great grounds where the other doctor had failed.” Jonas pulled a bottle of vodka out of his drawer, offering a glass for Gobaleski who obviously declined. Jonas still poured himself a shot glass full and poured the burning liquid down his throat. He continued, “The approach began to unravel, so to say. The subject’s brain started fighting the pleasant thoughts we were putting into him. This was even before we started to train him to be the weapon that you need. This has never been a problem with anyone before. The other patients just refused to fight, or died in the process of the experimented. This boy has curiosity. He is practically becoming self aware. This doesn’t usually fit well.

“What is the good news then?” Gobaleski sternly urged.

“The good news is the Doctor figured out what the previous doctor had done wrong. Now he put the subject in a place of peace and tranquility; so he feels safe and secure, but also a place to train him to be what we want him to be. This place harnesses his very ability; it gives him pride in what he does, so that his mind is at peace with itself. Putting a killer in a suburban life, simply wasn’t working.”

“So what about his other memories?” Gobaleski asked.

“Simply erased. We started from scratch, but are working in a more effective manner so that the timeline will be met. The Good Doctor has said that the boy is taking to the chip wonderfully. His mind is working properly, and everything should be finished at the end of this very month."

"The end of this month? Gobaleski asked, his voice rising a bit.

"It's a little past the due date I know, but you must understand."

"You must understand brother." This was a term used loosely with mob men that partnered up. "This boy had better work properly, or it's your head on the platter. You understand me?"

"Crystal," Jonas answered.

Gobaleski got up to leave. "Always a pleasure doing business with you Jonas."

When he closed the door, Jonas breathed a sigh of relief. He would definitely be glad when this whole thing was done and over with. What he would do with the money he received to better formulate his organization? What he would do indeed.

"The whole second and third floors of the facility are the living parts of the compound." Ty followed Bones outside the dining area, and watched as he showed him around. Bones continued, "The whole facility was about three square miles, and was nestled in the woods, of the Gronan Mountains."

This stopped Ty in his tracks. "What do you mean nestled in the mountains?" he asked. "I saw an ocean and a lighthouse outside my window just this morning."

"Merely a mirage. No, that is a too strong of a word. It's a holographic image, given in order for the occupant of each room to feel more comfortable with their surroundings. You like oceans, and lighthouses, and bright summer sunny days." Bones turned and started walking again.

Ty wasn't sure, but for as long as he could remember; he liked summer beaches. Not the populated beaches of the south, but the more serene beaches of the Northern United States. He just wasn't sure exactly how long that was that he loved those beaches. The memories felt fake almost. The whole world seemed artificial, as if he was dreaming. He couldn't quite place it.

Ty chased after Bones and said," You said the lighthouses are a hologram? What does that mean?" he asked.

"It means they're not real. From what we've seen in the last few years is that when people are held under comfortable living conditions, where their minds can grow and bloom, then they are simply faster at retaining knowledge." Bones simply finished the thought by saying, "I have lived in this world for the last fifteen years, and have enjoyed it thoroughly."

With that, Bones walked further down a very wide hallway. Bright white walls and white fifteen foot high ceilings to match, the walls and ceilings glowed with cleanliness. The floors were a crisp silver color that reflected the light from the ceilings as a mirror would.

Ty had no idea what Bones meant by, 'the last fifteen years in this world'. Maybe he considered this compound a world. Ty wasn't sure.

They kept walking.

Bones stopped at a huge door and swiped a keycard. The door slide open, and the two walked through. Inside he saw what made up most of the compound. A training area for what looked like special ops. Ty thought he recognized the layout of the city, but he wasn't sure. His mind didn't seem right. It felt like things would come and go as if he was losing his mind, or someone was adding and subtracting information at their whim. He felt played with, but decided to play along, just to see where all this went.

There was a mini city inside this area with four story buildings, stores with real things in the window, and roads and side streets and signs and cars, you name it this place had it. Ty thought it was pretty amazing, considering it was all still in a bigger facility.

"This is the nerve center, if you will, of the whole operation. This is what we are about," Bones said, waving his right hand so that Ty would look at the vastness of the whole area.

"Yeah," was all Ty would say.

"Yeah?" Bones repeated. "Son this is it. This is where you get off."

Ty looked at him curiously.

"Mr. Livingston, this is the direction we want you to go." Bones motioned Ty over to a door off to the side that didn't look like it went into any buildings. "Come on in here, I want you to see something."

Ty walked inside. He saw a large control panel. There were huge screens set up where cameras were marking out various parts of the mirrored city. Three men with black sweaters, black pants and shoes, and black beanies sat at the controls watching the screens and pushing various buttons at certain intervals. They also wore tight black gloves hiding both hands. Every so often they would say something into their headsets; Ty was too far away to make out.

"Gentleman, meet our newest trainee?" Bones said to the men.

They turned and said a quick, "Hey," and nodded in unison at Ty, then turned back around in their chairs to begin what they were doing before Ty or Bones even walked through the door.

"Come over here, Ty." Bones walked over to the control panel and motioned for Ty to join him. "I want to show you what we do in here."

Ty walked over to the control panel, and watched as one of the screens showed a person running through one of the streets. They didn't have any weapons that Ty could make out other than a sword strapped to their back, and throwing knives strapped to both thighs. They wore a mask, as well as a full body suit of total black combat gear. From what Ty could see, they were being very careful.

The person was very limber and even moved with grace as they ran through the streets, hiding in the shadows, trying to stay out of the street lights view.

"Right now it's night time in the city, but we can make it day with just a push of this button. I'm not going to push it now of course," Bones chuckled. "The person in the screen, that you are looking at, is one of our newest members. She is learning fast for only being with us two months."

Ty watched intently amazed at the physical prowess of the girl. She was being hunted he knew, yet she acted as if she was baiting the predator so she could get the drop on them.

She moved in and out of parked cars on the side of a street. The camera views would change on the various screens to give the men a better view, depending on what camera she was nearest to.

One man spoke into his headset, "P-4 she's on Commerce Street. You should be right above her."

Ty looked at Bones, who wore an incredible eerie smile. He motioned for Ty to keep watching.

Above the girl was a man dressed in all black on a one story electronics store roof. His face was covered in what looked like a metal alloy type material. His eyes shifted, from what Ty could see. The glowing yellow slits narrowed. The man moved like some sort of powered android.

The metal man pulled a rod from his back. When he pushed a button on it, the bows string came out of it, as the rod simultaneously bent to form a very formidable bow. Ty watched as the man, on screen, reached for an arrow that was slid into a pouch on his right thigh. He stuck it on the string, and pulled back gently. Two cameras were on the man, and two on the girl.

"He'll kill her for certain," Ty objected.

"Just watch," Bones whispered.

Ty couldn't peal his eyes off any of the screens, as the man held steady. He fed his sites until they were aimed right at the girls head. She was between the car and the store, on the street crouched down. She peered out from the side of the car, her back fully to the store and her soon to be assassin on top of it.

The man aimed for a few more seconds. He only had one shot at this. If he missed, he would either be dead, or the girl would get away.

Finally the man let the arrow fly. Ty watched as the girl slid out of the way of the oncoming missile, and fluidly launched a throwing knife from her thigh strap that took the man in the neck even before the arrow hit the car tire where her head had been. The man gurgled, and then flipped off the top of building. His head and the top of his back hit the car in which the girl was behind, and it flipped him toward the building like a ragdoll.

The girl checked the bodies' pulse, then walked away satisfied.

"She took out all the other men, placed in the world before we even got here. This man was the last one."

Ty found it hard to believe. He was silently routing for the girl, of course, not even knowing who she was, but to see someone die like that was just bizarre. Why would a training mission actually kill someone?

As if reading his thoughts, Bones said, "He knew there was a chance that he would die. It's what he gets paid to do." Bones continued, "We are training the girl. The man you saw is a special assassin, bred perfectly for this mission?"

Ty was confused. He was glad the girl was alright, but not sure why a man had to die to further a combat training exercise.

Bones smiled and looked at the control panel, as if satisfied. He leaned down and grabbed a head set. "That is all, my dear. Please disrobe, and come into the control room. I want you to see someone."

Ty's heart quickly fluddered and jumped. He couldn't believe that he would actually get to meet this girl who laid out such a perfect reverse kill.

The girl opened a whole different door off to the other side of the control room. Ty turned and saw a delicately featured Asian girl, probably in her mid twenties. Her features were soft, and not battle warn, as Ty would have imagined from such a stealthy killer.

"Ty this is Sumiko," Bones introduced.

Ty shook Sumiko's right hand, but got a glimpse of her left. Her ring finger was missing. Completely gone from what Ty could see.

Sumiko noticed Ty staring, so she said, "Yeah, it's healing nicely."

"What happened?" Ty asked.

"What do you mean?" Sumiko looked at him baffled.

Bones jumped into the conversation, "Sumiko, you seem to have a fan here." He quickly changed the subject. This young man here, was watching your last kill, and was thoroughly impressed. Weren't you Ty?"

Ty blinked a few times and said, "Yes. Thoroughly."

"So your name is Ty," Sumiko said, smiling. Ty couldn't get passed her beauty. She was a little over five and a half feet tall with long slender features. Her hair was a bit past her shoulder, jet black and shined beautifully even in the dimly lit room.

Even above all of this, Ty still was baffled over the enigma that was her finger. "I'm sorry, but I'm new here, what happened to your finger. Did you lose it in a fighting exercise?" he asked.

"No." Sumiko looked at Ty curiously, then at Bones. "Haven't you told him?" She looked back at Ty, "Your hand is bandaged. You're new here. Think about it." She shrugged as she raised her brows. Sumiko said again and nodded, "think about it."

CHAPTER 6

"Yeah, where's—?"

"You Detective—?"

"Yes," it was Detective Miller's turn to interrupt the front desk receptionist.

"Down stairs to the left. Follow the yellow line on the wall, can't miss it."

Miller smiled quickly, mostly to be polite, and took off down the stairs.

He came to a room that the yellow line led him and quickly opened the door. Roanoke was inside with Doctor Terry who found the discovery of the origin of the finger.

"Miller, glad you got here. Check this out. This is Doctor Terry; he's the forensic scientist who found a lot of info about the finger," Roanoke announced upon Miller's entrance. "I'll let him explain."

"Doctor," Detective Miller greeted in a nod.

The doctor took his rubber glove off and they shook hands.

"Well detective," the doctor started, "what we have is a very interesting discovery. I found through some research that the finger belongs to a young woman in her early to mid twenties. I found this out by the amount of bone marrow found in the bone of the finger.

She also derives from Asia, more prominently from Tokyo." Doctor Terry waved the detective over to take a look at his computer, where he had an x-ray of the finger on screen. "What more I found out, was that there are traces of copper and fluorine found under the nail."

"What does that mean," Detective Miller, questioned shaking his head.

"There are traces of that metal and that mineral in upper West Virginia in the Gronan Mountains. That is the only place near here that would vaguely be the place of these two materials together that close to the surface of the soil."

Detective Miller looked at Doctor Terry, then at Detective Roanoke. "This is interesting, and it gives me a good lead." Miller raised an eyebrow. "This is good," he said at last. "Yes, thank you." He walked toward the door.

"Miller, don't you need help?" Roanoke said, before Miller could get out of the door.

"Yes, I would. The Gronan Mountains stretch into Feelsburg, WV," Detective Miller remembered.

Roanoke's face lit up, as if he had a revelation. "Right they do."

"Put a team together, and give me a call. Twenty or so boys or more. I need trackers, hunters, you name it."

"You got it," Detective Roanoke said.

Miller left the lab.

Detective Miller had his head back, and his mouth open, when his phone rang. He jumped up with a start and looked at his watch. Ten 'til eleven. "Well thirty minutes of sleep in fifty hours isn't bad."

His phone rang the fourth time. He picked it up and flipped it open. "This is Miller?"

Miller, this is Philmore. The woman you told me to follow grabbed a cab back to the hospital where she picked up her car. She then went to a pay phone and called someone—in Feelsburg.

"So it all ties together. Good work. Listen. I've got Roanoke getting a team together. We're heading up to the Gronan Mountains, which is in Feelsburg. I think we're going to find the same thing. You want to join the hunt?"

"You know I do. I'll be there in ten."

"Alright my phones beeping, I got another call, see you then," Miller quickly said.

He switched lines. "This is Miller,"

"Hey this is Roanoke. I almost got the whole team together. We are you?"

Detective Miller looked around, considering he just woke up, he wanted to make sure he was in the same place when he fell asleep half an hour before. "I'm outside the precinct," he finally said.

"Okay. I'll be out there in about ten minutes, with the team. See you then," Roanoke replied.

"Yep, I'll be ready." Miller flipped the cell shut, and laid his head back on the seat. He sat up to look at his watch. "Alright, just a few more Z's," he said to himself, as his eyes drifted shut.

Mr. Jonas twisted in his chair. His arms folded again in front of him, he was thinking. He picked up the phone.

It rang and rang until finally The Good Doctor picked up. "Hello?" was the reply.

"Doctor. What is going on with the patient? Is everything going to plan?"

"Everything is perfect. This is a much better facility, I have him in. Here he can be monitored, and I have someone on the inside in which I trust greatly." With that the Doctor laughed, which made Jonas feel uneasy.

He didn't bother to ask any questions. "Well, if anything goes awry you call me. You got it?"

"Perfectly. Not to worry," the Doctor repeated his words from earlier their meeting.

Mr. Jonas quickly hung up. He couldn't stand working with the Doctor, or having the Doctor working for him. He was a means to an end, he thought.

Ty looked at Bones then at Sumiko. Then he looked at his hands. He ripped off the bandages very rapidly before Bones could think to stop him. Sure enough his left ring finger was missing. He couldn't believe it. It didn't hurt, in the least, which he couldn't explain, but the idea that someone took his finger really made him angry.

The men at the control panel stood up as if to offer Bones some support. No one was really sure what Ty was going to do.

Sumiko jumped in, "Look it's a means to an end," she said.

"A means to an end?" Ty asked emphatically. "How do you figure?"

Sumiko looked at Bones. "What have you explained to him?" she asked.

"Not that," Bones replied.

"Then I suggest we find a comfortable place to sit and talk," she urged.

"I would agree," Ty solidly stated.

Bones knowing Ty's past didn't want to push the issue any more. "Alright I know of a place—my office. Follow me."

The trio walked out of the control room into a secret hallway. Down the hallway about thirty some feet or so was a door on a left. Bones slid his keycard through the power slot. He pushed the door open and led them inside. He offered them both to sit down on comfortable plush guest desk seats.

The office was eloquently designed, with huge fish tanks imbedded into the walls all around the room. In the calm dimness of the office, they gave a gentle flowing blue color. There were all kinds of colorful exotic fish in the tanks from all over the world.

After the Ty and Sumiko grabbed their seats; Bones sat down at his desk and smiled. He folded his hands in front of himself with his elbows on top of the desktop. "Well," he started, "I suppose I should start by saying, that I'm sorry I didn't tell you sooner about your finger."

Ty's eyes narrowed.

"I think what Bones is trying to say is he didn't mean to be dishonest with you. This is not a bad place Ty," Sumiko began.

Ty shifted to look at her better as she spoke.

"See, I don't remember much from my childhood. Most people don't here, but this place is home to a lot of us who have no home. I am sure you've had to leave your home or maybe never had a home, either way you're here now, and I'm glad at least. Now I can have someone to train with." Sumiko raised her shoulder in a cute way as she sat in her chair, with her legs crossed leaning toward Ty, and smiled.

"Ty let me tell you about where Assassin's come from. Can I do that?" Bones asked.

"I'm listening to you. I'll take whatever knowledge you want to give," Ty flatly stated, more on the sarcastic side then anything.

Bones ignored the sarcasm.

"Many, many years ago, there was man named Omar Has'sir." Bones suddenly began. "He grew up in a small village outside of the Western City of India, called Geopolo. Omar did what he could to support his family, but growing up with a large family and a father who died at an earlier age, as the oldest brother; he was the one to fend for his family.

"Troubled by his newfound responsibility, at sixteen he marched into the city set on making his mother and siblings proud. Not knowing the ways of the city, he accidently got caught up with the bad crowd, and was thrown in jail for stealing. They chopped off one of his fingers, and told him that if he was ever caught in the city, he would be hung.

"Angry at the fact that they stole his finger from him, and that he was banned from the city, he set out to overthrow the leaders of the city for making it so difficult for poor families to gain a foothold to feed their children."

Ty narrowed his eyes even more when he found out Omar was angry at the fact that they stole his finger, because that was exactly how he was feeling right now.

Bones ignored the look and continued; hoping the next part would change Ty's perception on what the compound would bring. "Omar spent the next few weeks combing the city at night, looking for the outlaws. Those, that the city did them wrong. Some of them spent time in prison, some of them escaped from being hung or executed in one of the cities favorite ways. Once he found a solid—loyal, he set up meetings every night in different places each time, to throw off the law at the time. They would train under the moonlight, perfecting their skills.

"In that time, there were eight officials that ran the city, sort of like a board of executives or a senate. They were royalty living in the lapse of luxury. They went over their mission a hundred times, drawing it out in the dirt. When the perfect night came, they all met at their designated spots. When the moon was the highest in the sky, they struck. Sneaking into the individual houses, they destroyed the lives of these eight men and their families."

Ty listened intently, leaning a bit closer to Bones as he spoke.

"When it was all said and done, and the city heard of the murders of the eight royals, they rejoiced. When you thought there would be mayhem, there was peace. The city got together, and raised one leader to lead them, with a vote of the people. The land knew peace and prosperity for many years. This city adopted the lifestyles of the poorer communities around it and drew them in toward them, giving them a safe place to live. They opened, a rather large, trading relationships with these people, and with other cities, bringing more prosperity to the City.

"This was just the beginning for Omar Has'sir. His men's past transgressions were forgiven obviously. They devoted their lives to following Omar. His leadership led to the biggest revolution of the day, and they had nowhere else to go. To show their loyalty, they all chopped off their fingers, their left ring finger. Even back then, people would tie bands on their left ring fingers to show their devotion to their partner. These men's devotion was to Omar Has'sir. There was no ring to put on their finger; there was no other life these men could live. They were married to the sect.

"When Omar died, another man took over Has'sir's alliance of assassins, and when he died another man took it over. The name the group called themselves Has'sir's, and it slowly changed to what we know it to be called today—Assassins. Their popularity and prestige grew throughout the lands. People came from all over the world to join this group, for it was a good life to live."

Bones leaned very close to Ty, as the desk in between would allow and said, "Ty, we want you to be our assassin. We offer you a changed life. We offer you a chance to use your talents for us. If you join our sect, we will make you great. We will make you someone. You never will want or need again. You will never have to run away again."

The word's 'run away' sparked a distant memory in Ty's head. He did run away from something, he couldn't quite figure out what. Once he started thinking about it, though, the thought diminished quickly.

The idea, though of belonging to something, intrigued Ty greatly. The idea of becoming something different, in this mixed up world, he called his head, perhaps would be a great new plan for his life.

Ty looked down at his hand, the missing finger oozed a little blood, but the doctors did a great job in sowing it up properly. Plus this place did seem to hold some of the answers that he needed to know. Yeah he would stay here, for a little while at least. To see what he could become or find.

"I'll do it," Ty said at last.

This brought a great smile to Bones' face. "Good, good," he said. "We will begin your training tomorrow. Go and talk with Sumiko, on what's to be expected of you. This will be the beginning of your greatest dreams come true, my dear boy. Your greatest dreams."

Bones motioned the two to the door. "I have a good bit of work to do, so if you please... Sumiko will show you where things are in the rest of the compound, and make sure you are fully comfortable. We will see you tomorrow."

With that, Ty and Sumiko got up from their chairs, and walked toward the door. Once they were on the other side, Sumiko said, "Come on, I want to show you something."

They walked through hallways and long corridors, opening up many, many doors as they passed. Finally they came to this really large dome. Inside was that of a rainforest. This was no mirage, but real plants. The dome stretched as far as a hundred feet in the air, and maybe a thousand yards across. It had a moist stone path, for walking, and birds were seen and heard above their heads, as they walked inside. "Isn't this place wonderful," Sumiko said at last, gazing up at one very colorful bird.

"Yeah," Ty answered, staring at the same bird. "This is crazy,"

"It's like its own eco-system in here. Water comes out of the top every so often, on timers of course, and a mock sun rises and sets with the beginning and end of the day. I mean take a huge breath. The purity of the oxygen is amazing alone."

Ty did take that breath, and the pureness of air was amazing. He couldn't believe it. Trees stretched to the top of the dome, and there were beautiful flowers and shrubbery of all sorts. Tropical and not so tropical plants gathered over the dome's floor. The birds sang beautiful songs as they flew from tree top to tree top.

The two walked on the path admiring everything they could see and hear. "You know, most the time, I come here, especially after training. It helps me relax. It helps me appreciate the smaller details in life," Sumiko turned and smiled at Ty, who met her gaze.

"I can see that," Ty replied. "It is definitely relaxing, indeed. You've been here a while?" he asked knowing the answer, because Bones told him in the control room, but wanting to create small talk, and maybe find out more about this mysterious place.

"About two months I think. It's a little hazy how I got here though," she answered.

"Aha, for me too," Ty said. "A little hazy that is. So if you don't mind me asking, how did you get here?"

"Not at all," Sumiko smiled so eloquently. Well I'm from Tokyo, Japan, and I remember working at my grandfather's book store one night real late," she began, "he had an emergency, his brother—my great uncle, had a heart attack or something. So he left, and I closed up.

"We knew the streets were not as safe as they once were when I was a child, but it was only a few blocks to my house, and he thought I would be safe enough." Sumiko made a face at the next part of her story. "Of course, on the way home, I got jumped by three or so guys. I couldn't make out their faces in the darkness, but they were very strong—and fast," she added. "I couldn't break free, no matter what. I think there were about four of them, now that I think about it more.

"To be honest, I thought I was going to die. I thought they were going to do bad things to me; they kept sniffing my hair and face. It was really weird. Well all of a sudden, these other guys came out of nowhere, with masks and combat gear on. They seemed even stronger than the muggers. The last thing I remembered was the bad men getting beaten to a pulp, and I must have fainted; I don't really remember that part."

When I woke up—here, my hand was bandaged also. Bones said

that this was a special hospital. I later found out it was more complex than that. This was also a training facility. I later found out, my great uncle had died which made my grandfather have a heart attack, and he died, not long after. They were very close brothers, and my grandfather was the only family I really had, or can remember rather. I don't remember much about my parents, oddly enough." Sumiko looked up at another flying bird, as if trying to remember anything from her parents.

"So, even though Bones said that I could leave at anytime; I decided to stay and be trained. He told me the meaning of my finger, as he told you, and said that I could belong to a family now."

"What does he do with all the fingers?" Ty asked.

"That I'm not sure," Sumiko answered, then laughed, "I'm not sure I want to know."

Ty laughed with her, but quickly grew serious. "So you like living here?"

"I like it better now, that you're here," she said, stealing a smile and a blush from Ty. Sumiko continued, "To be honest, it's odd that Bones would suggest you learn of this place from me."

"How so?" Ty asked.

"Because, guys and girls are usually not aloud talking too much, or being seen together for long periods of time, especially in private like this place."

"How many people are here?" Ty wondered.

"It's hard to say, they come and go."

"And go?" Ty repeated in a question.

"Yeah, once they complete their training, they are sent out into the world to do actual missions, I guess. This place here is a huge glorified training facility for assassins, more or less." Sumiko shrugged as if the concept should be obvious.

"I got that much," Ty replied. "So why do you think he wants us to spend time together?"

“Well I don’t know. I’m sure we’re being watched. Bones thinks that relationships will make the sect soft. ‘We are more brothers and sisters than anything,’ he likes to say.” Sumiko stopped on a nearby dry bench along the path and sat down. Ty followed. “From what I got out of him, is that we are going to be working together. Somehow, we will learn to train together. It’s weird. The things I can do here, I could not do before from what I remember. I didn’t think I would learn the art of fighting as quickly as I did. The weaponry is unique. I’ve never used a weapon before in my life, yet it comes so naturally here. Bones says that he knows talent and knows how to hone that into what he needs. He says that you have talent.” Sumiko smiled.

Ty looked away in thought, then back at Sumiko. “Well we’ll soon find out I guess, tomorrow.”

“Yeah, good luck with your first training session. That one is always hard. I nearly died my first time. Don’t worry though you’ll be alright. The facility has ways of bringing you back around.” She smiled again.

“Great,” was all Ty could muster.

CHAPTER 7

Miller heard a tapping on his truck window. He woke from his slumber to see Philmore and Roanoke, and about twenty some men and women all milling about. He wound down his window.

"Are you sure; you're ready for this, and you shouldn't go home and get some rest first?" Was the first thing that Detective Miller heard.

"No I'll be fine," he answered. He looked at his watch. He got about fifteen more minutes of sleep. "Let's go," he said.

Roanoke passed him a thermos of hot coffee through the window. "Here, you're probably going to need this."

"Thanks," was the reply.

"Black—just the way you like, it," Roanoke said. He then turned toward the men and women behind him and yelled so all could hear. "Alright people! Load up in the police van. Make sure you have your gear and are completely ready. This suspect is entirely armed and dangerous. He has already taken a finger from a victim. This victim may still be alive; we're not sure. We do know he has already taken three lives, so again, exercise extreme caution. Our first stop is forty-one Roanoke Road."

One man yelled out of the crowd, "Hey that's your name."

Detective Roanoke scowled and turned back toward Miller. "This is your smartest group of people," Miller snickered.

"Something like that," Roanoke said quietly, so not even Philmore could hear.

Soon they were heading up to Feelsburg, West Virginia, where the Gronan Mountains stretched as far as the eye could see. Miller led the brigade, with Roanoke and Philmore trailing behind him, the police van bringing up the rear. It proved challenging trying to find the address on the note. Roanoke Road went on for miles, without so much as a mailbox. There were no power lines to even admit that anyone lived anywhere near here. The road soon turned to dirt and Miller kept on trekking through it. Finally the road looked like it was going to dead end. After about fourteen miles of driving, the dirt road finally came to an end. Detective Miller got out of his truck and slammed the door. The brigade behind him caught up to him and also stopped.

"Son of a . . ." but Miller never finished. When Roanoke and Philmore heard it, they knew it would be a bit longer until they found this mystery house.

Nurse Darnell was driving, driving up a mountain. She came up on what looked like a van, but the dust from the dirt road inhibited her from seeing the police insignia on the back of it. She finally spotted what kind of van it was, but she was too close. They already saw her. She quickly turned her car around on the narrow dirt road and began driving as fast as she could in the other direction. She couldn't believe the police were tracking that note.

She picked up a pre-paid cell phone that she bought on her way up there. "You are not going to believe who is on your doorstep—the police. I'm trying to evade them now, and draw them away from you. I would take defensive measures if I were you. Alright see you in a few hours." She was hoping she wouldn't need more time to try to lose the cops.

Ty laid on his bed with his hands behind his head, listening to the sounds of the mock ocean. It was relaxing even though it was reproduction of the real thing. Suddenly he heard a knock at his door. He got up and opened it to see Noel standing there. "Hey," then he stopped. He was a bit more surprised than he thought he would be.

"Hey, yourself," she said in her sweet little accent. She looked at his left hand. "I heard you spent the day with Sumiko," she announced a little out of the blue.

"Um ... yeah. She took me to see the rainforest dome. It's very beautiful."

"Yeah." Noel looked at the floor. "Um ... yeah, well ... I just wanted to say welcome, and I'm glad you're here."

"Thanks," Ty sincerely said.

"Yeah . . ." was the reply. Noel looked back up at Ty. "Um ... good luck with your training tomorrow."

"Okay, sure thanks. Did you go through it?" he asked, seeing the conversation's odd pauses were making him feel uneasy.

"Um ... yeah, I did. It was pretty cool," Noel said.

"You didn't almost die, did you?" Ty thought he would ask someone else while she was here, so as to get another person's idea."

"Um ... personally, yes I gotten pretty close a few times, but something's different about this place, you know? It's like your senses are more attuned somehow. When you step foot into the training area, your whole mind is more alert automatically, it's weird."

"Oh, well that's good to know, I guess. Hopefully mine will be just as alert." Ty just remembered to be polite and realized they were standing there in to doorway talking. "Did you want to come in; I have a sitting area. You could tell me all about your experience, even how you got here."

"Oh, um . . ." Noel looked right then left down the hallway. "I would really love to, but I shouldn't. We're not supposed to be talking for this long.

"Come on, who's going to know? I want to hear your story," Ty urged.

"Tell you what, why don't you meet me in the rainforest dome tomorrow after your training. I can tell you then."

"Alright," Ty smiled. It's a date.

That drew a very large grin from Noel's face, who ran out of the doorway and down the hall before anyone spotted her. Ty watched her skip away. She was so adorable.

Ty was a little nervous, about the next day. He couldn't imagine getting any sleep that night, but even as he thought it; he drifted off and had the most bizarre dreams consisting of dark men, fangs, and assassinations.

Bones sat, staring at a group of monitors in another control room outside his office. He was alone in the room as was his request. His eyes darted at the six various monitors showing a different view of the outside world. Even in the darkness, the night vision cameras set up outside the compound, gave enough viewing ability so Bones could see anything and everything that moved. Motion sensors were set up all through the outside of the compound. He was very disturbed after receiving the phone call.

Bones sat there for a long while, staring at the various monitors over and over. He saw nothing. He switched the shots to that a little further out from the camouflaged cameras placed on trees. He still saw nothing moving, nothing out of the ordinary. He thought for a moment he saw something, but it was a deer. It suddenly ran off as if spooked. He switched to the cameras around the dear, and his eyes grew wide. He saw men, at least a dozen or more, dressed in all black.

Bones slid his roller chair away from his desk to a filing cabinet behind him. He opened the drawer and pulled out a large book that had all the camera's labeled specifically. "This camera is about a mile away from the house," he said to himself aloud. "This isn't good at all, this really isn't good." He grabbed the phone.

The Good Doctor woke up from his slumber hearing his phone ring. He checked the number and knew exactly who it was. "What is it?" he asked a little more abrupt than he would have liked. "Yes, what is the problem?" The Good Doctor waited for the issue. "I swear to you, I have everything under control. Let's just see how it all plays out." He paused again, listening. "Relax. I have everything taken care of. They're all under my control. Do not worry about anything. Goodbye."

The Good Doctor turned back around to see his beautiful Olga sleeping soundly next to him. He checked his watch. It was almost time for his feeding anyways. He got up from one of the beds in the hospital and changed out of his night gown. He ventured down stairs, and out the front entrance. The moon produced brightly in the sky. The Good Doctor preferred this lighted sphere in the sky, as opposed to its partner.

The Good Doctor walked down the long lane toward the streets. Who was going to be his next victim?

The van and a few of the men and women, Philmore and Roanoke followed the mysterious car. They wondered why a vehicle would be on such a deserted road with no appearance of houses anywhere for miles.

Detective Miller and about a dozen others from the team took off through the woods past where the road had ended. They walked for a few miles, tracking footprints that seemed to just run them in circles. Finally as it started to get dark the team was about to head back toward the dirt road.

Just then one of the trackers saw something in the distance through his night vision. From this distance he couldn't be sure what it was, but he told the rest of the team in a whisper. They all headed in that direction, fanning out about ten feet apart in a V shaped arc. They came closer, and many of the team saw what it was. It was definitely a house, or more or less, a cabin in the middle of the woods. There was no path—no road that led up to the cabin. Miller looked up, and saw there was a brief clearing in the trees around the house that might have meant air support could get in and out. He had his own night vision goggles on, and couldn't see any tracks that would have indicated anyone stood or walked near the house at all.

His team spread out and surrounded the small cabin. Each one ready for whatever was inside. When Miller gave the signal all of them burst in the back and front doors. The ones at the windows didn't break the windows, but merely stood up and shone their lights and guns at the inside. The one room cabin was empty.

A small homemade wooden table, which looked more like a stump bench, than an eating table, sat in the center of the cabin. Other than a small cooking stove, a few old looking pots, and plates, there was nothing or no one around. The walls were made out of rustic logs, which looked as if it was at least two hundred years old or more. They were practically falling apart from each other. There was nothing else around. One of the trackers noticed a four, and a one nailed to one of the logs by the outside of the front door.

Miller picked his phone out of his pocket, and called Roanoke. When he finally picked up, Miller said. "We found the house. There's nothing here; how'd you make out?"

"The car that we were chasing veered off through a side path. You wouldn't believe it. This person definitely knows their way around these woods. In other words, we lost them."

“Dead ends the whole way around. Alright, pull the men out; we’re going to meet at the rendezvous on the dirt road. See you in about an hour.” Miller clicked his phone shut. He just wouldn’t take a dead end for an answer. There had to be a reason, this house was put on that note. He just couldn’t see why, other than a short safe haven. Perhaps a meeting place. He walked outside, and looked up. The tree leaves all around the house were windblown in a circular motion. This gave the idea that a chopper had to of touched down right here. He remembered what Gerald Funk had said on the road about thirty-six hours ago. The team was heading out of the house, when Miller went back inside. There had to be a reason that chopper that picked Ty up touched down here.

He looked around, but saw nothing out of sorts, although the whole house was out of sorts in this part of the woods, as far as an adequate living area for anyone. He looked at the pot on the table. The whole place was incredibly dirty, with leaves and years of dust gathering all around, yet the pot was spotless. It was as if it was new and just put there. He tried to pick it up, but it wouldn’t move. It was nailed to the table. He tried with both hands, but he could not pry the pot free from the table’s grasp. He tried wiggling the pot to loosen whatever was holding it down, and when he did the pot turned. Not out of giving away, but automatically, Miller felt.

The table gave out a hydraulic wheeze, as it started moving downward. It moved slowly but surely, and revealed a hole, with steps that led down to a basement of the house. With all the noise from the table, the whole team was back inside the house, by this time, looking down the hole.

“Let’s go,” Miller ordered not even looking at the team.

He was the first down, the hole. The bottom of the steps to the ground was about a twelve foot drop, so he had to hang from his hands and hit the ground as soft as he could, which was still harder than he would have hoped to land. He quickly got up and looked in both directions. It was incredible. It was some sort of warehouse facility. Totally dark, but with the night vision, he could see that the room was at least a hundred feet all the way around. He noticed a track going off into a darkened tunnel. He turned, as the rest of the team jumped to the ground, and looked around. Miller saw vehicles, huge army type vehicles, parked along the far wall of the warehouse. Pillars holding the ceiling at bay inhibited his view from seeing everything, but other than the vehicles, this warehouse was empty of any persons.

The last of the team entered the underground warehouse, as Miller clicked his phone up again. He called Roanoke and told them where they were. Roanoke would be there around an hour. That would give Detective Miller enough time to send a few guys to scout ahead. If a track was needed, the trip was probably long. If it was, he would have to see if they could get one or more of these vehicles working, so they could get to the end of this tunnel. It was the only plan he had.

The dark chilling breeze felt good on the Doctors exposed skin. He didn't feel the cold at all. There weren't many people in this city, but the people that were here, were very superstitious. The Good Doctor would play with that a bit. He walked through the town almost without limping. His new found location of the hospital was good to his infirmaries. The secluded town and area alone led him to do his hunting more carefully without worrying about being seen by anyone, he couldn't easily kill. He almost felt like a young man, but better. He felt powerful. He was the hunter. He smelled the air. The humans were the prey.

We walked through the darkened streets of night, looking at the rubble of buildings. The snow on the ground lay thick, but he left no footprints to be tracked or seen by anyone.

He stuck his nose in the air, and sniffed again. He smelled the sweet aroma of fresh warm blood, just a few yards away. He followed the scent to an old town house. Half the house was torn to shreds, no doubt from the war.

The Doctor pushed on the door, but it wouldn't move. There was someone inside; he could feel it. He could smell it. He could smell them. There were a few. The closer he was to his destination; he could smell all the better. There were at least four flavors of blood in there, all different types. He smelled the air again. A man, a woman, and two teenage girls if his nose didn't let him down, and it never had. He walked around the side of the house, where the rubble and debris lay all strewed throughout. He climbed over it with ease and not with much of a limp now. The smell of fresh blood gave him, strength. He found a small sliver inside. He crept as silently as he could through the two story house. He walked from room to room, but saw no one. Then he put his nose to the floor and smelled. He smelled it. The blood was underneath him. He began looking at some sort of object in which to rip the floorboards apart, and then realized, there must be an easier way to get down there. He looked from room to room, and found a hole barely big enough for a child to fit through in one of the corners. He knelt down and took a long sniff, and smiled. He could hear the steady pulses of three of the victim's but the fourth was more sporadic. They were awake. He sniffed quietly, and then took a long whiff knowing for sure that it was one of the young girls. He would feed off of her first, he thought, then the others.

He would feed well tonight gaining the fullness of his youth.

CHAPTER 8

Ty woke up to the sound of Bones' voice through the blank monitor. "Are you ready, my dear boy?" he asked more emphatically than Ty would have liked.

Ty woke up groggily. He estimated; he only got a few hours sleep, if that much. He was anxiously awaiting his test of wits, and strength. He heard a knock on his door, and answered it naked to the waist. It was Noel, whose face lit up when she saw his broad chest. "Um . . ." she stammered, "You're supposed to follow me to the training area," she smiled.

Ty looked down at his own chest and replied, "Well tell you what. Let me get dressed here, and I'll be ready in a quickie."

"Sure," Noel didn't take her eyes off his chest or take the grin from her face. "Take your time, I'll be waiting right here."

"Thanks." Ty smiled and closed the door softly.

He threw on the same clothing from before, the same style at least, but different clothes. After pushing the shoes onto his feet, he reopened the door. "All ready," he said. "Lead the way."

She led him down the same stairs as the day before to the main floor of the facility and through the number of the spotless corridors that led into the training area.

"So we're still up for our date after the training right?" Ty asked, hoping not his chance for more answers about this place.

"Sure, if you don't need to rest. I will be waiting in the rainforest dome for you," she answered looking back at him as she led the way.

"Okay, I'll be there as soon as I can. We'll have to see how this goes," Ty stated, a little unsure on what was about to take place.

"You'll be fine, I have faith in you," Noel said, looking back and offering a comforting smile.

They made it up to the door of the pre-training locker room. Noel motioned Ty inside, and waved as he closed the door. Ty turned to see Bones standing with that same goofy grin on his face as when he first met him.

"How's your finger holding up buddy?" Bones asked.

"You mean my lack of finger," Ty scorched back.

Bones put his hand up in surrender. "Come," he said at last, "I want to show you your suit."

Ty walked over to a locker with his name on it, "Ty Livingston."

Bones opened the locker door, and showed him a combat suit with straps all around it for various weapons. The suit was made with a Kevlar material, with hard exo-skeleton armor. Ty couldn't help but smile at the site. Bones then showed him a mask. A fully functional mask that once the wearer put it on, it would mesh with the connection nerves, and act as Ty's own face would. It enacted him to see in regular, night vision, or infrared, whenever he thought it. It had a hundred thousand millimeter scope built into the eyes that enhanced his vision remarkably. Whenever Ty would think to see something closer, it would narrow in on that very object and pull it to a few feet from his face. It would be something from three miles away to ten feet. The mask also had an exo-skeleton made of adamantine plates that fanned down his face to bend around his chin and cover his neck. This meshed well with his suit, and made him look like a fighting terror.

His weapons were simple. Laid out on a black cloth on a large table were two katana swords to be strapped on his back, twenty throwing knives, to be strapped strategically around his body so that no matter what position he was in, he could easily get to any of them. He had two throwing boomerangs. The only catch was these were razor sharp on all sides and only able to be caught by the adamantine suit hand that threw them.

The most mysterious weapon, he was given were three tiny marbles that would be strapped just under his arm. When these little marbles were clicked into position, they gave out a light about three times brighter than the sun for a split second. Just like a flash bang grenade, but much more powerful, these little marbles would blind anyone looking into them, giving the user a few minutes to disappear. If the enemy was not staring at the marbles, the tiny electrodes the marbles gave off, would give the enemy the appearance that just a few seconds went by, when in fact a minute or more went by. This was done with a special electro-magnetic pulse that would actually hit the nerves in the brain and give the enemy a personal lapse in time.

Ty was amazed at everything Bones had shown him, but still a little nervous.

"Do not worry my dear boy. We don't bring out all the guns, your first time. We break you in first. The idea is to see your enemy before they see you. There will be five men; you must kill them in order to pass this test. Should come easy to you."

Ty shifted his feet. He didn't know what Bones meant by that comment. Ty couldn't remember his past life, and had an inkling of an idea that Bones could. "I have to kill them?" Ty questioned.

"Yes, my dear boy. In order for you to pass your first test, the men must die. Do not worry; they are prepared for what they have coming to them. The men know it's your first time, so they actually think they have a chance, but I know better." Bones smiled and tapped his index finger against his temple.

"You see, even if you never fought before, which we all know you have." Ty shifted again, every time Bones made a reference to Ty fighting or even killing anyone. "We will be more or less, downloading fighting techniques in your head. Your suit and mask is like a computer. You download a program or some sort of application, and the computer holds the knowledge. It never forgets it, until we decide to erase it to make room for newer knowledge. Your suit and mask are built with connector that connects the wireless waves to your brain. It may surprise you, but you will know what to do, when you need to do it, guaranteed. I will be watching the whole thing, and you should walk out of the training exercise unscathed." Bones smiled and raised his shoulders as if the task was all so simple.

"Take a few minutes and regroup. Try your clothes on, they should fit to your body style, and try your mask out. Strap your weapons in. When you enter the training arena; we will give you a few minutes to get used to everything. Try to exercise everything your suit can do in those valuable minutes. Remember Ty, your suit is an extension of yourself. Assassins have come a long way since the times of Omar Has'sir. We have more technology. You'll be fine." Bones gave him a pat on the shoulder. "I will bid you farewell, and see you on the other side. When you are finishing putting everything on, you may exit to the door on your right." Bones motioned to the door at the far end of the training locker room.

Bones then left through another door to go to the control room leaving Ty alone with his thoughts, and his powerful suit and weapons.

When Roanoke, Philmore, and the few trackers that went with them, met up with Miller, and his group they briefed him on what they saw, which wasn't much.

"We didn't get a good look at, the vehicle at all," Roanoke started.

"The dust from the dirt road totally took away any view we would get of a license plate, let alone the make or model of the car.

Philmore started, "I was behind Roanoke the whole time, so I didn't get anything either, the van was in front of us, and you can only go so fast in a van on that type of road."

Miller looked down at the floor his hands and suit dirty from the grease from the vehicles. The team put together temporary lighting, made with short term batteries so they all could preserve their night vision batteries. "Well, we do have a lead here." Miller said at last. "That's better than anything as for right now," Miller said, looking back at the trucks, his hands on his waist. "We have a few larger army combat trucks that can hold the team. I sent a few scouts into the tunnel, and they came back a little while ago saying it goes on for at least a few miles. Judging by this track, it's got to be three or more."

Roanoke and Philmore looked down the tunnel and at the tracks that went into darkness. "We ready to go soon, then?" Philmore asked.

"Yeah, the team is just finishing the last of the three vehicles up. They have to jump it with the other vehicles. Then we're ready to go," Miller's replied.

Ty's suit fit perfectly. It almost attached itself to his body as soon as he put it on. He couldn't explain it, but it did feel like an extension of himself. He felt more aware, more alive than he ever had. When Ty put on his mask, he jumped at the force that attached itself to him. He was shocked at the mere power that his mind could produce, even without moving. He couldn't explain to himself why his mind seemed to almost feel the dream like state that he was in. It was as if he was dreaming, as if everything he had ever remembered, ever known was false—a figment of his imagination. After much thought, Ty finally came to one conclusion. That meant he could do anything. He was the king of his mind, the king of his dreams. His body shook, as that thought came to his mind. He looked across the room at a locker, and to the name tag on it. He focused, and zoomed in on the name he could barely see. It became as if he was standing right at that locker, "Noah Gustav," he read. Though no one could see it, he smiled under his masked helmet.

Ty strapped his weapons all each to the right places they went, definitely not forgetting the three marbles. He was sure they would come in handy at some point. He took the swords from their scabbards, and admired the handy work. He saw the name "Has'sir" etched into the handle, gold inlayed. He put them back into their holders, and strapped them onto his back. It was as if his suit was alive, because it grabbed the scabbards and held them tight, for easier removal of the sword. This suit was definitely awesome.

When Ty was finished getting dressed, and admiring his suit and weaponry, he looked at the door. His test awaited. He marched toward the door. He was ready. The door flung opened, and he looked at the various streets, and side streets. He looked at the buildings, and the fluorescent lights. Ty really couldn't believe it, but this place actually looked like a real city at night—without the people of course. With his enhanced suit, it felt so much more real. Ty still felt like he was in a dream world, but that this suit was somehow a key to unlocking it, and letting him step into a real world or something.

Ty walked around the city, looking at the various parked cars on the side of the road. He looked up to see a mock full moon and stars. Even the sky looked authentic and real.

"We'll give you another minute, Ty before the boys will enter." A voice came from inside his mask ear piece.

"And I have to kill them?" Ty questioned one last time, just to be sure of the task set before him.

"Ty we've been over this. In order to pass the test, you do have to kill all five enemies. Their lives are now in your hands, and are now forfeit." The voice continued, "You must understand, Ty that in order to be an effective assassin, you must learn how to kill. You must do it effectively and efficiently to accomplish your goal."

"Alright," Ty said into his mouth piece built into the adamantine mouth guard, cushioned with foam alloy.

"Alright, it's go time buddy. Show us what you got," Bones spoke, through the ear piece. "Make us proud."

"Will do," Ty growled.

This suit, Ty knew was part of the answer. He just had to use it. He quickly ran down a side street. He was careful to stay out of the street lights and the lighting that shown from store fronts. He ran down another side street. He couldn't see anything, but lights, cars, and buildings in all directions. This city looked familiar. Ty looked at a building, and cocked his head. He saw that same building before. He turned around and looked at the store across from it; it was a mom and pop's store.

Ty looked at the name, "The General's Store," he said quietly to himself. He knew that store. When he needed to fix something, he used to go to that store. He couldn't remember for what. He walked up to the door, and turned around. There was no one in sight. He opened the door to the store, and walked inside. The store looked very familiar, Ty was sure he was in this store at some point, or the real version at least. Ty rounded a corner aisle saw hammers and mallets hanging on the shelving to his left. Ty looked to the right, and he saw the rope and chain section. He stopped and closed his eyes. His mind wondered to a different place, a place where he used to be happy.

"Mr. Yotz," Ty spoke to himself, referring to the General's Store owner. "I came in to buy a bike chain for my bike when I was fifteen," Ty spoke out loud. "Mr. Yotz always asked me if I had a car for when I turned sixteen. I stopped coming by when I turned sixteen."

Ty walked down another aisle then heard something. He quickly stopped moving, and looked up. Someone was on the roof. Ty moved quickly ducking under security lights of the General's Store and the street lights shining in the front. The store was closed at night so only those lights shown which gave it a dim glow and plenty of shadows.

Ty stopped and hid behind a center aisle display piece. He listened, but when he stopped the moving on the roof stopped. He crept to the end of the aisle; he was in and listened again. Ty moved slowly, listening feeling with his suit, letting the power consume him. He closed his eyes. To the average person that meant taking away a sense, but to Ty it meant making his other senses stronger. He listened deeply to the man's pulse. He was now inside the store. The man was being very, very quiet, but Ty heard him as loud as if he was a child knocking down a glass vase. Ty knew exactly where he was.

Ty moved to the other aisle with the silence of a hunter stalking his prey. He opened his eyes. If he heard correctly, the pulse was coming from two aisles away. Ty crept into the next aisle, not making a sound. He moved slowly, but surely toward his target. He crept into the next aisle, and saw the man peaking around the other corner, crouched.

Ty snuck up behind him. He figured taking out his sword would make too much noise right behind the man, so he took one of his throwing knives from his side pouch. Ty snuck silently closer, and quickly grabbed the man by the neck with his left hand pulling him back, giving him a quick view of the man's neck. Ty shoved the knife into his neck with the other hand in one fluid motion. He laid the man down softly. All that could be heard from the killing was a brief grunt from the unsuspecting victim.

Ty moved to the door. He was down on his stomach, and could see no movement from the outside. He thought that if this was the General's Store, then his old house was a few blocks down that side street, diagonal from the store.

Ty was amazed at how his memory was returning to him. He stopped and looked back at the silent man lying on his back. Blood flowed in the dim lights, under the shelving. "I must kill them all." He said aloud, but more to give himself comfort. Bones said that I should be used to it, what did he mean, by that. Ty thought to himself.

Ty thought that he might find more answers once he made it back to his mock house. He crept slowly out of the store. When he was sure that the outside was clear he moved slowly toward the side road. Down the side street a few hundred feet was his house. The streets weren't nearly as lit up and Ty was grateful for that. He stood on the sidewalk, and looked at his old home. The old shudders, that his mom told his dad to fix, and the old mail box that was taped with duck tape because it was hit every Halloween by vandals with baseball bats.

Ty looked around, and then walked toward the door. It was just how he remembered it, and his memories were becoming stronger. The door was unlocked, and Ty crept in slowly. He saw the dining room first, and the stairs he would always run up after he was done with school, or playing baseball with ... Ty left his mashed up thoughts stop. With . . ., he thought. He would remember that later. He was happy he got this much of his memory. He moved up the stairs, and through the hallway. He saw his room, picture of a sports car on the door. Everything was the same, it was odd. Ty pushed the door open slowly, and went inside. He saw his model air plane; he built when he was eight hanging from the ceiling. He saw his bed, and his desk with his laptop on it, the headphones draped over the edge of the desktop.

Suddenly a man came out of nowhere with a huge sword, or it seemed huge for this small room. Ty quickly reacted and not a moment too late, because if he had been any later, his head would have been gone for sure. The swipe led the attacker to hit the wall, above his bed. Plaster and dust fell from the slit wall, as the, would be, assassin pulled his sword free. Ty pulled out one of his own katanas that seemed as light as a feather. He blocked the next swing more out of instinct. "Focus!" he yelled at himself. The man kept pressing. Ty blocked another, and then another swipe. Ty was always on the defensive in this small room; he quickly realized that he would have to push the swordsman out the door. Ty ducked low, and came up high with his own sword causing the man to react fast as to not get sliced in the stomach. This gave Ty a moment to go with a few offensive thrusts that pushed the man back into the doorway.

Ty moved fast, and surprising for not ever really using a sword. He felt his suit, focus tightly on the job at hand, as if it was doing most of the work and letting Ty go along for the ride. Ty pushed the man back and back toward the stairs. Ty then saw his opportunity, and he might only get one shot at this, for if the man realized his plan, it would not work again. Ty went low again, practically going on the defensive again. It was all part of his plan. He took out a throwing knife from his ankle strap, and jammed it into the man's calf. This let out a large howl from the man, and Ty came up pushing, not with his sword's blade, but with the hilt, catching the man totally by surprise and pushing him down the stairs. The man tossed and twisted, and hit wall at the bottom hard. Ty flew down the stairs, and before the man could react to the fall or the pain in his stabbed calf, Ty shoved a katana tip into the man's throat.

At this moment, Ty was breathing heavy. He killed a man in his childhood home—in his mock child hood home. Ty couldn't believe what he had done. He took the sword from the man's neck and in one quick motioned cleaned the tip, and put it back in his back scabbard. Ty leaned up against the wall breathing heavy.

Ty stood at the bottom of the steps, and looked into his old dining room. He closed his eyes, and a picture came to his mind as clear as day. He saw his father screaming at his mother. His mom was crying. Ty felt hopeless, his adopted parents had never fought in this way. He tried to calm his dad down but, his father threw him backwards flipping Ty over his chair. He saw his father take a swing at his mother knocking her off her chair toward the wall. Ty cried out, but he couldn't even hear his own voice. He saw a fork lying beside him, and picked it up. He lunged at his adopted father, and in one motion stabbed him in the eye. He then turned toward his mother who lay unconscious lying very still against the wall. In a moment of passion, in a moment of anger; he rushed to her, but she is not breathing; she still wasn't moving. He gripped the back of her head, and slammed it over and over into the wall, breaking plaster and drywall in his rage, blood spattering all over. Then he himself collapses and falls to the floor.

Ty's mind focused back to the present, and it all came together. He had remembered blacking out, but had no idea what had happened until he woke up in the hospital with the detective breathing down his throat. Ty threw the table and it crashed against the wall. His perfect world came crashing down all around him now. Someone was playing with his mind. Someone was messing with his head. Someone was using him as a puppet.

Ty looked at his front door. In his rage; he marched out of the door looking for his next victim.

CHAPTER 9

The Good Doctors phone rang. “Curse,” he accidently spoke out loud. “Why did I ever bring this cursed phone on a hunt?” He looked at who was calling, and flipped it up. “Yes my dear Olga,” he sung his voice completely changing. “Do not worry, my child, I’ll be right there.”

He smelled the air, and realized that the steady pulses were more sporadic now. The family was awake. “Hmm,” he whispered. “I’ll have to come back for you some other time.” He sniffed the air one last time and ran out of the house, faster than lightning faster than humanly possible.

He made it back to the hospital within a few minutes, and was up to the room in under a minute. Olga was standing by the computer that was hooked to the young man’s head.

“Oh, so glad you made it back. Did you go out for a midnight stroll?” Olga asked.

“Um…yes my dear. You know, just to clear my head,” The Doctor lied. “Now what is your pretty little head worrying about?”

Olga showed him the screen. Not only was his heart rate and blood pressure sky rocketing, but if it picked up any more, he would actually wake up out of his comatose state. That wasn’t even the worse part. His brain functions were off the charts. His brain was going against the implanted chip, and the machines being hooked up to it.

"Move out of my way!" The Good Doctor screamed as he pushed Olga away. He sat down at the computer and began clicking. "Come on you. You will not do this to me, not while I am this close," he mumbled. "You will not win, my dear boy, you will not win."

The detectives and the team were driving slowly in three vehicles down the dark tunnel. Only the lights of the vehicles could be seen. Darkness flooded the tunnel for what looked like miles ahead. No one could see any bit of light, or reflection of a light other than the metal of the tracks. They pressed on with caution, driving more over an hour. The first truck had the most trackers of the team in it. They had their night vision goggles on looking every which way for anyone or anything devising an ambush, but they saw nothing. It made them all anxious. That was their worst enemy at the moment—the enemy of uncertainty.

Ty looked to the left then to the right not seeing any one. He knew that the men were being told where he was at like they did with Sumiko. That made him all the angrier. His blood bubbled through his face, as he pressed on through the city, fully ready for anything. He didn't even bother hiding any more. He actually walked dead center down the middle of the road making sure all the street lights picked him up.

Bones looked at the monitors and couldn't believe what he was seeing. Ty was acting very stupid, and going against everything his suit was telling him to do. Stealth was thrown right out the window. Other than the beginning instruction, it was against the rules for Bones to interfere with Ty, or anything that he did. He couldn't say a word into his earpiece until the last of the enemy men were down.

"Where are P-2, P-4, and P5?" he demanded.

"Their all about a hundred feet away and closing in. They should all reach him at about the same time if they keep heading in the direction their going. What do you want us to do?" one of the men asked, checking the monitors, making sure that he was giving accurate information.

"Let them come," was Bones reply. "I am curious to see how this all plays out. Ty is our most gifted student. I want to see his plan for this."

"Sir, his blood pressure levels are off the chart, anger is fueling him."

"He has a lot to be angry about. I believe he has remembered, some of his repressed memories," Bones calmly spoke, allowing his voice and his nerves to settle. "These next encounters could prove interesting. Tell the men their headed in the right direction. Tell them to move quickly but silently. Tell them that they should reach him within a few minutes. Let's see what happens."

The men relayed the messages, and then watched the screens. "This may be better than TV," one of them said.

It took all for Ty to not yell out, "Come and get me." He wanted to, but his suit was advising him not to. He was already going against its wishes by not taking the best planned action in such a situation, but his faith that the suit would see him through, calmed the sentient computer suit down. They were one in the same, two separate yet working together entities—Ty and his suit.

Ty closed his eyes and knelt down in the middle of the street. He knew that the men would be on him shortly anywhere.

Ty cocked his head with his eyes closed. He could hear the pulses getting louder, and louder. The pulses slowed. The men were stopped. They were watching him now. No doubt from rooftops as the last one had with Sumiko. Ty looked up on the nearest rooftops. He looked to both sides of the street. Wait one of them was grown level. Ty heard his pulse the clearest. He was the closest.

Ty moved with lightning speed, and disappeared down a side street. He jumped over a mock dumpster, and over a small four foot wall. He darted in and out of small parking lots, until he came in full view of his target. He reached behind his lower back and pulled out the boomerang. Carefully, and silently he crept up behind the target and behind a building to conceal his view. He slid out from the corner and from about thirty feet away; he launched the razored weapon. It flew through the air, fast practically too fast for the naked eye to spot. If Ty had not had the helmet mask wouldn't even been able to see it fly end over end through the air. The target barely turned half way and the thing took his head clean off. Before the man's head or his body hit the ground it came back and took his right arm as well. Ty caught it before all three body parts hit the ground. His head bounced, and rolled off to the side of the road.

Ty, satisfied with his kill, listened. He could hear the other pulses doubling back. The man did not have time to scream, and Ty knew that he didn't make a noise. They were being told where he was at. Ty would forgive the men in the booth, because they just made his job easier. He moved off to the side of the street out of site. The one was hopping onto rooftops of the closer buildings. The other side of the street the buildings were further apart; so the other man was on ground level.

Ty didn't have to move, but he did wait.

The one on top of the building got to him first. Ty slid so he was directly under the building where the man was. He listened to his pulse beating fast; he could hear the man's heavy breathing through his own armored suit. Ty moved so that he was directly above the one story building staring up. He could not see the man and the man could not see Ty, but that was how Ty wanted it. He measured the jump. He drew out his two katanas and crisscrossed them. He crouched low, breathing one deep breath. Ty jumped. He met the man at eye level and with two simultaneous swipes at the neck and waist; the man's body also fell in three parts.

Ty quickly turned, and hit the roof to his belly just as the other man was coming up the street. The man was trying to be silent, but it really wasn't working for him. Ty saw the bow rod tied to the back of the torso part of the man on the roof. He grabbed it from him and pushed the secret button, which spit out the tight bow string. He grabbed an arrow, from the back of the torso's quiver, and took aim. This man's pulse was also fast and narrow. Ty could tell the man was anxious—nervous even. In the trained assassin's heart he knew that his comrades were dead. He pulled out his sword, and moved off behind a car.

Ty moved to his masked eyes to infrared and could see the man perfectly. The man was couched moving slowly. Ty pulled the arrow back and waited. Sure enough like a turkey in the hunt, his head came out from behind the car, and an arrow went through his left cheek coming out the other side. The man fell to the ground.

A voice came to his earpiece. "That is good Mr. Livingston. Welcome to our world."

"You have some answers for me, I presume," was Ty's quick demand.

"If you speak peacefully," was the reply.

Ty thought about it, perhaps for too long, for Bones' comfort, but his answer finally was, "Alright peacefully, if you tell me everything." Ty could hear the sigh, and the pulse of Bone's through the earpiece, steady a bit. Ty smiled. He would enjoy this new found power. Definitely enjoy it.

"Well, then the stats are resting; everything seems to be going down to normal. I should make the call to see what went wrong on the inside," the Good Doctor said, breathing a bit easier now. "It will take me a bit to hack into his brain and see what went wrong, I may find out more the other way, I'm not sure. I just cannot yet break into that evasive strand of DNA." By this time the Doctor was talking to himself.

"I think it should be alright. It probably was a small glitch, like before, but you have it under control," Olga said, smiling and twisting uneasily. She changed the subject back to the midnight stroll. "You can wake me up if you need to go out for a midnight walk' it is okay."

"Yes, well, certainly I am entitled to my degree of privacy."

That put Olga back. She had known the Doctor but a short time, and although his methods were unorthodox at times; he did show her the attention she had needed through this trying world. Perhaps he was just stressed. "You know perhaps I can give you something for your stress that may calm you down," Olga quickly responded when the thought came to her mind.

The Doctor thought for a few moments, pondering the request. His thirst burned his throat. He had not fed, in a few nights; he had been so consumed with his work. It was Olga that interrupted him, albeit for a good reason. Still, nevertheless, he could find other assistance. Perhaps more attractive ones, he thought. He turned to regard, Olga. "Yes there is something you can do for me my dear. Come here," the Doctor smiled.

Olga blushed and walked toward him. If she only knew what he had in store for her, she would have ran the other way.

Ty took off his suit, and in a few minutes he was in the control room.

"No weapons?" Bones asked not taking any chances.

"None." Ty reassured the man standing before him. "If you do not lie to me, and tell me everything, then I won't have a reason to kill you."

"Alright come to my office. It's private, and I will tell you everything in there."

Ty followed Bones to his office, the same way he took Sumiko and Ty the day before.

As they entered, Bones offered Ty a seat. Bones took his customary place behind his desk and breathed out a long breath.

Ty raised his right brow, and leaned back into his chair as if he was about to be lectured by a nagging parent.

"Well, I suppose I should start from the beginning. This is not a real world as you might come to expect." Bones paused.

Ty shifted in his chair. "Please go on," he said in a stern voice.

"Well, I know in the mock city that you remembered a lot about your past, well your fake past. I... um... I really shouldn't be telling you this at all, but I have not seen the real world in about fifteen years."

"What do you mean?" Ty asked.

"I am hooked up to a monitor in a comatose state just like you. This world is inexact."

Ty blinked a few times and shifted back the other way in his chair. "What are you talking about?" His eyes narrowed.

"A man came to me one day, about fifteen years ago. He asked me to be part of a project—an experiment rather. The project was the experiment." Bones mumbled as if repeating some sort of irrelevant rhetoric. "There was a large sum of money that I would get paid by the end. The only thing is it would take fifteen years of my time on the natural planet. However, I would be fully comfortable." Bones waved his hand around his office. Ty agreed it definitely was relaxing and a nice work environment. Bones continued, "At the end I would be brought back; and given the money and leave. I couldn't speak of it to anyone."

At that moment Ty realized something about Bones. "You were the man in the car outside my house. You hit me with the car when I was crossing the street."

"Indeed," came the reply. "I was supposed to follow you all through your life." Bones went on. "You see Ty; there were other's before you. Most of them orphan kids, I helped with them also, but they didn't make it. They didn't possess the emotionality of killing in them. They simply would refuse. We thought by getting kids who had nothing, and putting them through this comfortable living environment that they would kill for us," Bones spoke as if the subject was easy to take hold of.

Bones kept going. "So my superiors deemed it necessary to grab you. A person who already had killing built into their DNA." Bones leaned forward placing his folded arms down on the desk. "Ty, you're twenty-five years old in the real world, not seventeen.

Ty blinked many times. He was thinking this was just a dream, and in essence it was, but he knew in his heart, what Bones was telling him was real. It was too bizarre and explained so much of what he was feeling not to be real.

"If it makes you feel any better, most of the men you killed in the training area, were computer simulations, made to look real."

"Most of the men?" Ty asked.

"Right, two of them were real people tied to the same program you and I are," Bones answered.

"I'm twenty-five?" was Ty's next question. He had so many.

"Yes, you are." Bones paused before he started on the second part. "Ty, there's something about you, we can't quite place. You are being created not only to be an assassin, but to be a weapon of some sort. I, myself am not sure exactly what for, or to kill what. From the preordained training exercises, I would imagine you are supposed to kill a very formidable foe.

"You were a street thug, with a bad attitude when we found you. You killed some people in your life. We found out."

"How many people, have I killed already?" was Ty's next question.

"Eleven is what I was told. You caught at the age seventeen were thrown into a maximum security facility, tried as an adult. It wasn't until a buyer by the name Jonas pulled you out, saying that if he could experiment with placing certain memories in your mind; he could make you an adequate person in society. The jails and state prisons were busting at the seams, so they obliged. You went along with it, until you tried to kill the people trying to drive you away. The vehicle wrecked and you were unconscious. They put you in a hospital to help you regain your strength. Doctors worked on you, from there with their experiments, then all of sudden the doctors disappeared. Someone took you out of the hospital, unconscious and you ended up at some other facility, I am not sure of.

"Ty, I am coming to the end of my fifteen year contract, and it was looking like you would be the one. Grant, it you began to have black outs, and killed people, even in your perfect little world that was implanted in your head. This threw Jonas for a loop, and he was about to pull the plug. A man by the name The Good Doctor got a hold of you and changed all that. He thought by putting you here, in this perfect peaceful little area; he could meet the deadline and make you into the assassin that you needed to be."

"So the assassin part of the story is real? Wait does that mean I have my finger in real life?"

"Um...you should, as I should too. Hopefully." Bones laughed, but this was clearly not a laughing matter for Ty, who felt as if his best friend stabbed him in the back.

Ty thought about his childhood best friend and remembered his name. "So what of Derik?"

"Your friend was artificial intelligence put there to give you good dreams—more or less. The doctors gave you the AI parents, and gave you your simple school life to replace your bad memories. We thought that if they would first keep you from killing random people, and then give you a list of targets to kill, because killing is already in your blood." Bones threw his hands up for emphasis, "I mean look at the training exercise. You are a pro for not having any memories of killing at all. I wouldn't think I'd ever say this to anyone, but you are a natural at taking peoples lies." Toward the end, Bones was practically yelling for emphasis to get his point across, and he knew that he had hit home.

"So is anyone but you and me real in this place?" Ty asked.

"Well other than the two, you killed in the training area, Sumiko and Noel area the only other two that are real. Noel showed promise, so she actually is being kept. Sumiko is at another facility, in the real world, and that I am not sure where. She is here, but running through the same experiment, she is somewhere entirely different than you. They would not tell me where. Oh before I forget. You remember Nurse Darnell?"

"Yeah, the nurse in the hospital."

"Yeah well, she was also put into this program to watch over you. The note she gave you, everything was so she could aim you in my direction."

"Note?" Ty asked. "Oh the note. Yeah, I must have dropped it."

"Yeah, we knew you did, and wouldn't know where to go, so we had to take other measures. Never mind about all that. That brings me to another point. Nurse Darnell actually called me a few nights ago or so, and said that a few detectives were hot on your trail. It would seem that this one particular detective has had a run in or two with this Ms. Darnell."

"So."

Well, it would seem that we've never seen an AI show quite this much attention, in finding a person. This Detective Miller she kept talking about with her phone call. He's really pressing the issue in trying to find you. The AI wouldn't have been put into this whole program to act like that. There may be more real people in here then we've realized. We're not sure."

Ty leaned back in his chair. He didn't know quite what to think or how many people he killed. He remembered getting angry in the training exercise and blacking out, but were those just emotions, or were they chemicals making him make those decisions. He's felt played with from the start, but now that he realized his whole remembered life, was fake, he didn't know how to feel now.

"Well you say all this about me being created to be an assassin, and kill, kill, kill type thing, but what am I going to kill when I am brought out of this illusive world?"

Bones put his head down, and rubbed the back of his head, then looked back up at Ty and sighed. "Okay this may take you by storm, but I am hundred percent telling you the truth. You are being bred to kill vampires."

Just then a buzzard went off. "Sir?" Came a voice from Bone's speaker phone.

Bones pushed the button to speak, "Go ahead," he said.

"Sir, we have company. Your needed down by the tunnels right away."

"I'll be right there," Bones let go of the button. "Ty, how bout you get that suit on and go for some more practice."

"Sure thing," Ty got up and walked toward the door. He had a new outlook on this concocted life now.

CHAPTER 10

The Good Doctor wiped his mouth delicately, savoring the taste. His eyes rolled back into his head as he sighed in ecstasy and snarled. His cell phone rang. He rolled his head and his eyes twice around as he picked it out of his pocket. "Yes," he growled.

"Doctor, what experiments are you running over there?"

"Why, whatever do you mean?" the Good Doctor asked.

"There has been an issue. The boy is self aware. Plus you knew that consequences could occur, had you put more humans into the program without fully monitoring them."

"Everything is under control on my end." The Doctor's voice became very dark. "Do not forget whom I work for, or my responsibility to the sect." His face cringed with anger. He put a finger to his forehead to wipe off some splattered blood. Looking at the red liquid on his finger; he licked it off while talking.

The voice straightened in the phone. "I am very aware of whom you are, as I would hope you would remember whom my father is. Do not forget who you work for. Do not mess with progress. This may be our greatest weapon we have."

The Doctor walked over to the body lying on the cold table. "I am well aware at what is at stake. I have the best interest of the sect at heart. That is why I am running these experiments. Do not bother yourself with what you do not know or cannot begin to comprehend."

"Everything is a go on my side. Get your side together on this, or I will speak to my father of this treachery."

"The boy will be pulled out of the program when he is ready. He is not to know the purpose he was created for. I will make him into our finest weapon. "

"What of Gobaleski?"

"Gobaleski will not know of my doings."

"See to it then. You make sure you pull the boy out in time. Make sure your inside man doesn't tell of us or the secrets he knows."

"Not to worry," was the Doctors reply and his most frequently used phrase as of late. "My inside man thinks we are all on the same side. Everything will be finished in time. Everyone is under my complete control." The Doctor closed his phone and growled under his breath. "Too long we have waited. It is time dear brothers to arise to a new nation. A world ruled by the only one worthy to rule it."

The Good Doctor checked the monitors. Everything was going as planned. Nothing was out of the ordinary. He left the room of the boy to check on the other patients.

Detective Miller, Philmore, and Roanoke moved slowly in the cabs of the three vehicles. Teams of eight to ten were in the backs of each truck, guns poised on anything that moved in the tunnels. They seen and heard nothing for hours, and were wondering how far this place really was.

Instantly one of the team members fell over in the first truck. The rest of the team hadn't realized it until a bit later, but when they did alarm rang out. The first truck stopped, and the team in the back of that truck took account of the damages. The member was dead, with an instant shot to the head. Blood poured out of the wound, like a faucet. They all made silent hand gestures at the trucks behind them to beware.

"What do you want to do?" The driver asked Detective Miller in the cab of the first truck.

Miller leaned out the open window to assess the damage. "How bad is he?" he whispered to the nearest tracker.

"He's dead sir. I don't know where the shot came from," the tracker whispered back.

Miller leaned back into the cab. He knew the shot didn't come from any of their men, because they were all trained fighters. It definitely was a silenced weapon, because in this tunnel any louder shot would definitely be heard. He looked at the driver, "We're like sardines in a can, ready to be picked off." Detective Miller paused. "We do this old school," he said at last. "I'll take a few members with me. Get a few members off the each truck and we'll walk along side it, using it for cover. They're like sitting ducks up there. I would say about five members stay on the trucks at all times, but stay low." Miller breathed out; when he was finished, and looked at his phone. He had no signal. Obviously. He opened the door, and slowly slid out of the truck and went back to Roanoke's truck—the second truck.

Before Miller could open his mouth, Detective Roanoke started. "We know where the shooter is."

Miller looked around thinking; he was out in the open. "Where?" he asked.

Roanoke pulled him close." He's right on top of us.

Miller started to look up, and Roanoke pulled him closer. "He's in the roof of the tunnel. Literally right above our truck," Roanoke whispered.

"But the ceiling is concrete. This is one big concrete sardine pack." Detective Miller spoke a bit louder

"He has a door that he slides open, and closes. The way the tunnel is laid out; we wouldn't have seen it, but a few of the guys in our truck said that they saw a hatch slide closed. The shooter is in hiding right now. We don't know how many of these secret doors there are. What's your call?"

"Well," Miller started, "I think what we should do is grab a few guys from each truck to walk on both sides of each truck. We'll leave about five guys to stay in each truck. Driver's obviously stay inside the trucks and drive as slow as we were going. Each man watches the back of the man in front of him. We work as a team at this."

"There's another thing," Roanoke whispered. "We have a Military ladder inside our truck. If we stacked the thing from the back of the truck where it sits here, we could probably get a few guys to go up top, and take a few of these guys out."

Miller looked around again. "Do you think that will work?" he whispered.

"It can't hurt. It may help even the odds a bit," was Roanoke's answer.

"Alright get on that." Miller went back to let Roanoke, and his team know what they were doing.

Immediately, Roanoke got his team together to work the ladder to the top. He was definitely going up with them. They moved quickly slapping the ladder in place. Roanoke was the first up. He grabbed an automatic assault rifle, before strapping it around his back. He looked a little funny heading up with a detective's suit on, but he did just that. He tried to move the hatch but it was jammed, no doubt from the other side. He began hitting it with the butt of his gun, but to no avail. He was running out of options. He had no idea where these guys were, or what they were doing, but he could be a sitting duck at the top of this ladder like this if he didn't think fast.

Roanoke looked at his gun, "Armor piercing rounds," he said to himself and then looked back at the tunnel's secret door. He stepped a few rungs down on the ladder, and let it all fly. He emptied a clip into the door, making the concrete fall to the truck and members below. No one was seriously hurt, although a rather large block nipped Roanoke's arm. It cut his sleeve and scraped him, but he would be alright.

The assault rifle did its job, and punched a hole in the tunnel ceiling big enough so that a person could fit through. Roanoke didn't waste any time. He packed another clip into the gun, and climbed the rest of the way, gun in hand. He popped his head into the clearing, then ducked down real quick as his training devised. He looked up again slowly. It was incredibly dark up there. He ducked back down and motioned for one of the team members to throw him a light. He caught the flashlight and peaked back up. He shown the light all around him and saw nothing. He saw no one at all. He climbed up the rest of the way, and then crouched down to motion for others to join him. When the top of the tunnel was filled with about six men and a woman, they pressed on. They scouted ahead, knowing that it wouldn't take very long for Miller to rally the troops and get them ready to move.

Moving in a forming V as how they were trained, they stretched end to end in the tunnel. They saw a lot of nothing, but darkness and flashlights. There was no one up here at all. The man must have shot once then booked it back, but back to where? They pressed on.

Detective Miller had the trucks moving in the formations he wanted. Every man watched the other man's back. He even put a guy in the passenger seat of each truck to watch the driver, as the driver had to focus on making it to the destination. They drove for what seemed like a good solid forty-five minutes until they came to a brick wall. This was strange, because Miller was certain people used this tunnel just a few days before. He pushed forward, tapping on the brick wall with his gun. It wasn't solid. The mortar hadn't even fully settled yet. This wall had just been set in place. The inside men, definitely knew, Miller and his team were there; he was sure of it. This could also be an ambush. He moved the men into position back on the trucks.

Miller then stepped up on the first running board step of the side of the truck. "I want you to blast through that wall, and be ready for anything that is on the other side. We're going in guns blazing. We're riding this all the way."

"Alright, just give me the signal," the driver said, looking at the wall.

"Will do," Miller got off the running board and told the second and third driver to just stay on the tail of the truck in front of them.

Roanoke stopped his men. His team came to a dead end. He trekked real slowly toward the concrete wall of the tunnel. "This can't be the end of the tunnel," he whispered to the nearest member.

He walked slowly toward it, and noticed a grated door, leading into what looked like a garage type area. He was about to turn to give instruction and he heard a shot, then another. Two men fell on both sides of him. "THIS IS WAR!" he screamed. "SHOOT BACK!"

The team began firing into the darkness of the tunnel behind them. This was definitely an ambush.

Detective Miller gave the signal just as the firing started up above. He didn't hear the first few shots due to the rev of the trucks engine. The driver pushed forward speeding up as he went. He crashed through the wall, and the bullets began to fly from both ends.

The truck crashed through to a well fortified garage and ambush. Death was in the air. The truck sped on and crashed into a concrete fortified area. Out of nowhere, men with battle suits jumped into the back of the truck. The truck behind the first truck tried to shoot at them, but the melee wouldn't allow it. They totally took the team by surprise. It would take an act of God to get out of this.

Bones walked into the locker room as Ty was placing the last of the throwing knives in their strapped holsters. His mask in place, Ty narrowed in on Bones as he closed the door.

Bones walked over to Ty. "I was going to wait to give you this until your second training session, but I suppose this as good a time as any. Your suit is a very powerful machine that is pretty much unstoppable. These weapons," Bones handed him two Mac 10s, "are made specifically for your suit. They are only to be held by you. For as long as you are in this world of course." Bones breathed heavily hearing the sounds of gunfire already. "Ty, this suit makes the bullets that shoot out of this gun as fast as you can shoot them. You pretty much have an unlimited supply." Ty looked down at the weapons.

"It's all scientific, despite the falsehood of this world. I will explain later. Press them against your suit anywhere."

Ty pressed the guns against his suit, and once he did the suit grabbed them with straps holding them in place. "Whenever you need the weapons, you just pull them and your suit will let them go. No one can touch them, but you. No one can rip them from your suit, but you. No one can shoot them, but you." Bones' words gave Ty a grand smile.

"I do hope this makes up for… what has been done to you. May we get out of this world alive, eh?" Bones smiled.

Ty met that smile and grabbed his guns. "Let's do it," Ty said through his suit.

He walked out of the locker room, and passed a few doors. He walked down a few long corridors following the sounds of gunfire, and pulses. He could hear them louder as he went. He came to a door; he knew just what was on the other side. The guards of this facility might be fake, but Ty needed them to distract the enemy, until he could get everything under control.

He kicked the door down and sprayed.

Roanoke hammered at the grate trying to bust it open. He heard the fighting and when he saw a truck wiz past; he worked more fervently. Finally the grate broke free. He turned to see the wall of team giving him room to hammer it down. Another went down, but they held strong, even pushed away from Roanoke a little.

Roanoke crouched, and put his head upside down through the gate. He looked in all directions. Enemy soldiers pounded away at Miller's team. He didn't see Miller or Philmore, but hoped they were alright. He saw black combat suits, jumping on top of trucks stopping them in their tracks; these men were stronger than normal humans. Roanoke then saw one in particular stronger than the rest. Shooting without abandon, purely hitting the team and none of the floating enemy soldiers; he moved with grace and style. He saw the man, in armor, crouch down. A team member shot at him, the bullets flying over his head. The super human, moved like no one Roanoke ever seen. He dodged all the automatic bullets, and when he turned, Roanoke realized the team member was good as dead. The super human walked up to the man strapping the automatic-duel weapons, he held to his suit. He grabbed the gun from the member's hand, threw it aside, and threw him against a truck's front windshield. The tracker's body broke the window instantly. The superhuman didn't stop there; he moved over to the truck dodging the bullets from the driver with his quick moves. He whipped out two sharp looking boomerangs and threw them. Both of them hit their targets, the driver shooting at him, and the man; he just threw through the window. They stuck into the back of the cab, but the super human held up both his hands, palm out and they came twisting back into his grasp instantly. Roanoke would definitely need a huge plan to take this guy down.

He pulled his head free from the ceiling crevice, and realized his team was all dead. Guns were aimed right at his face. Roanoke put his hands up, and surrendered. "Nice," he mumbled under his breath.

"Miller over here," Philmore motioned toward a side door. "It would help us get to the source of this charade. Maybe even find the murderer. Miller moved closer to the door, hoping to not direct attention to himself. He slid through the door with Philmore undetected.

"Alright," Detective Miller said. "Let's find this murderous kid, shall we." They had no idea; they were heading in the wrong direction. They moved through the corridor, to the end of it to that door. It was locked with a keycard. "Let's do it," Miller whispered. He shot the keycard reader. The door stayed stationary. Miller looked confused; he truly believed that would work. Both he and Philmore tried pushing the door open, but it wouldn't budge.

"Well," Philmore sighed, thinking and looking around. "There." He pointed to a heating shaft. "Might as well."

Sumiko sat in her room, with her headphones on, her head back against the pillow. She wouldn't have heard the shooting anyways, because it was in the basement of the facility. A knock came to her door, more forceful the second time. Finally it burst opened causing her to jump and turn. It was Noel.

"The facility is under attack," Noel told her.

"What do you mean under attack, what's going on?" Sumiko asked. "Where's Ty?" was her second question.

"Do you even care about him?" Noel asked completely out of the blue.

"Um…what are you talking about? I just asked where; he was. What's going on Noel?"

"Sumiko, I don't want you to hurt him anymore."

"Hurt him, what are you talking about, Noel? Where is Ty?"

"The facility is being invaded. Ty is down in the lower level garage fighting them off."

"Oh no, I have to get to him. I'll put on my suit." Sumiko jumped up from the bed and fiddled around with putting on her shoes.

"No," Noel simply said.

"No? What are you talking about Noel, I am trained. I must fight beside him to save the facility." Sumiko turned to face Noel, and her eyes nearly bulged out at her head. She heard the sound, but really didn't recognized that she was shot, until she looked down and saw the blood pouring from her lower abdomen.

Sumiko fell to the floor. "Why, Noel?" was all she gurgled as she closed her eyes. The last thing she saw was the end of the gun.

CHAPTER 11

I can't believe we're climbing through, a heating duct," Miller whispered to Philmore who was right behind him.

"I know this kid has got to be in here somewhere," Philmore whispered. "It just wouldn't make sense, with how he was taken though. I'm not sure if he's here on his own free will, or he was taken by force."

"Oh you mean, what Gerald Funk said on the road?" Miller turned his head while still crawling

"Yeah, something doesn't add up. We better find some answers soon." Philmore whispered.

The Detectives crawled through the heating duct as silently as they could, but it buckled in some points and made loud creasing noises in others. They still pressed on determined to find the suspect in three killings probably four they believed.

Noel looked at Sumiko's still body. She breathed heavily, and she didn't know why. The gun still smelled of fresh powder. She walked over to the body, and was about to pull the trigger one more time, but then she decided against it. She didn't see Sumiko's chest rise or fall, so she presumed her dead. She moved slowly out of the room, hoping no one heard the gun shot. More in likely with the activity in the basement, everyone was already down there anyways. She left the floor and moved downward to Bone's office. She had to make a phone call.

In a darkened, sub-basement in Tokyo, Japan, a girl's body laid on a table. Her stats flew through the roof as she convulsed violently.

A dark figure was sitting in a chair by a computer clicking around, when he heard the heart monitor speed up then weaken in brevity. He stopped his clicking and turned. He got up quickly and rushed over to the girl's body. Making sure all the connections were in the right places; he clicked at a computer near her head on a table beside. He brought up a machine checking the functionality of the brain chip; he placed inside her. Everything was working fine. He then clicked up another list of commands, which brought him a brief summary of what happened in the last few moments. His eyes nearly fell out of his head. His blood instantly boiled. He grabbed his phone.

The Good Doctor was sitting in his chair when his phone rang. Surprised at the number he answered it. "I take it everything is going as planned," he said, methodically.

"You did WHAT!" the Doctor gasped. "My dear child why would do such a thing. I do not have control over that particular soul as of this moment."

The Doctor paused as he listened to the weak explanation.

"You be ready, I'm brining you out of there." I will have to bring him out to. I've been watching the brief battle, and he's doing very well to my standards. I believe he's ready. The Illuminati are not going to be happy with what you've done my child. I am not happy with what you've done."

He paused as he listened.

"You can't fix it—." The interruption was uncanny, as the girl went on rambling.

"You listen here child," The Good Doctor cut in. I am the reason for this experiment, and now you have sped things along rapidly. I must adapt, and make changes. Be ready, I will bring you out shortly." The Doctor heard the beep and looked at his phone. He then placed it back up to his ear. "I have another call; you could guess who it is. Be ready, we will talk more of your treachery when I bring you out."

The Doctor clicked off of that phone call, and onto the other one. "Yes Takeo. What might I do for you this fine hour," the Doctor asked.

"You probably already know the reason for my calling. It would seem that you cannot keep your dogs under a leash. This will surely banish you forever from the sect," Takeo nearly yelled over the phone.

"My dear Takeo, why don't you take a look at what I'm sending you now?" The Good Doctor clicked on his computer to bring up the last few moments of footage of a camera in the basement. The footage showed Ty, dressed completely in his Kevlar combat suit, moving almost faster than the camera could allow the naked eye to see.

A few moments of silence then finally, "This proves nothing. Your betrayal—."

"I have not betrayed anyone. The girl was acting on her own free will. I will bring her out and deal with her accordingly. The footage shows our greatest weapon, moving as if he has been doing it for years. This is only the second time picking up the sword. Can you imagine what he can do, with the training from our sect of our finest warriors?"

"He is merely human." Takeo spat over the phone. I could crush him easily."

"Perhaps now, but perhaps not in a few weeks of solid training. He moves with the grace of one of our own. He is powerful than most I've seen. Don't you see Takeo; once we turn him, once he is a pure bread, there will be no stopping him."

Takeo nearly spat again. "You do not know, all that will be required in this ritual. The boy is useless in my mind."

"But not in the mind of your father. Not in the mind of me. I was given the responsibility to head this whole experiment, and everything is going as planned." The Good Doctor smiled, even knowing that it could not be seen by Takeo thousands of miles away.

"Not everything is going as planned. My weapon has internal bleeding, thanks to one of your dogs going awry."

"Do not refer to my children as dogs, a third time dear Brother or I will personally bite out your tongue for such blasphemy," The Good Doctor growled.

Takeo knew he had pressed his luck a little too far. "What do you suggest I do then, Brother!?"

The Good Doctor caught the prude way he said the last word, but he decided to offer his insight anyway. "Why don't you give her some of your blood?" The Doctor acted as if it was a simple solution.

"You mean turn her?" Takeo hissed at the thought.

"You have to do it anyways, might as well do it now. The main weapon is ready to be brought out. Turn the girl now while she is in need of it and get it over with."

Takeo pondered the issue. He looked at the girl still convulsing. She wouldn't last much longer, not in her normal human body.

Just like a bright light went off in Takeo's head he said, "Your weapon is nothing without his suit. What do you propose happens when he comes out and is merely a human?" Takeo thought he had the Doctor in a check mate.

"You let me worry about that when the time comes. You will know soon enough." The Good Doctor explained. The truth was; he did have an experimental plan that had never been done before. He was sure it would work. "You worry about your patient, err, I mean subject, and I will worry about mine. Give her your blood, Takeo. I've seen the damage. She needs it. If you don't turn her now, you will just have to do it later. It might as well be now while she needs it to live," he repeated. You know our bodies heal much faster than the humans. Do it now before it's too late. Her vitals have just dropped again."

Takeo turned toward his screens and watched as the girl's body convulsed less, now. She was weakening and would soon die. How would that look to his father if he turned the Subject early? Yet, if he let his subject die after two months of research, how would that also look? His one subject he was in charge of showed more promise than all the other subjects in the experiment other than the Doctor's prized boy. Yes he would have to give her his blood, to heal her and perhaps to make her stronger, than even the Good Doctor's prized experiment.

"I'll do it." Takeo hung up the phone.

The Good Doctor sat back in his chair with a perfectly satisfied grin.

Noel stopped when she left Bones' office. She had no idea where he was and frankly she didn't care at the moment. She heard a noise off to her side. Not her side, but rather above her, she then figured out. She looked up and cocked her head. The sound was moving through the ceiling. She followed it for about twenty feet until it stopped. She looked at the sound curiously. "Could it be that we have rats," she said to herself smiling evilly.

Noel took off running to the training area where the locker room was located. She quickly put on her suit, boots, mask, weapons—the works. She strapped her two Uzi's to her suit. Her suit was made just like Ty's, but formulated to fit her body in all its curves and contours.

Noel rushed out of the locker room, and ran to where she heard the sound. She heard nothing for a few moments, so she decided to walk a few extra feet where the sound seemed to be heading, and then she heard it. It was shuffling of some sort. Her weapon of choice was two duel adamantine whips that were made especially for her, thus the Doctor's orders. She unwound them from her waist and began swinging them side to side all around her in twirling motions. She whipped at the ceiling and took some of the plaster away. The smacking sound stopped the shuffling. "Come out, come out wherever you are," she said, tauntingly.

She whipped again and again, taking away more of the plaster. She saw a gaping hole in the ceiling, where a heating duct was about ten feet above her head. She swung those long whips again at the same time and took two clean lines out of the duct. She smiled when she heard a cry of agony, and saw blood dripping to the floor. She licked her top lip. "Gotcha," she smiled.

Noel swung the whips again and again taking out huge lines of the duct work, hearing screams of pain every so often. Finally in their dismay and because the duct was becoming weaker from the slashes; the two men tumbled out onto the floor, right on top of each other.

Noel couldn't tell who was bleeding more or from where. She bit her lower lip at the site. "Hello boys, so nice of you to drop in," she smiled then frowned at her own stupid choice of words.

Ty definitely moved with the grace of a Vampire especially for not being one. His duel katanas lashed out chopping everyone down in his path. He turned and dodged a bullet, just in time, then replaced both his swords. With both hands working in unison, he grabbed two throwing knives that were strapped to his chest, and threw them both hitting the unfortunate victim in the main artery of the neck taking him down instantly.

Then Ty remembered the marbles that Bones had given him. He

hadn't used them at all yet and was anxious to learn what they could do. He grabbed two of them, turned and clicked them in place with his fingers, and threw them in each direction. Three seconds and a very bright light splashed the room, causing the remaining few team to cringe at their eyes in pain. Ty moved with speed as he took out his two swords, and swept around the room slashing at the unfortunate victims, killing them before they hit the floor. His swords moved faster than anyone could have realized. Not that any of the targets could see their impending doom, because of the temporary blindness.

There was one man left. He was on his knees held, by two strong machine looking men, with power suits. "What should we do with him?" one of them asked Ty.

Ty looked at the man still cringing at the bright light, totally blinded for a few more minutes at least. Ty looked at his bloody swords, and was about to do a crisscross scissor slash, when he stopped. "Something's different about him," he noticed. "Take him to Bones; I want to see what he says." The two moved away as did the rest of the facilities powered human team.

Ty was left alone again looking at his bloody swords. So many emotions flowed through his brain right now; he wasn't sure what to think. His mind told him these men were not real; he just killed without abandon. Yet, part of his mind said that he shouldn't care either way. It was as if his conscience was being torn apart fighting with itself about a moral dilemma.

"They are only human," Ty found himself saying. He shivered at what he just said. Where would a thought like that come from? he thought. "I'm also human," he answered himself as if he needed to hear himself say it. He found a nearby body and wiped his dripping swords on their clothes, then replaced them and walked toward the door.

"Ty, where are you at?" It was Noel's voice, on the facilities' intercom system.

"I'm about to see Bones. I have a prisoner being sent in. I want to know about him," Ty answered.

"I have found some wondering rats myself. Bones is in the interrogation chamber. I'll meet you there."

"Wait, where is the interrogation chamber; I've never been there?" Ty quickly asked.

"I'm looking at you right now through a camera. You want to go straight through the door you are facing now, take a left down that hallway through the door straight ahead. It's the first door on the right after that. Any more questions love?" Noel quickly asked.

"What'd you call me?" Ty quizzed. Ty couldn't help, but notice a change in the voice vibrations of Noel.

"Nothing," came the reply.

"Wait. Where's Sumiko? I figured she would be down here, fighting?"

"Ty, there's been an accident involving the rats I've found. I'll tell you more, when you get here." Ty heard muffled moans in the background. Deep down he hoped Sumiko was okay.

Ty walked out of the basement-garage area, and left the dead bodies of the team members behind. He followed Noel's directions to the letter, and quickly opened the door to the Interrogation Room; or rather it opened for him when he got to it.

Ty walked inside and saw Bones, and Noel. He saw the two powered human soldiers that he told to take the man in the blazer suit coat, and two men battered and bloody laying at Noel's feet. The room was large, and wasn't like a traditional police style interrogation room. It was surrounded by thick concrete walls with no windows or mirrors. It had no furniture, just a drain in the middle of the floor that was getting its use, considering the two bleeding men were draped over it.

"Well it seems your guy looks a bit better than mine," Noel smiled a more evil grin than anything Ty had ever seen from her.

"Where's Sumiko?" Ty asked again mostly staring at Noel's prisoners, than at Noel.

"This one killed her," Noel answered, pushing Miller to his face in front of Ty's feet.

Ty bent low and picked him up by his hair. "You killed her?" he whispered, so that no one in the room could barely hear except the man he was talking to.

"I don't know what you're talking about. You're the killer here," Miller grunted as bold as he could, considering the beating he took from the whips.

Ty became angry. He shoved Miller's face into the ground over and over, until Bones stepped in. "TY!" he shouted to get his attention.

Ty stopped.

"There is something wrong with this picture," Bone's quickly exclaimed.

"What are you talking about," Ty said, looking up from his crouched position, glaring at Bones.

"Something doesn't quite add up. I found Sumiko in her room with a gunshot wound to her stomach. These men were running through the heating ducts, not even close to her room. There isn't any way they killed her." Bones continued before Ty could cut him off. "Plus there's something peculiar from these men. With your suit equipped, can you not feel it?" he offered emphasis to get the point across.

Ty looked down at the man. He did feel something different. He couldn't quite place what it was, but his pulse did seem stronger. He dropped the man's head and walked over to his prisoner. His pulse felt stronger too. Ty walked over to the other bleeding man, his pulse felt strong also. He looked at his two guards, still holding the prisoner. Their pulse, Ty could still feel, but not near as strong.

He looked at Noel, "What did you do with her?" he asked.

"What are you talking—?"

"I will ask it once more, and I assure you only once. We both know I could kill you without a moment notice before you could even blink. What did you do with Sumiko?" Ty began walking over to Noel.

Noel backed up, and yelled something in a foreign language; he couldn't understand. Before Ty could get to her to even grab her, her body hit the floor. Ty cocked his head and bent down to feel her pulse, but he didn't need to. She was dead.

CHAPTER 12

Her eyes embraced the darkness as soon as they opened. The flashing lights above her were not welcoming, however. Noel blinked away the spots they left behind on her retinas. She got up and immediately fell back onto the cold table. Tubes and wires were going in and out of her body from her head to her legs. She rolled her eyes, and began pulling them out one by one. Her puncture wounds healed instantly. She slid off the table and onto the floor. Noel was only wearing a skimpy night gown. She looked down at her nearly exposed body. "Oh this will not do," she said to herself.

Noel wondered the darkened-flickering hallways holding her hand up to her face as if she was blocking out a bright light or the sun. She felt dizzy all of a sudden and suddenly realized how long it had been since she fed. She didn't really know how long she was in that program. She felt her head and part of her hair was missing on her temple. She felt the stitches, and knew that was where the Doctor had put the chip. She moved in and out of hallways searching for the Doctor. She thought to call out, but ruled against it. The dizziness was getting stronger. She put her hand up against a nearby wall to steady herself, and held her other hand to rub her forehead. "Doc..." that was all she could mutter before falling from the exhaustion.

Ty stared at the empty "dead" shell of Noel. He took off his mask, which let out a grunt from Miller, and a noise from Philmore and Roanoke who had seen pictures. Ty looked at all of them and gave them a look to shut them all up. He had no idea what just happened with Noel. He didn't even touch her, and she fell over completely gone from this world. He studied her face and body for a moment trying to decipher the enigma of it all.

Suddenly he heard Bones' voice. "Ty we shouldn't kill the prisoners."

Ty barely noticed anyone was talking to him let alone what Bones' said. "What?" he muttered.

"We cannot kill the prisoners. They're human." Bones reiterated a little louder and clearer.

Ty looked up and then looked at the three men. He knelt down to Miller's body lying, bleeding on the interrogation room's floor. "If this one makes it through the night, it will be a miracle in itself," Ty said.

"We have doctors that might be able to help in the facility," Bones emphasized.

"They are not real; they won't be able to heal these men."

"They took care of your finger," Bones reminded.

"You said my finger may not even be gone in the real world, so why would it hurt me in this fake dream world?" Ty rebutted.

Bones was quiet for a minute. He paced around the room. "We have to get out of here then. We have to find the Doctor. He'll know what to do."

"Okay. I'll agree that we have to get out of here. I am getting sick of all this false dream state crap that I don't need, but I don't even know if we can trust this Doctor. Someone's been messing with my head on the other side, and I want to find out who and why." Ty continued, "You say I am supposed to be this assassin. You feed me a nifty story. Then you say I'm supposed to kill vampires." Ty made sure that

Bones was looking at him when he said, "Since when do vampires even exist. It's urban legend. Have you ever seen a vampire?"

Bones looked down at the floor. "No I haven't," he sincerely answered.

"See," Ty said. "You say that I'm supposed to kill these vamps, but who am I to say that someone isn't trying to brain wash me into thinking that some government official is a vampire, and I kill him?" Ty stood up. "Like I said, someone's been messing with my head all along. If you hadn't set me straight when you did, then I would still be in the dark. What we need to do is get out of this dream world and get to the real one so I can find some answers, namely where I really come from." Ty was ranting he knew, but he was angry with the predicament. He was angry he didn't have a chance to kill Noel before she died, or left, or whatever she did to make herself non-existent in this world. Ty breathed out a long breath.

"Everywhere where there's a camera we can be seen, by him." Bones lowered his voice in a whisper. There are no cameras in this room, but there is in my office."

"Why would we want to go to your office?" Ty simply asked.

"Because that is where the only phone in the facility is that I can keep in touch with the Doctor. If I somehow could hook it up to my computer, I might be able to create a short window of opportunity that we could wake out of this dream state. We could all get out."

"I really hate to pipe in here, when you all seem to be brainstorming," Roanoke started.

Both Bones and Ty looked at him, forgetting that he was the only one of the human invaders that didn't get hurt. "What do you got to say?" Ty asked bluntly.

"Well for starters, I would like to know what's going on. I've lived in this world my whole life. I had three wives and four kids in my lifetime. There is no way I am living in a disillusioned false world. This is the real world. I'm afraid you all are going to be under arrest."

Ty looked back at Bones, then at Roanoke. Ty cocked his head and lowered his brow as if trying to comprehend all that was said. Not only was the man on his knees held by two very strong super humans in full battle gear, but he was disillusioned as to what was going on, as he himself put it.

Ty pointed at the two guards, and looked at Roanoke. "Do you understand that, you are in no place to be giving orders to anyone?"

Ty knelt down so he was eye level with the man on his knees. "Do you understand . . ." Ty paused as if wanting an answer and his name.

"My name is Seymour Roanoke, and yes I understand where I am, but you must understand that you killed people."

Ty stood up. "This is true I have killed people. Some of them real some of them not, I suppose. Tell me Seymour Roanoke, but do know that you are probably laying somewhere on a cold hard table with wires hooked up to your head and some chip in your brain made to think that this beautiful world you live in is real?"

"One this world is not beautiful as long as people like you are in it, and two it has never crossed my mind. This is all I know. I know that that you need psychiatric help. If you let me go, I could get you the professional help you need."

Ty simply became angry at the last comment. He kicked Roanoke hard in the face.

"Ty!" Bones shouted.

Ty turned. "Hey he asked for it. Do we have to take these rats with us?" Using the term Noel used for the men just seemed fitting at the moment.

"Ty I once believed that this experiment was worthy. That I was going to get a lump sum of money at the end. I don't even know if that is going to happen anymore to be honest." Bones walked around while he talked. "The thing is that killing is wrong. It's against the law in this world and in the other world. These men are human, and leaving them here would kill them."

"They could go on with their lives," Ty put in.

"No. If there isn't anyone overseeing the experiment, their life source in the real world will not be. Something could go wrong with the wiring. They're being fed through tubes. Something could and more definitely will happen if we leave them here."

It was Ty's turn to pace around the room. "I see your point, but I really don't like them very much."

"Ty it is more in likely a fair chance, these men are cops in the real world. They were picked because of their instinct. They went after you, a killer, because it was what they had been trained to do." Bones followed the pacing Ty with his eyes as he spoke.

Ty stopped, and looked back at the men. They all were bleeding now, because he was almost certain, he broke Roanoke's nose with the kick.

Ty turned back to Bones, and said. "Let's do it."

Noel woke up a second time in the hour, this time a little confused at where she was at. Her hands were handcuffed to a wall handrail in one of the rooms. She almost preferred the blinking strobes. This room was completely dark. Despite her having loved the darkness, her predicament left her feeling dismayed. She usually could break handcuffs, but she was weakened by her lack of feeding for the last few weeks. The Doctor has only given her drops of blood in her IV.

Speaking of which; he opened the door to her room. "Hello, my dear child. I do hope you feel alright." If the Doctor was looking or could be able to have seen it, he would have seen a darkened scow on Noel's face.

"Why are you doing this?" she demanded.

"Why?" the Doctor repeated. "Why you ask? Because my dear child, you neglected your responsibilities. You left your love for this human to stand in the way of your duty."

"But you were going to turn him."

"Are going to turn him," the Good Doctor corrected. He paced back and forth as if teaching a class. "You see my dear child; you are being punished for your transgressions. You are being chastised from your evil doings."

Noel was speechless. The Doctor continued, "Your life is forfeit."

"NO!" Noel cried. "I can fix it."

"Fix it you say?" The Good Doctor was toying with her. "Oh yes, you will fix your mistakes. That, my dear child, has already been set into motion."

"Well can you undo these locks? I need sustenance. Just a drink of blood to do this task," she pleaded.

The Doctor laughed and hissed. "You will have no blood until the end of your duty. Your weakened state will be a reminder to you of what you've done." The Doctor walked up to Noel and bent low so his face was six inches from hers. "You will be weak, when Ty finds you and whatever clan he brings with him. You will be weak, when Ty looks for Sumiko."

Noel started to protest, when she heard Sumiko's name, but a slap reminded her of whom she was. "You will be weak when you stay with him, watching his every move. There is more training. Your anger you build for me, will only fuel his own fire. I need you Noel." The Good Doctor stroked her cheek with the back of his hand. "I need you to do this. When it is all done, you will get your sustenance, but not a moment sooner than that."

The Doctor slammed the door on his way out. Noel pushed the thoughts of feeding on any human she came into contact with until he was gone. She knew that he could read thoughts of vampires if he was in the same room, but doubted he could after he left. She struggled for a moment, but that soon faded and she lay in a heap on the cold floor. She felt a chill bite her spine. She usually didn't feel the cold, but with her lack of feeding and her task before her, she felt it more now than ever. Noel shivered, her bottom lip started to quiver. Her eyes flicked this way then that in the darkness. In that same pitch blackness of the room, Noel started to cry.

Ty and Bones led the way to Bones' office. Ty had a hold of the scruff of Roanoke's collar and dragged him along. The two super human's dragged Miller, and Philmore along behind. Bones opened the door and was the first inside. He knew that there were two cameras in his office and had no idea if anyone was sitting at the monitors or not, so he had to be careful. Bones sat down at his desk and quickly opened his drawer. He grabbed a small screwdriver, and started unscrewing some of the screws underneath his laptop. He worked fervently, until he had them all out and pried it off. He then took a different screwdriver, and took the cover off his phone. He then grabbed a pair of pliers and began pulling some wires out of the Mother board of his computer and did the same with the phone, pulling wires apart exposing the copper. His face showed sheer determination. He took the wires from both, and began twisting them together. Bones then powered on his computer, and opened a black screen in which he fed it commands. The computer would pause at times, and then give Bones the knowledge that he needed as he quickly typed and clicked.

Ty waited patiently, and the three men just lay in heaps on the floor, awaiting their impending doom.

All of a sudden, Bones stopped. "What is it?" Ty asked, looking over his desk.

"This is weird." Bones said, looking baffled at his computer. I have learned a lot since living in this world, and have hacked this computer so many times, yet I never saw this command before."

"You're talking to someone who flunked out of computer class," Ty stopped. "Well at least in this fantasy world," he finished.

Bones just kept looking at his laptop. "This should work, but that command is foreign to me. It wasn't there before. I've looked at this option many times, just in case the Good Doctor wouldn't let me out. I know this wasn't here before. I've been over this computer. It didn't exist."

"Well, let's keep going with it," Ty advised. "I want to get out of this world and into a real one; where I have control over my thoughts and memories."

"Right, Just a few more seconds," Bones said as he told the computer what he wanted to do. "There. Pick up the phone, and it should work."

"Just pick up the phone?" Ty asked.

"Just pick up the phone," Bones repeated.

Ty looked curiously at the phone then at Bones. "Alright." He took a step toward the phone on Bones' desk. Instantly when he picked it up he collapsed to the floor.

Bones felt for a pulse, but didn't feel a thing. "Let's hope that worked," he said to no one in particular.

Ty awoke with a start. His mind felt like it was flooding with information. It felt as if someone had filled it with thousands and thousands of images, and then started playing them all in front of his eyes. One by one every split second was a new image. Ty cringed and closed his eyes, but they were still there. Finally after a few long seconds, they stopped.

Ty opened his eyes in disbelief gasping for air, and holding onto whatever he could find. His mind felt new; it felt fresh. He wasn't sure where he was, but he could tell this must be the real world, because the dreaming sensation left him. He felt the chill of the room as real as day. It was night.

Ty sat up, and immediately was jerked down by the wires and

tubes going in and out of his head and body. He took them out slowly, feeling each one exit his body. It took all he could, not to scream out in agony.

After Ty was done with that ordeal, he remembered to look at his left hand. He was horrified at the site. He thought the real world would leave him with his real digit because he felt no pain, but his finger was still missing. It left ring finger was completely gone. He screamed out in anger. He felt no pain, but still the missing finger greatly angered Ty. He was dead set on finding out who done this to him.

He got up from his bed, and once he stood all the blood rushed to his feet. The overload, made him stumble and knock over a tray of crude looking tools. A drill that was still plugged in fell to the floor beside him. Ty felt the left side of his temple, and sure enough there was a sown hole there. "What did you do to me?" he muttered under his breath. Ty felt his face, and felt about a week's worth of growth. He shook his head. "I will find some answers," he said quietly to himself.

He ventured out of the room, and into the flickering hallway. When the breeze nearly took his gown, from him he realized what he was wearing. He had to get more clothes. His head throbbed loudly in his ears with each step that he took on the cold floor. He moved slowly holding onto the wall as he went. He almost stumbled a few times, but he was determined to find some answers from someone. Most of the rooms were boarded up, and Ty knew he didn't have the strength to pry the boards free.

Ty fell to the floor right in front of a room that was not boarded up. He let himself rest there a bit face down on the cold floor. His body became numb from walking in his bare feet. He heard a tiny whimper coming from the other side of the door, which made him sit up quickly, as quickly as his body would allow. He listened on the other side of the door, and it was definitely short soft sobs.

Ty opened the door quickly to surprise the person from the other side. He was in no mood for a battle at this moment. He could barely see in the darkened room, so he grabbed a hold of the wall to help himself up. He felt for a light switch, and when he finally found one, it did no good anyways. It didn't work at all.

"Who's there?" came a voice from inside the room.

"Who's that?" Ty answered the question with another question.

"Ty, is that you?" the voice asked.

"Noel." Ty's voice dropped knowing exactly who it was. "So you're not dead," Ty noticed trying to feel his way around the room; trying to find out where the voice was coming from.

"No," Noel answered in the darkness of the room. "This is obviously no dream. This is the here and now, the real world."

Ty finally figured out where she was. "So then I can kill you now… for good," he said grabbing a small piece of piping nearby, with absolutely no remorse in his voice.

CHAPTER 13

Sumiko awoke with a gasp. She breathed heavily for a few seconds, unsure exactly what had happened. Her skin hurt as if it was on fire. Her whole body ached with a pain she had never known before. She could feel something hot traveling through her body, burning her inside. The pain made her cry out.

A man quickly got up from his desk, spinning the chair out of the way. He rushed to her to hold her down as she tried to squirm and get up. "No, you must rest!" Takeo forcefully said. "You have had quite an ordeal, please rest."

After a few moments of calming; she finally settled down, and began to breathe slower. She had a slight pain in her stomach that she could feel above the rest of her aching—on fire body. She then remembered the gun, and quickly fought against Takeo's hands pushing them away so she could look at her stomach. It wasn't bleeding at all. She lifted the sheet and sifted through the layers of gown, she had on, but there was absolutely nothing.

Takeo knowing what she was going through her mind quickly explained, "You were bleeding internally for a while, but I believe it stopped."

She turned to him. "What do you mean I was bleeding internally?

What just happened to me?" she asked demandingly.

"I know you were shot," Takeo said. "I thought you were going to die, so I inserted something into your IV, to take the edge off. It was either that or you would die."

Sumiko lied back on her pillow. She noticed a lot of wires, and the IV running to her forearm vein. She followed that tube to the IV bag. "What did you put in the IV," she asked.

"What do you remember?" Takeo took her question and asked another.

"I remember getting shot," she bluntly said, breathing deeply at certain points because of the pain her body was going through. "Can you give me something for the pain? Are you a doctor?"

"I am in a way; but there is nothing I can give you for the pain. There is no amount of medication that can take that pain away," Takeo replied.

"What do you mean?" Sumiko asked. "Certainly you can find something for the pain, morphine anything. What is happening to my body? It can't hurt all over if I got shot. Why is there no outside wound? I know I was shot."

"Do you remember who shot you?" Takeo calmingly questioned.

Sumiko tried to remember, but couldn't. Her memories from the last few months were all a blur from what she could tell. She remembered the room she was in, and the gun going off, but nothing at the moment around that. "No, I cannot," she finally said, grunting at another attack of heat coursing through her body. "What is happening to me?"

"Do you remember what happened before two months ago?" Takeo asked.

Sumiko thought through the pain. She breathed heavily. "I remember walking home from my grandfather's store and getting mugged. Then I remember waking up in a nice place I didn't know. I remember a guy looking at me over my bed; it wasn't you though;

it wasn't this room either." Sumiko looked around. She was in some kind of sub-basement of a building. Everything looked sanitary enough and professional as if she was in a real hospital, although she figured she wasn't. Takeo said he was a doctor, but didn't really look like the doctor type.

"Do you remember a girl name Noel?" Takeo pressed.

"I told you I . . ." Sumiko paused. "Wait," she said, trying to think. She took a few seconds. "I do remember a girl named Noel. She hated me. She hated me because . . ." Sumiko grunted the coursing heat pain away again. "She hated me because of a boy. He was younger than me. His name started with a T," she said.

"Good. You are remembering certain points this is good."

"What's your name?" Sumiko asked staring up at Takeo.

"It's Takeo," he said.

"It wasn't you."

This drew a slight chuckle from Takeo. "It certainly was not," he said.

"You're Japanese then, like me."

Takeo laughed aloud now. "I am like you in more ways than you think now. Do you mind if I fill in some blanks for you?" he asked, leaning over her bed.

"Please, do. With this pain, I really don't want to go anywhere right now."

"You'll probably have that pain for the next twenty-four hours or so, then it will dissipate and you will be changed forever."

Sumiko laughed, although it wasn't really a laughing matter. "Twenty-four hours or so? My life will be changed? How do you know so much about what is going on with my body and you can't give me anything to take away the pain," she questioned.

"Because what you have isn't a disease. It's a necessary process."

"A process of what?"

"Sumiko, are you familiar with kyuuketsuki?" Takeo asked, referring to the Japanese word for Vampire.

"Vampires!" she chuckled. "Yeah, in books and movies. Urban legends and all that."

Takeo moved away from her bed and sighed. "Well it's a little too late for urban legends now," he mumbled under his breath.

"Excuse me what?" Sumiko asked, grunting away another heated attack.

"Sumiko, do you remember a man named Bones?"

Sumiko thought for a moment then answered suddenly, "Yeah, I do. He was the one who was in charge of the men that rescued me from the muggers. Yeah, he trained me to fight, and all that. Do you know him?"

"Indirectly, yes." Takeo said. "Tell you what, how bout I tell you a little bit about what happened with you in the last two months, and you keep an open mind. Okay?"

Sumiko lowered her eye brows a bit confused at what Takeo was about to say, but she agreed.

"You see," Takeo began. "After you were mugged, I found you in an alley bleeding, nearly dying."

"Okay, but I don't remember—."

"Open mind, please," Takeo reminded.

"Alright, go on."

"I thought you were a vampire believe it or not, so I took you back here"

"Okay, why would think I was a vampire, because they don't exist."

Takeo shot her a look, and she stopped. "Open mind right," she said as a reminder for herself.

"After I ran tests on your blood; I quickly learned that you were human. So I had a dilemma. One I have never been wrong about telling between a human and vampire before. There was something different about you."

"I bet you say that to all the girls lying in your hospital room, thing," she laughed.

Takeo ignored the comment and continued. "I didn't know what to do with you. So I consulted with my father on this issue. He was very grieved to find out that I brought a human to the underground lab."

"Wait, wait, wait, wait, wait," Sumiko quickly cut in. "Who is your father?"

"You will know in time."

"Second you keep referring to me as human, which would make me think that you are not that."

"Neither are you anymore," Takeo bluntly said, because he saw his story, of what happened, not sinking in.

"Then what am I?" Sumiko asked playing along.

"You are at the beginning stages of the next phase in evolution." Takeo looked deep into her eyes. "You will know for sure of your power and what you are by this time tomorrow."

"What now?" Sumiko still couldn't believe any of it.

"Do you remember Bones' story about Omar Has'sir?" Takeo asked, trying to take a different approach.

"Yeah, of course I do. That's the whole explanation why I've lost my finger." Sumiko held up her left hand, ring finger gone of course.

"That marks you as an assassin. Your finger is gone because it denotes that you belong to our clan and our cause."

"Yeah, okay that isn't what Bones said, unless you mean the clan of assassins."

"Your friend Bones, doesn't know the whole story. He only knew what we told him. Allow me to explain."

Sumiko put a hand behind her head, merely to get comfortable, but it looked like a sarcastic gesture as if she was going to be here awhile listening to ramblings.

Takeo ignored the gesture and told her the true story of Omar Has'sir. "Omar Has'sir did live as a farmer's son on the outside of Geopolo around 45 A.D. Omar wrote a journal of what happened to himself all through his life, as a boy. This diary is dated back to this time period. When we found it buried deep underground in his tomb many years ago, we knew that this man had to be the father of us all."

Sumiko kept quiet and listened not sure what to think. Takeo's sincerity took her by surprise, but vampires were hard to fathom.

Takeo continued, "Omar didn't document, how he became a vampire, however. This we are not sure. There were a few pages, ripped out in the very beginning of his journal that we are still looking for.

There was no interruption from the girl, so Takeo continued without delay, "Omar became irritated with farm work all of a sudden. The bright hot sun of India made his skin very sensitive. He couldn't think straight. Suddenly he grew very pale and sick. His parents called the local doctor, and he said he was poisoned and wouldn't live long. His family took him to the local church. They told them that Omar was unclean and full of demons. So his family banished him from their home at the age of sixteen. He moved toward the city, but he didn't look like everyone one else. His skin was pale as snow and his hair as black at night. He had to steal to stay alive."

Sumiko listened more intently now. This was not Bones' version, but it definitely was an interesting one.

"Omar's body began to change as the time went on. Normal food as a human would eat, didn't sustain him. He began to have an uncontrollable thirst, and at night he would go looking for anything to satisfy it. A few months later and close to death, unable to keep anything down, out of anger and resentment toward society and his parents; he attacked one of the sheep on their farm. He bathed in the blood, and when some got into his mouth and slid down his throat, he said his stomach leaped for joy in his journal.

"Omar drank until he was full. Then his father came out with a sling shot to ward off the attacker. Omar says in his journal that his father's eyes grew incredibly large at the site of him. Omar was a monster. He was a ravishing monster unable to control his urges or his monstrous appearance. Fearing for his life, and not wanting his family to see him like this he ran off.

"Omar came upon a brook not too far away, and when he looked at his appearance he nearly fell over unto death. His whole appearance had changed. At the age of twenty, he looked like he was fifty. His hair was long and unkempt. It was black as night. His face filled with wrinkles. Omar lived in the wilderness for five more years, learning to control these urges. He fed off of the nearby animals, mostly attacking wild animals and not getting to nearer to the farms around the area.

"Omar knew there had to be more like him, so he ventured into the city one night and went to a local tavern. He stayed in the corner of the bar bringing a jug made out of skins, filled with blood, to sustain him so as to not grab a drink and get sick. He stayed all through the night.

"Then after a few nights of his observations, a fight broke out. Omar Has'sir sat in the corner trying to avoid it at all costs, yet it swung his way. He took a few punches, but felt no pain. This intrigued Omar, so he began to swing. His hands grew claws in an instance, and his fangs became longer. He scratched at one patron drawing blood. When he smelled the sweet scent of the blood of a human, he attacked without abandon. He bit and scratched anyone, he could find. In a matter of minutes the fight was over, the only one standing was Omar. Shocked and dismayed at what he had done, he ran from the bar frightened. He didn't mean to kill all those people.

"But Omar didn't kill all those people. On the eve of the next morning, they came back to life. Their thirst for blood was irrefutable. Most of them was caught and hung. The ones that did escape ran toward the forest.

"Soon they caught up with Omar, having no recollection of his turning them. They were confused at their new found power and thirst. Omar became their leader and their savior all at the same time. They built homes in the forest, only venturing into the city at night to feed. Omar realized soon that this was too risky, so he set up rules, a ten commandments of the vampires, if you will.

"They would only feed to satisfy themselves. They chose who they wanted to kill. They went after the evil men of the city. In order to sustain humanity from the animalistic vampires, they had to follows these rules. The ones that did not were killed. You see Sumiko; we have come descended from Omar Has'sir. Although he is our father, vampires have evolved into what they are today. Most have full control."

"Unfortunately for Omar, another leader rose to power. He became jealous of Omar's exploits, and began his thirst of power. At first Has'sir rebuked the vampire, calling him out of the group. He banished him finally and the man left the group to hide in the forest. A few years later, he returned with a rather large army. Omar wrote in his journal that they descended from the trees with the wings of birds and the teeth of lions. They were the next phase of evolution."

Sumiko shifted to her side, and squinted away another heated attack. She listened intently to the whole story.

"This man was called Sargon. He was the leader of a group called the night ravens. He is my father."

Sumiko's eyes nearly tumbled out of her skull, had she opened her lids any more. "He's you're . . ." she stammered.

"You'll know more about that in time. For now you need to rest."

Sumiko blinked a few times, not really comprehending everything that Takeo just told her.

"I know you may not believe me. I don't even know why I told you the story; I guess I thought you should know. You see Sumiko; I had to inject you with my blood in order for you to live because you have a gift that I have not seen in any human before you. The burning is my blood making its way through your veins. As soon as it has run its course, the thirst will begin. I will teach you how to control it, and to not make yourself known. It is for the betterment of our people." Takeo put his head down expecting feedback and sarcasm.

Sumiko said nothing for a few moments. She stared at Takeo, then at the ceiling. She didn't know what to think about his story or about anything. Her body felt as if it was being ripped apart, but if Takeo was right, it would end within the next day. She looked back at Takeo and said, "I need time to rest I guess then."

This brought a great smile to Takeo's face. "You do just that." He was satisfied that his story hit home.

He left the room and gently closed the door.

"Yeah, I'll do just that on my own, weirdo," Sumiko mumbled under her breath as she pulled the IV free from her arm. She looked at the door. "Forget you, I'm out of here."

"NO, TY PLEASE NO!" Noel screamed. It was all she had left.

Ty stopped in mid swing of the copper piping to hear her cries.

"Please," she cried realizing that she had his attention and she wasn't dead yet. "I didn't mean to kill Sumiko. I was under some sort of spell. It was as if someone was controlling my thoughts," she quickly got out.

When Ty heard those words, he lowered the pipe. "What do you mean?" Ty questioned.

"I don't know. It was like someone told me to do it. I couldn't stop. I honestly didn't want to. She is such a nice girl."

Ty noticed the word "is" in her sentence. "What do you mean is? Sumiko is dead," he said.

"I think she is alive," Noel started. She was gasping for air at this point. "I'm sorry, I'm tired." She continued, "When I came out of here, a man I was working with, called the Good Doctor, found me."

"The Good Doctor?" Ty repeated.

"Yeah, he was working on the experiment that put you in the program. He put me in there too. I was supposed to monitor you, but when I got out he turned against me. He said that I failed my mission, because I started to fall in love with you. I shouldn't have; I know that now. So he made me do things that I didn't want to do. I know you love Sumiko, but he made me hurt you like that so there was no way you could even begin to love me." Noel began to cry.

The words "love" were strong for Ty to fathom. He wasn't sure what to think of everything. He dropped the piping and leaned up against a nearby table before he fell. "You love me?" he gasped with short breaths.

"I do." Noel looked up at Ty in mid sobs. "I really do. You're not like anyone I've ever met. I am so sorry." She buried her face in her hands and sobbed loudly.

"What about Sumiko?" he asked. "Is she still alive?"

"The Doctor said that she was before he cuffed me to this rail. He knew that you would find a way out of the program soon, and would kill me. He said that was punishment for my transgressions."

These words stung Ty greatly. All his life evidently he had been a killer, taking from society things that he thought he needed. It had been in his life the whole time. It even followed him into his fantasy world that was created for him. If he hadn't dropped the pipe before; he definitely would have then. He was truly sorry for the killing of everyone; he had ever come across. Ty had no idea who that was however. His life was mashed up with memories from the fake world. He could hardly remember anything from his real life. He was in the program too long.

He grabbed the piping again. Noel cringed, and pulled away. "Don't worry," he said. "I am not going to kill you. I'm going to try to pry the handcuffs free."

She held her hands apart as best she could, and looked away. Ty jammed the pipe to the cuffs. Thanks to that and the cold air, they broke after a few seconds of hard pounding. After he realized her hands were free, he collapsed on the floor from exhaustion.

"Oh Ty," Noel slid over to him. She held him close and sincerely cried. She closed her eyes and pulled his head against her breasts, and kissed the back of his head. She opened her eyes, and saw the back of his neck.

Her mouth was very dry. She hadn't fed for a while.

CHAPTER 14

The Good Doctor was driven to the Illuminati castle gate, a little after midnight, in Dublin, Ireland. The gate opened a few moments later, and the limousine drove up the long driveway to the main door. Along the way, the Good Doctor remembered the huge statues of various abstract characters and gargoyles. "It's good to be home," he muttered to himself with a sly smile. The driveway cut off, around a large fountain with a statuette of a beautiful female vampire atop it. With water coming out of her mouth, the site was gorgeous to be hold. The driver stopped and the Good Doctor got out of the car.

He didn't wear the lab coat as he had worn for so many years. He looked better for the wear. He looked younger, more vibrant. He wore a long silk trench coat. It was black as coal on the outside, and red as blood on the inner lining. It flowed as he walked to the door, as a cape would.

The Good Doctor walked up to the door, and despite the house looking historic, it had a state of the art security system. The Doctor pressed his finger to the door bell, but unlike regular door bells this one's needle pricked his finger drawing blood. The high-tech computer system read The Good Doctor's DNA through his blood and opened automatically.

The Doctor walked through the main foyer and the dining hall licking the prick on his finger. Vampires mingled about in their finest attire; all staring at the veteran Illuminati member. The Doctor made his way into the Illuminati meeting chamber. Entering the chamber, the Good Doctor saw the twelve of the thirteen Illuminati sitting around the large rectangular table. They all wore the same silk robes as was worn by the Vampire Illuminati. These were the most powerful men of the vampire race. No matter if someone was a vampire for a week or born a vampire. They knew to respect the Illuminati.

"I see you are well," one of the Illuminati, named Magnus, greeted the Good Doctor. They all stood as was the custom when a member came back from a trip or a long time away from the house. They were again the complete thirteen.

"Indeed Magnus. I am feeling very spry these days," the Good Doctor greeted.

"Join us around the table and tell us of your experiment. How goes it?" Magnus questioned.

The Good Doctor ascended the four steps where the table rested and joined the others. They all sat down together. "This has been a trying four years," the Doctor started. "So many experiments, so many flaws."

The Vampire Illuminati put their heads down in a grim response.

"Yet, we have found a warrior among them. A boy by the name of Ty Livingston," the Doctor continued.

"Where is he? You have not brought him with you. Let us see this new found warrior you have bred for us," a man by the name Dakhanavar said.

The Good Doctor looked at Dakhanavar and expressed, "the boy is not yet through with his training session."

"He is still in the program?" a vampire by the name Lazarus asked.

"No," the Good Doctor replied calmly. "He is in this world. His training was cut short by my other experiments; so I figure it best to fully train him on this plain." The Good Doctor looked around the table. "Not to worry gentleman, by the time he makes it to our doorstep, his training will be complete."

"How do you know he is the one? What if he fails," an Illuminati vampire sitting to the Doctors left, by the name Jacob asked.

"Trust me he is the one," the Good Doctor simply smiled. "Trust me."

Noel fought back the urge. She could feel Ty's pulse through his neck as he lay close to her chest. She had full view of the back of the neck, and her vampire senses brought his veins to the surface. She began kissing him softly at first, then more rapidly—more passionately. She sucked on the surface of the back of his neck without abandon. Ty looked up, and their lips immediately attached in a kiss of passion. He cupped his hand around her face, and she pulled him closer than he even was before. Tongues moved in and out, sliding delicately with each other as their kissed progressed.

Ty pulled apart first. "I'm sorry," he started.

"No I'm sorry, I shouldn't have . . ." Noel really couldn't find the words to say.

Their eyes locked for a moment. So much had happened to them both in the last few hours that they didn't know whether this random kiss was because of the memories that were flooding their minds, or if it was because they really did care for each other.

Noel never kissed a human before. It was odd for her, especially with her being so thirsty. She could practically taste Ty's blood through his lips, but refrained from biting. She had never been that close to a human and so thirsty for sustenance and still reframed.

Ty wasn't sure what he thought. He loved Sumiko, or the memory of her, but now he didn't know if that was pre-ordained memories put into his head to tell him what to feel, or if it was real. He knew now that he was in the real world. The feelings the emotions—the pain was all so real. It was fresh. Even the pleasure he felt from that long succulent kiss, was all so real. More real than anything he could have remembered. There was something different about Noel, though he couldn't quite put his finger on it. In all her vulnerability, in all her beauty, there was something underneath; he just couldn't quite grasp.

"We should probably get going," Ty finally said to break the awkward silence. He could tell that Noel was pondering the last few moments in her head also.

"Right," she said. "Where should we go?"

"I'm not sure. I want to find this Doctor character. We should look for Sumiko."

Ty's sudden use of the word "we", told Noel that she may have won a part of his heart over. She wasn't sure of her feelings exactly right now. She pushed all the emotions aside.

"Yeah," she said. "We should find some clothes to wear. I think we're somewhere in Siberia right now, during the winter of course. You're probably cold."

Ty chuckled a bit. "I'm probably cold. You have on about the same amount of clothes as I do. You're probably cold too." They grabbed each other and helped the other up. They walked out of the dark room, holding each other for warmth, and because they both weren't quite steady on their legs yet.

They walked down the long flickering hallway of the creepy hospital. Most of the rooms were boarded up, so they just passed them on. They walked through double doors—the doors that were still in place, and moved on through looking for any type of blanket or clothing they could put around themselves.

Finally on the same floor, they saw a room giving off an uncanny amount of light. The lights flickered, but not as much as the hallway. They moved toward the room. They immediately saw a lap top set up on a table in the center of the room. Also on the table, were clothes to fit Ty and Noel on separate folded piles. The duel moved toward the clothing and quickly put them on. The clothing was identical although tight fitting to fit the contours of the different body structures. Black in color, the material Ty couldn't place. Noel knew it to be an exotic material made from the silk glands of a certain vampire bat. A rare bat found in certain caves around the world. The tight clothing fit their bodies perfectly to give it a comfortable measure of movement as well as a perfect warm temperature.

The two shivered the last remnants of cold away after placing on their boots. Then they looked at the screen. It had "press any key" written in bright blood red letters.

Ty pushed the 'enter' button.

The computer came to life, as a picture of a face appeared. It was the Good Doctor, dressed in his black silken coat. His eyes were a sharp black, and his hair dark as night itself. Noel hadn't remembered the Doctor looking like that when he stood by her lecturing her while she was cuffed to the wall. He must have been feeding to gain such strength so fast.

"My dearly beloveds," the Good Doctor started. "I take it you found your clothing fitting and keeping you warm from this very cold climate, you find yourselves in."

Ty looked at Noel who returned the look. They looked back at the screen.

"I recorded this message, on the return of you two; what I like to call the solid plain. It is in fact the real world for you Ty who might be still confused at the idea." The Good Doctor continued, "Ty I know that you probably feel misled."

Ty's eyes scowled low.

"This was all done so that you could feel the truth. This life that you found yourself in; this dream state that you were in was merely a testing ground. The local authorities were going to hang you from the noose, figuratively speaking of course."

Pictures flashed up on the screen of Ty's life in the real world. Pictures of him were shown on America's Most Wanted. Security camera footage and pictures were shown on screen of Ty brutally stabbing store clerks in the dead of night. None of them were the store clerks in the dream world either. This was actual footage. Short news footage of a nationwide man hunt to find this killer played across the screen for a few seconds. Road way cameras showed Ty, even a bit younger, breaking into someone's car, killing that person and hot wiring their vehicle. The computer showed the choppers narrowing in on the running Ty, from a sky view in a suburban neighborhood. Ty merely gasped aloud when the police and swat shot him over and over in the chest. Ty lifted up his shirt, and saw the scars. He figured them from the various wires that were placed inside of him, but knew now their true origin.

"I should be dead." Ty shook his head.

"Keep watching," Noel said, not taking her eyes from the monitor.

The footage showed another news cast of a man short and bald with bigger men behind him, entering the hospital, with news cameras and microphones in his face. Upon an interview, he told the cameras that he would fix the boy, taking away his need for killing, in an experimental procedure. The name that flashed up at the bottom of the screen was Mr. Levi Jonas.

Ty's eyes lowered again. "That is probably the man we need to see first."

Noel said nothing.

The Good Doctor came back on. "You see my dear boy, we saved you," he said on screen. "We gave you a new life. Your will to kill has not been broken, although a bit jaded. I would hope and still assume that Noel is still alive, but not before you gave off a few words of her demise."

Ty's face lowered, and he looked at Noel. She grabbed his arm and held him close. He bent down a bit, and she whispered in his ears, "It's okay Ty; we'll get through this together now."

Ty smiled back.

The on screen Good Doctor went on, "In return, we still need you to kill. Do not worry; you are a changed man now. We will not ask you to kill pathetic weaklings, but we will give you the target. Your training is not yet complete, however. Your journey will lead you to the end result. Me! When you make it to my doorstep, you will have passed the test." The Doctor went on, "I would assume you will be looking for Sumiko. Take Noel because she knows where she is. She may not be as easy to find as you would think, but I know you can do it. When you are finished with that quest, come find me. When you passed the test, you will receive your answers you crave and your rewards.

"Before I forget; I left you a little present. You'll know what it is, because when you need it the most; it will be there."

Ty looked baffled at the screen. "What do you suppose he means?" Ty asked Noel.

"I'm not sure," she answered sincerely not knowing.

"For your informational purposes," the Good Doctor began again. "Bones and your three friends the Detectives you met in the program are all fine and dandy." The Doctor chuckled at his own choice of words. "If you find them, they may unlock some of the answers you seek, if you so choose to take that path."

"I would suppose you only have a few moments, before you have to," the Doctor paused for a few seconds. "Well RUN!" he shouted on screen. Ty jerked at the sudden loudness that filled the room. The screen flickered when the Doctor yelled, and suddenly went blank.

Ty saw lights coming from outside that looked like a vehicle was pulling up. In the sheer dimness of the inside of the hospital, seeing any outside lights proved easy even from a few floors up.

Ty moved behind the table to the window, for a view of the outside. He realized that he was three floors up, but he could see the men getting out of the car. Through the open window he heard them say, "Alright scour this place. I want that Doctor's head on a pike. If you find the boy's body, tag it and bag it. Let's move," the shorter bald one ordered. Ty realized that it was Mr. Jonas in the news footage.

Ty turned to Noel, who was using the table to lean against. Her body completely weakening by the lack of blood she had in the last few weeks. Ty's eyes grew, "We got to run."

Sumiko was enthralled with the story that Takeo told her, but she just couldn't believe the "nut job". She pulled out the rest of the wires that so delicately was put into her arms and face, and cringed at the feeling.

She slid off the bed, and immediately hit the floor. "Right, my legs," she mumbled to herself. "Should have checked to see if they could be used, stupid girl."

Sumiko got up, and leaned against her bed. The throbbing—burning coursing through her body was practically unbearable, but she had to keep moving. This place was comfortable enough, and Takeo seemed sincere and all that, but something was really weird about him. She had to get out of here.

Sumiko limped toward the door, and placed her ear to it. She heard nothing. She opened the door slowly and peaked outside. Unlike a normal hospital with all the bright lights; this one was very dimly lit. It was comfortable enough to see, but the lighting still gave it that eerie feeling.

She edged her way out of the room. Everything seemed normal, other than the lighting. She saw a nurse walk steadily by her, and she quickly hid behind the in-dent of the doorway. The nurse kept walking as if on a mission, not even giving Sumiko a second look.

Sumiko looked at her own clothes, a very modest gown down to her knees. She grabbed a hold of the side rails on the walls, and kept moving. She tried not to draw attention to herself, so she grunted away the pain and kept her eyes low. Doctors and nurses moved in and out of doorways talking and laughing as if this was a real hospital. Sumiko just didn't get that vibe. She wondered down the hallway a few hundred feet until she finally came to the nurse's station. She opened the door slowly looking back behind. All the doctors and nurses walking about didn't pay her any mind. She wondered inside, and no one was in there. She gazed around, and everything looked normal enough, except for a pitcher sitting on counter. She noticed a red fluid inside. She opened the fridge, and in side were bags and bags of what looked like blood. Sumiko closed the door quickly.

She wondered inside a door, where a locker room was. Sumiko looked down at her gown again. All the lockers were unlocked; so it didn't take her long to find a nurse's uniform to fit, shoes and all. She put it on gritting the pain away with her teeth. She made it to a mirror and noticed the uniform. She tied her hair back, with a rubber band. Now she looked like all the other nurses walking the hallways.

Sumiko flattened out her new clothing and bit away the pain, as she walked as steadily as she could out into the hallway. She moved to an elevator, no one was inside. She looked at the various floors and instead of going down to the right floor the elevator only could go up. She pushed to go to the surface floor. The elevator stopped on the next floor, and in walked a doctor and a nurse. They were talking in an unknown language that Sumiko couldn't understand. Then the doctor nearest to her looked down at Sumiko and sniffed once at her. Sumiko gave a rather unpleasant, but courteous smile, and the doctor looked away. The three got off on the same floor, and Sumiko kept looking behind her until the doctor and nurse walked away. She moved rapidly through the lobby entrance, until she came to the main doors. She looked behind her once, and saw that no one was looking her way. She left the building and hit the bright morning sun just peaking the buildings tops. She was in a city, she recognized as Tokyo. She felt comfort in that thought. All she had to do was find the way to her house. Everything would be alright.

Sumiko started to walk, but the pain over took her. She fell to the ground. Most of the people walked around her, but there was one older lady that stopped to help her up. When Sumiko turned to look at her to thank her, the ladies eyes nearly bulged out of her head. She ran screaming in Japanese. Sumiko recognized the word "witch".

Sumiko walked with her head, down and cut down an alley to another street. She found a window of an abandoned building, and when she looked in it she gasped in horror. Her eyes were black as death itself.

CHAPTER 15

Bones was the last to leave the fake world behind. He excused all thoughts of ever getting paid. He quickly assumed that wasn't going to happen. When he awoke though, he wasn't lying on any table with wires hooked up to him. He was lying in an alley, in the middle of a city. He knew this must be the real world, because the throbbing head ache he had was more than anything he had ever known. Bones got up slowly leaning against the brick wall of the nearby building for support. He looked around; it was just entering the evening hours. Things were getting very dark.

"Wow," Bones said to himself. "It's been fifteen years since I've been in this world." He shook his head in disbelief.

Bones moved out of the alley into the street lights. He was wearing a tattered suit coat. He knew he had to change. The people who weren't safely tucked away in their homes quickly rushed past him, bumping into him, nearly knocking him down. He quickly regained his footing and got a good look at the city. From the darkness fast approaching; he could see the buildings and actually could make out where he was. It had been a while, but Bones remembered he was a few blocks from his house.

Bones moved cautiously. He didn't truly understand the rush of everyone as they bustled past, but he kept moving in the direction he was sure of. He took a left down a side street after a few blocks and made his way to a suburban area. His home was nestled back in a bit on a dead end cul-de-sac.

Relieved that he had found his home; he wondered if it would have changed over the past fifteen years. His tiny lawn was taken care of from developments ongoing service. They took money automatically out of his account. He left everything for his friend Ronald Billings to take care of while he was gone. Bones laughed at the fact that he seemed to have dropped off the grid for the last fifteen years, and really didn't have anything to show for it.

Bones entered his doorstep, with the crest of night upon the city. He heard a scream he thought was right behind him. He quickly turned, but no one was there. It must have been in the distant. He grabbed his hidden key; he couldn't have imagined he would remember where it was, and unlocked the door. Sheets covered most of his furniture with a layer of dust on top. The electric didn't work, because he had it turned off before his experiment, so there were no lights to turn on. He slightly remembered keeping a spare flashlight nearby in a kitchen drawer, and sure enough it was still there. It was empty, of course, of any batteries.

Bones rubbed his forehead. He laughed at the fact that his left hand held its ring finger still. He was getting used to not having one that it was weird for him to get back into the swing of things, with one.

He stumbled in the darkness toward his office. Bones kept a few candles in his desk drawer. He grabbed some matches, and lit them. That showed a little light. He took one of the candles from room to room, inspecting his house. He was really famished, but he didn't leave anything in cupboards.

Everything was how he remembered it, but one thing seemed out of place. His computer from his office in the facility was lying on his living room coffee table. Bones thought this odd, because it couldn't have been possible to bring a tangible item out of the program.He walked up to it and saw that an on screen message said "press any key". Bones hit a button, and an on screen footage of the Good Doctor appeared.

"Hello Doctor Bones. Can I call you Doctor Bones?" the voice asked. "Or would you prefer Mr. Leroy Bones? Well I suppose it doesn't really matter because I cannot hear your answer, and this was pre-recorded upon your return to the land of the living." The Doctor laughed to himself. "I just wanted to congratulate you on a job well done. You were wise to plan a way out. Ty's training is not fully complete, but I do hope this money compensates you well enough for your duties."

Bones eyes widened to see the screen go to another page, and show that one billion dollars was being dropped into his account.

"I do hope you find that satisfactory. If I was you, I would start out by purchasing a new suit." The Doctor laughed again. "That one you have on has been through the ringer no doubt. I would be careful. I know you have a grateful heart, but there are some men that might want to talk to you. If I was you, I would draw out some of that money before they freeze your accounts. I took the liberty of giving you a special card. I created it myself. It's in your pants pocket. This will allow you to get out more than the minimum amount of money that is in your account. That is the amount that the ATM actually has at this hour. I would then move some place warm. I would do it now." The screen went blank.

Bones folded up the laptop, grabbed a small satchel bag and simply ran out of his house. He had to get to an ATM fast.

Detective Miller woke up in his bed. His bottle of gin sat beside him on his night stand. He rubbed his eyes, and fell back on his pillow. He had the weirdest dream. His mind was racing at what he just saw. He's been obsessing over this killer; it was hard to believe that this rich guy just swept him up to use for some experiment. He even dreamt about him now.

He grabbed the bottle and took a swig from it rather than pour it in the glass; he had to numb this head ache. Miller looked outside; darkness was pretty much blanketing the city. Detective Miller picked up his phone and dialed his captain.

It rang for a few seconds until the voice mail came on. Miller hung up. It was entering the night times, and he had to get rid of this head ache. He plopped down in his bed and drifted off. He could see his captain in the morning.

When Roanoke woke up he was on a bus. He was slouched over in the back. There were only two other people on the bus, a homeless lady, and younger man that looked more like he grew up on the streets than in any actual home. Detective Roanoke couldn't shake this nasty headache, he had. He looked out of the window; and had no idea where he was, or what day it was for that matter. Last thing he remembered was falling asleep, in his bed. He had no idea how he woke up on this bus.

He remembered having this weird dream though, of him being a detective. He loved detective movies, and it was his long time fantasy to be one and figure out clues, but he had no idea where that elaborate dream came from. He was a door to door salesman from Detroit. He definitely wasn't a detective by any means.

The bus stopped and the thuggish looking younger man got off the bus. Roanoke decided to wait until the next stop to get off. He sat there for a few moments until the homeless looking woman came up to him. She reeked of booze, and grime. She sat in the seat in front of his.

"Are you Roanoke?" she asked.

Roanoke looked at the woman curiously for a bit, and then answered, "Yes. Who are you?" he questioned.

"That's not important. A man paid me three hundred bucks to tell you to get off at the next stop. He said you should wake up by then. So I'm telling you." The woman got up and sat in the same seat she came from.

The bus soon stopped and Roanoke walked up through the bus looking at the woman as he got off. His head throbbed as he stepped out in the cool air. "What is this?" he asked himself.

Not long after that a black SUV pulled up. The passenger asked, "Are you Roanoke?"

"Yes, why?"

"Get in," was all that was said.

The door to the SUV swung open, and Roanoke having no other choices and fearing if he ran, got in the vehicle.

Philmore awoke with a start, and he wish he hadn't. He was in a dark basement, with a bright light shining directly in his face. At least three men walked around him yelling at him in Russian. One man cold cocked him in the face. The brass knuckles he wore made it worse. Philmore was sure he lost a tooth or two. Blood splattered on the floor in the hit, and he cringed at the pain. This just added to his migraine. Philmore had no idea where he was or what was going on. All he remembered was he was a detective in some lucid dream. He just lost his job as a bank teller yesterday, so he had no idea what this was about. Philmore was a nobody from nowhere. He definitely wasn't anyone that needed to be tied to a chair, and beaten.

Ty and Noel ran as fast as they could down the hallway; as fast as their aching-exhausted bodies would allow. They held each other up as they ran around corners. Panicked looks in their eye; they were worn out and confused.

They heard the door to the hospital open abruptly, and voices saying, "We'll check the room first to make sure."

"If he's not in there, search the whole hospital. Turn this place upside down; I mean totally upside down. I want this Doctor, and I want this kid now."

Ty recognized the voice, and it was confirmed. He had to get out of this hospital, but his aching body wouldn't allow him to move any faster and Noel was leaning on him plus half holding him up from falling.

They moved down a flight of steps wanting to avoid the floor they were on, considering Jonas was probably headed that way anyways with his men. Ty and Noel ran down the hallway of the second floor nearly tripping as they went. If their exhaustion wasn't taking over, the flickering lights dizzied both of them for two separate reasons.

Something wrapped itself around Ty's leg and he went down hard, dragging Noel with him. As he turned to see what it was it disappeared into thin air. He gave it a weird look, and then looked out across the hallway in which they ran from. They were out of the way of the stairs so no one should see them unless they walked down this particular hallway. Ty got up and helped Noel to her feet.

"What was that?" she asked.

"I have no idea; did you see it?"

"For like a split second. It was like something encased your foot for a second then immediately disappeared."

"I know, that's really weird," Ty said breathing heavy, brushing himself off from the fall on the grimy floor. "Let's try going down this hallway, and see if there's another stairway that will lead us out of here."

"You lead the way," Noel said panting herself.

They ran down another hallway and suddenly stopped. The double doors that led the way into the other hallway were boarded up. The worst part was that above that door was an "exit" sign.

Noel nearly cried out but good thing she didn't, because just at that moment, they heard voices coming down the adjacent hallway.

Ty looked at Noel, eyes wide. "We got to get through this door."

"You have any ideas?"

Ty looked at the door; the boards were old looking. He may be able to break them, but he wasn't sure. He pushed on them, and they budged a little, but just wouldn't quite give way. "If only I was a bit stronger," he said.

At that instance, an armored covering came down on his arms to his hands stopping to cover his fingers. He looked at the new sleeves that appeared out of nowhere, and then looked at Noel mouth agape.

"That might be . . ." she started to say, but just couldn't finish.

Ty's arms felt strengthened. He walked up to the board and pulled one free. He punched another, and with his adamantine armor covering his hands, he didn't feel it at all. The two inch thick board broke instantly. Ty looked at his hands.

"This is cool. I don't know what just happened, but it works. Ty spent no time at all removing the final three boards blocking the door, so they could get through. They kept going. Ty felt the thing wrap around his leg again. He stopped instantly almost tripping Noel. Ty looked down at his feet. The armored Kevlar and adamantine suit was covering his feet and working its way up his legs. It got to his torso and stopped.

"This is my suit I had in the dream world."

Noel's mouth simply dropped. "I know," she said. "How did it get here?"

"I don't know, but I like it. It's like rebuilding my legs, making the stronger. I feel the strength taking away the pain. Come on, I'll help you." Ty nearly picked Noel off the floor, as they moved on. His suit was empowering his every step.

They followed the exit red line drawn on the wall all the way down the next hall. They made it to a stairs and stopped instantly.

There were two men at the bottom with guns. They looked up. "There they are," one of them shouted.

The other got on a walkie, and radioed Jonas, "Boss we spotted them."

"Head them off," the reply came from the radio.

"We're going up to the second floor."

Ty and Noel took off running. Ty nearly yanked her arm off pulling her along, but she needed the extra motivation, because her legs were about to give out at any minute.

They took off down another side hallway on the second floor, and ran until it dead ended.

"There is no place we can go," Noel said, nearly gasping for air.

"There's got to be." Ty breathed out.

Ty looked around. All he saw were boarded up rooms, and a boarded window at the end of a hall. Ty looked down at his legs.

Noel looked where his eyes were and immediately knew what he was thinking. "It won't work."

"You heard the Doctor. It will be here whenever I need it. I haven't even begun to max out the abilities of this suit."

"Yeah but you could do more in the programmed world. It's like when you dream and you jump off a big building and you don't really get truly hurt, just a little in real life," Noel pleaded.

"Yeah but this is only a floor up. I can do it."

"There's got to be another way; you'll break your legs, you're only human," Noel didn't want to let it slip that she was a vampire yet, and could have kicked herself for referring to Ty as a human.

He didn't seem to catch it right then. "Look there's guys with guns coming right at us. I got to do this now."

Ty didn't take any more time arguing. He swooped Noel up in his armored arms and backed up a bit. He took a run and turned at just the last minute to hit the brunt of the boards with his body. The turn also blocked Noel from any debris that might fly her way. The board broke simultaneously, and flew out of the way at the fast moving Ty.

Once his back hit the boards, armor covered it completely in a split second, blocking him from feeling any pain or catching any splinters. He had just a moment to think and twist his body so he hit the ground and not Noel first. His legs took most the shock, but the jolt of hitting the ground, made Noel fly out of his hands and hit the macadam driveway of the hospital. She slid a small ways before hitting her head against a car's tire. Ty rolled and rose immediately on his feet in a dead set run, but stopped when he realized Noel was no longer with him. He didn't feel any pain from the jump; his legs actually felt stronger as the suit seemed to be recharging them.

Ty ran to her, wanting to know the extent of her injuries. Her face and arms were scraped pretty bad from the sliding. She was knocked unconscious from hitting the tire. Ty looked back realizing his full torso and back was covered by the armored suit now. Everything but his head was fully encased. Ty picked her up gently. He looked at three SUVs that were parked outside the hospital. "Good grief, this guy brought a ton of reinforcements," Ty said aloud to himself

"There they are!" Ty heard someone yell from the window. They spoke in the radio.

Ty took off running down the long driveway. Noel was bleeding pretty badly and completely unconscious. Ty hoped that she would make it through the night. He silently cursed himself for making the jump, but he seriously had no other choices.

It didn't take long for most of the men to come out of the hospital in full sprints to their vehicles. "If he made that jump, I want him alive." Ty heard Jonas telling his men.

Ty got a quick idea. They want me alive huh? He thought. Then let's see what this suit is made of.

Ty gently put Noel in the bushes before anyone saw, half way down the drive path to the hospital. He still had a ways to go before reaching the main gate so he decided to do this here.

He then turned around to face his attackers. He could see the lights coming around the turn. Ty thought of his face being encased by the mask helmet, and he instantly felt a tingling in his spine. The full suit covered him now head to toe. He looked down at his chest, and realized that his razor-silver boomerangs were there. Ty felt around his back and realized both his swords were there; he actually felt them forming into a solid tangible item as he reached for them. He looked across his body, and each throwing knife was in place.

Ty waited as the first car came around the corner. He held his arms out as if holding two guns. There was nothing in his hand. He pushed his trigger fingers as if pulling back triggers, and slowly the beginning of his MAC-10s appeared in his hands. Ty smiled under his mask.

Soon his pulling of his fingers hit a solid object, and bullets flew. The first SUV swerved up over the embankment and hit a tree. The wooded drive path may prove a well fighting area indeed. Ty never left off the trigger; the guns would never over heat. He sprayed the bullets back the SUV until hitting the gas tank. Nothing happened. Ty looked in disbelief. He thought sure that would have blown up the vehicle. He looked at his guns. Men started firing back, and reinforcements arrived as soon as the other SUVs and Jonas' car caught up.

Ty jumped out of the way attaching his weapons to his suit. He dodged behind a tree. Looking across the drive path he saw the slight blackness of Noel's clothing. He had to move this small battle away from her to keep her safe. He picked both of his razor boomerangs off his chest and came out from under the tree. With a throw of both of them, men jumped and nearly screamed to get out of the way. The one boomerang took the arm completely off of the one man, who let out a squeal of agony. It would have taken his neck from his shoulders, had the man not dodged at just the last second.

Still it was his gun arm, and Ty was grateful to see the weapon hit the ground.

The other sank deeply into the glass on the passenger side of the SUV. All Ty saw through the darkness of night was blood splattering the other parts of the window. He called them both back in an instance.

At the same time, a man jumped out from behind a tree too close to Ty and Noel for Ty liking. The man shot once then twice at point blank range at Ty's temple. It was if Ty's suit knew the man's thoughts before they even came to mind. Ty dodged once then twice, then uppercut the guy to let him fly a few feet before landing too close to Noel who was lying very still in the underbrush. Ty was on him like a hawk, and that is precisely what he looked like, flying in the air sword drawn. Needless to say, the man did not keep his head on his shoulders for more than a few seconds in the mayhem. With a splatter of blood he fell where he stood. Ty turned satisfied that he didn't come close to harming Noel.

The blood and gore coming from the man's exposed torso seeped and ran close to Noel. Her body unknowingly turned toward the blood. The body of a vampire grew aimed her toward the seeping blood, as a plant grows toward the sun.

Noel began to drink.

CHAPTER 16

Ty fought with the power of a vampire with his suit in full motion. The longer he wore it; the longer it recharged him. The men came at him with a hectic swarm, and Ty swatted them away as flies. One they shot at him without abandon. Ty dodged and twisted his body in a way that the bullets didn't even touch him. He ran up on the SUV and flipped onto Jonas' car. Jonas was still inside with his driver. Ty took out his sword and ran it through the windshield killing the driver before he could react. He jumped down off the car, and punched the glass shattering it instantly. Jonas grabbed his gun out of his chest holster, and Ty snatched it out of his hand as a parent would snatch a rattle from a babies.

Jonas jumped and through his hands up in surrender. Ty eyed him through his suit, measuring the amount of anxiety in his actions. This man was sure of himself but at this very instance was a nervous as anyone could be.

Ty took the car door from its hinges and threw it on the side of the path. "You were the man that experimented on me," Ty said as he grabbed the man out of the car and pinned him against it.

"Yes, I am. What is it to you?" Jonas asked trying to keep what little control of the situation he had left.

"What's my name?" Ty asked.

"I don't understand." Jonas replied.

"Do you think of me as some sort of freak that you can snatch away and run experiments on?"

"With all due respect, I am not the one you should be seeking. There is a man who is in charge; his name is Mr. Gobaleski. He was the one who paid me to set all this up."

Ty measured the anxiety in Jonas' voice and realized he was telling the truth.

"First, who is this man who calls himself The Good Doctor?"

"He is the only scientist I found that was willing to take one such a case as yourself. You are a killer born and bred so we find. We thought to change that. Mr. Gobaleski hired me, because he never gets his hands dirty. He hired my organization to find the scientist and doctors who would do such an experiment on you and pay big when it worked. He is creating a weapon. The weapon is you, and judging by how many of my men lay dead, I would say the weapon is complete."

Ty took the compliment in stride. He was pretty powerful, and he couldn't explain why. He was again confused. He could tell he was in the real world, by the way he felt, but had no idea how his suit got into this world.

"Why me?" Ty asked. "Why did you or he choose me?"

"Because you have no living relatives that we know of. Because you are a killer by trade. You do not go soft and you jump right in there. You grew up on the streets hard as anyone could. You don't shy away from getting your hands dirty." Jonas changed the subject. "I am surprised to see the battle gear; my men didn't say anything about it when they were chasing you. Where did you get it?"

Ty shook Jonas and lifted him a good six inches off the ground. "I do not think you are the type of situation where you get to ask any questions, do you?"

Jonas reluctantly shook his head.

"What do you know about vampires?" Ty asked.

Jonas' eyes grew in size. "Of course," he said.

"Of course what?" Ty asked, pushing his back up against the car squeezing him a bit.

"That is what Mr. Gobaleski wanted you for. He never told me."

"What are you talking about?" Ty was growing impatient with this cat and mouse conversation.

"I have never seen one, but apparently I've heard stories. It started in Tokyo. This street gang were calling themselves vampires a few years ago. Then you didn't hear anything from them. I sent my men out all through Russia and Siberia at night to look for these so called vampires, and they always came back empty handed. Yet some of my deliveries were attacked and never made it to the buyer. If anyone would ever escape, they swore it vampires by the legends they've heard when they were children.

"Every time I asked Mr. Gobaleski what he wanted you for; all he would ever say was a weapon for his army. I believe it all makes sense now. You are supposed to be his vampire hunter." Jonas' eyes grew even wider. "That's what you were doing all along. It all makes complete sense."

"What do you mean, doing it all along?"

"I knew there was something different when I saw the footage. You weren't killing humans. You were killing vampires. You worked for someone. Vampires are real, my boy. I've never seen one in the natural, but you were being honed into the ultimate killer."

Ty was taken back. First Bones said something about it, now Jonas reaffirmed it. "But you've never seen a vampire yourself, and none of your men have actually seen one?"

"Never," Mr. Jonas repeated his answer from before.

"Until now," a voice came from behind Ty. It was Noel standing as tall as ever.

Ty turned abruptly, and Jonas' eyes nearly popped out of their sockets when he saw the girl. He prayed in Russian. Ty looked back at him, but by that time; he was already dead. Jonas collapsed to the ground as Ty left him fall. He just simply died.

Sumiko rushed to her home as fast as she could. She couldn't believe what she saw. The pain was overwhelming her with each step; her whole body burned. It felt like the skin was peeling off the bones. She nearly screamed, but didn't want to draw attention to herself. She tried not to make eye contact with anyone as she went. She brushed abruptly by pedestrians on the street, but just kept moving.

Finally she made it to her Tokyo apartment and ran inside quickly. The elevator was too risky to take, so she ran up the steps to the fourth floor. After sprinting three steps at a time, she made it to her floor crashing the door open and took a dead run down the hall. She made it to her door, but nearly cried out when she didn't have her key. She was fiddling around, thinking she may have put one somewhere in the hallway in case this ever happened, when the door burst open.

"May I help you?" the middle aged woman asked.

Sumiko nearly jumped out of her skin and technically it felt as if she was being plucked out of it. She looked up, but only for a second. Sumiko thought for a split second and decided to play blind.

"I'm sorry; I thought this was my apartment." Sumiko through the pain, tried to seem confused like she didn't mean this woman any harm. She would do anything to keep the woman from looking into her eyes. Sumiko looked everywhere, but the woman's face.

"I'm sorry, honey, please come in, I can pour you a pot of tea or something."

Sumiko didn't know what to do, but something inside her drew her to this woman. She knew that this was her apartment, so she went on inside.

"Please make yourself at home. I'm surprised you'd be out and about especially with being blind and all."

Sumiko looked at the woman then, but she was in the kitchen getting the tea, and her back was turned. Sumiko thought for a moment, and then decided to play that card. "Yeah, well I've been getting along okay I guess. I am really sorry about the mix up. I thought I was on the fourth floor, but someone was talking to me, and they must have pushed the wrong button on the elevator," Sumiko lied.

"It's quite alright. I don't get many visitors anyways, or entertain anyone. All my kids are in college. You actually look pretty similar to one of my daughters. Her picture is on—," but the woman stopped herself. "I'm so sorry, I didn't mean that."

Sumiko tried to figure out what she was apologizing for and then realized. "Oh no it's fine, really, it's quite alright." She was having a hard time choking back the pain.

"Do you feel alright?" the woman asked bringing her the tea. "Careful, it's hot."

Sumiko took the tea and began to drink. "Yeah, I'm fine. I just feel a bit under the weather today."

"I noticed your eyes aren't the normal color. Is that due to the blindness? Your also wearing a nurse's uniform, do you work down at the hospital? I'm sorry, I probably ask too many questions," the woman apologized.

Sumiko smiled. "It's fine." She thought really fast for an explanation. "I was in an accident; I don't really like talking about it."

"Oh I'm sorry dear to press. Oh here I am being rude. I haven't even told you my name. It's Ren."

"Oh water lily," Sumiko noted giving reference to the names meaning.

"Yeah, my mother loved the water, so she decided to name me after her favorite flower. Is the tea good?" Ren asked.

"Oh very satisfactory," Sumiko said, but in essence she was feeling very sick. The tea turned her stomach, like nothing she ever felt before. She set it down really fast on the coffee table, not really paying attention to the fact that she was supposed to be blind. She grabbed her stomach and bent her head toward her knees, and began to rock forward and backwards in a steady motion.

"Are you alright dear?" Ren asked, getting up from her chair and setting her own tea down and running to Sumiko's aid. Sumiko at first thought she was poisoned, but the woman seemed too sincere to do such a thing. She mumbled out the words, "I don't know."

"Here let me get you a towel." Ren got up to go to the kitchen, but Sumiko grabbed her arm.

Sumiko lunged at the woman, knocking her to the ground. The woman yelped out in surprise, and Sumiko couldn't stop herself. It smelled too good. Before she realized what she was doing, she sunk her teeth into Ren's neck puncturing skin. Sumiko began to suck the Ren's life force from her very body.

Bones wondered with his bag and his laptop to the ATM. He looked around him and saw no one. The darkness of night was in full swing. Bones heard a short scream behind him. He turned, but saw no one; the streets were bare. Bones put the card that he found in his pants pocket and pushed in his pin. The number still worked. He then went to draw out one million dollars. After a bit of processing, the money started stacking up at the bottom of the ATM. Bones lifted the tray and kept grabbing it, stuffing it into his bag. Finally the money stopped after a few minutes his bag was completely full.

"This should hold me over," Bones said to himself. He took off running down the street. He had to get to a hotel as soon as possible. He stayed away from alleys, and tried his best to stay in the light as best he could. Finally he made it to an old looking inn. Bones wondered up to the four story building and grabbed at the doors. They were locked. He pulled, and pulled and even knocked on the door. Finally a rustic looking man came from out back and waved Bones off. Bones then grabbed at a wad of cash he had in his satchel bag and showed it to the man. The man then grabbed his keys and opened the door.

"Oh thank you sir," Bones politely said.

"Yeah, don't mention it." The man said walking back behind the clerk's desk. "Room forty-seven is available. That'll be three hundred bucks." The man said abruptly.

"Three hundred bucks?" Bones repeated. "But you have a sign right behind you that says, 'get a room for the low, low price of fifty-nine, ninety-five."

The inn host turned around. "Oh that's for the morning hours, not after dark. After night comes, and the doors are locked, the price jumps. Listen if you don't need the room, you can leave right now."

"No, no, no, no, I'll take the room. It's alright." Bones counted out the twenties until they equaled three hundred dollars, and handed it to the man.

The man turned around and grabbed forty-seven's room key and told Bones to, "Sleep tight."

Bones merely took the key and gave a half smile and rounded the corner to the stairs.

Upon entering the fourth floor, he walked down the hallway and looked for room forty-seven. Finally he found it, and unlocked the door. He checked to make sure no one was in the hallway before going inside. He first got a whiff of the smell. It nearly took him off guard. The bed hadn't even been made up from the last tenant, and the walls were all stained yellow in blotches all the way around the room. Bones cringed having left his dream world, and his comfortable bed and luxuries. Although fake, they definitely outweighed this place. Still he patted his bag. Nearly one million dollars would satisfy him.

He made his way further into the room, and looked in the bathroom. He wished he hadn't. The toilet was overflowing with a brownish-yellow fluid. The sink was all rusted over, and the shower had holes in the wall, that Bones was sure he could see into the next room. Bones made a face.

He walked out to the room, and sat on the bed. His suit was tattered. He would have to get another one. Heck, he could get a whole different wardrobe now. He folded his arms in front of him, and breathed out. He wondered what happened to Ty, and the three detectives. He wished he knew if they were all alright. Fighting sleep, because of not wanting to lie down on the disgusting bed, he soon couldn't win over it and his eyes finally closed willingly.

Roanoke said nothing for a good long time, while sitting at the back of the SUV. Two men sat beside him, and two in the one in the driver and passenger seats. It was too dark to tell who they were, or what they wanted. Roanoke figured he didn't have a bag over his head so that could be a good thing—or a bad thing.

"So, what's this concerning?" Roanoke asked, but he didn't get an answer. He might as well been talking to the wall.

The vehicle drove for a long while, exiting the city, and following the water line of the river, up the mountain. It finally stopped at a huge gate that opened, as soon as it saw the SUV pull up. The vehicle continued down the lane, and came to rest in front of a very large-beautiful house. Roanoke had never really seen someone's house that looked like this, up close before. His mouth dropped at the site. The river rested behind the house flowing past, just adding to the elegant beauty of the mansion.

The men got out of the SUV, and the one man pulled on Roanoke's arm. They were very rough pulling him along, and forcing him to move faster than his legs were willing to go.

As they brought him inside, Roanoke nearly tripped many times. The brought him through the front lobby, and into a side room to stand in front of a desk.

A man sat at the desk, tall and powerful.

"I'm Mr. Gobaleski," he said to Roanoke, in a deep voice.

Roanoke shrugged his shoulders, as if the name didn't ring any bells. "I'm sorry; I don't know any Gobaleski's. I'm not even sure where I am to be honest with you. Is this concerning a vacuum I sold you or the steak knife set. I think I would have remembered selling that—."

"Enough!" a boisterous yell came from Gobaleski. "You don't know me, but I know a lot about you. Tell me, the last few days you spent most of your time in a program. You played a detective in this program. What do you know of this boy who is called Ty Livingston?"

"Um… well, I'm not sure." Roanoke was stunned that this man knew all about his dream, or was it a dream. "Um…" Roanoke began again. "I don't know whole lot. I only saw someone named Ty for a few moments. I believe me and two other detectives were looking for the boy also."

Gobaleski folded his arms in front of himself, letting his elbows rest easily on the top. "This intrigues me. Did you find him?"

"We did," Roanoke answered. "I'm a bit confused that I thought that was just a dream."

"Let me be frank with you. That wasn't a dream at all. You were placed in a program to live out your life for a few days. Your fantasy of becoming a detective was granted during this time. Now I want to know everything that happened when you saw this boy."

"Well to be honest, not much." The man standing behind Roanoke gave him a hard slap in the back of the head. Roanoke turned quickly to take note of his attacker, but this made Gobaleski yell again.

"What happened exactly!?"

"Well, we went underground to this big underground type of building, type thing, and we fought our way through. I went up through this roof thing, and fought my way through that way down through this garage type area. I saw this kid, Ty with this battle suit on. He was beating our team to a pulp. I had guys grab me from behind, so I didn't really get to do anything as far as battle anyone." Roanoke stopped thinking he was talking too fast, or too much.

"Please go on." Gobaleski said smiling.

"So after this Ty guy made short order of the team, he was about to kill me, in my dream of course. But he decided not to at the last minute and told the guys to drag me to this big concrete room. So Ty started arguing with the chick, and I was really out of it by then. He threw these marble type things that were really bright, like a flash bang grenade you see in games and what not. Well I was still getting my eye sight back from that, but the chick ended up dying; I didn't see how, but she was rude, so I was glad of it. She was a hot little thing but rude nonetheless. So then, they said how they could get us out of this world, and I thought they were all talking batty. Then this Ty guy dragged all three of us to this other room, with a fish tanks all around it, and this other guy started ripping his phone and computer apart, and that was the last I remembered before waking up on the bus. I must have dosed off or something. I'm not sure. I just don't see how this dream would mean anything."

Mr. Gobaleski held up a hand for Roanoke to stop his ramblings. "Tell me Mr. Roanoke, do you remember the other detective's names and the man who was ripping his computer and phone apart."

"Yeah, the other detectives were Detective Miller, and Philmore. Uh… the guy with the phone thing; think his name was Bones. I think."

"Excellent. Tell me one more thing. This girl that died. This girl have any special features about her, other than being attractive?"

"Yeah," Roanoke said, looking to the ceiling as he remembered.

He looked back at Mr. Gobaleski. "She had these two shiny whips hanging by her side. She wore a tight little-leather suit thing, but I do definitely remember those whips. They looked like they were made out of metal. I don't see how they would bend, but whatever; dreams will do that, I guess."

"Tell me," Gobaleski continued. "Do you remember her name?"

"I think they called her Noel."

"Thank you Mr. Roanoke, you may go," Gobaleski said. "Gentleman," Gobaleski then looked to the men on either side of Roanoke. "Please take Mr. Roanoke home for me would you?"

The men took Roanoke out of the office.

A man came out of the shadows, behind Gobaleski's desk. "I think she is the one," the mystery man said to Gobaleski.

"Do you think she is?" Gobaleski asked, without turning to regard the man.

"I am sure of it. The girl killed my brother twenty-five years ago, you don't forget that, and no one has whips that look like that. It's her, I'm sure of it."

"Well, it would appear as if your boy is quite powerful now wouldn't it?" Gobaleski questioned, still facing forward, changing the subject.

"Yes. A little coaxing through the program seemed to do him some good. I think I'm going to enjoy our little reunion." The mystery took out a brief case of money from behind him and laid it on Gobaleski's desk. "Payment in full," he said. "For finding the boy and making sure he is safe. There's a little extra in there, for also finding that girl. Although, I would admit, I got the better end of the deal." The mystery man smiled, but Gobaleski didn't notice, opening the briefcase of money on his desk. The shadows prohibited anyone to see it anyways.

"Yes. It would seem as though your boy took out quite the handful of these men in the program? You know the Good Doctor raised a powerful army of droids to defeat him. It would prove well, that this weapon is complete. I sent Jonas to pick him up for me. I'm almost anticipating meeting this boy myself."

"You and I both," the mystery man laughed.

"So you'll just take me home. Do you remember where I live? Roanoke asked while walking to the SUV that brought him there. "Because I don't think, I live anywhere close to where you guys picked me up." He turned when no one answered, and saw a gun aimed, point blank, right at his forehead. He barely heard the shot before falling on the pavement.

CHAPTER 17

Philmore awoke again, for the second time. His face was numbed with pain. He looked up and pulled back from the bright light shining in his eyes. He had no idea what was going on; the confusion of the men yelling in a language he didn't speak just adding to the mayhem.

He was slapped again across the face. His head went with the blow. His head was more a jack in box on springs attached to his neck, than anything else. Finally a man came down the steps, with another man right behind him. Philmore tried to see who it was, if he would recognize anything, but the light inhibited his site from seeing anything other than black silhouettes of the men who were beating him. The man was careful to stay outside of the light to keep his appearance a secret. The man behind him stayed also in secret.

"My name is Mr. Gobaleski," the man said at last. "It would appear that you were in a dream world with a certain Detective Miller, and Detective Roanoke. Is that true?"

Philmore squinted to make anything out on the man, but he didn't even recognize the voice, and he definitely didn't know any Gobaleski. "So someone speaks English in here." This guaranteed another punch to the face from one of the men standing near the chair. "Allow me to rephrase. Yeah, that's true." Philmore's speech was muffled due to his swollen jaw and lips. "I know I'm not a detective. I knew it was fake. I can't believe you people just beat me, without personally asking me anything in English first. I don't speak what ever language your guys are speaking." There was another punch to the face. This time Philmore lost another tooth; he actually saw this one fly and hit the far wall.

"Aha, he seems smarter than the other one, and a bit loose tongued," Gobaleski reacted, turning to the mysterious man behind him. He turned back to Philmore. "Tell me Mr. Philmore, but what is your account with a certain individual named Ty Livingston?"

"My account?" Philmore asked. "The world was made up. I thought I was dreaming the whole time, but obviously that wasn't true considering your making such a big deal over it." This drew yet another punch to the mid back, causing Philmore to grunt, and turn to see the man standing behind him. Philmore also got a good look at a gun tucked in his front belt, sticking out over his shirt. He turned back around.

"I would suppose it is a big deal, or you wouldn't be going through all this trouble to find this boy, or have me strapped to a chair and beating me over and over to tell you what I know."

Philmore started to nonchalantly slip his hands out of his ropes behind him, without drawing attention to himself, from the guy standing right behind him.

"Aha, see, we can all get along when we all understand each other," Gobaleski said smiling, even though Philmore could barely make it out.

"Right, well, I know we chased this guy for a few days. We finally narrowed it down to this compound thing. We went underground. I rode in a truck, and this Detective Miller rode in one. The Detective Roanoke, you referred to went above. Me and the Detective Miller fellow, snuck in through this door in all this mayhem of the battle.

Battled armored suited guys were coming out of the walls it seemed. Just massacring the team, we brought with us." Philmore stopped to spit blood from his broken teeth. "Sorry about that. I suppose it's the hospitality, I've been so gratefully shown." Philmore noticed Gobaleski putting his hand up to stop the man from behind from smacking him again.

"Please continue." Gobaleski seemed intrigued.

"Well, we couldn't get through this key carded door. So, in my suggestion, we went above to try to get through the heating vents. This girl came out of nowhere, and started taking massive chunks of heating ducts out with these whips. She bloodied the Detective and me, and we fell out, but obviously I'm fine now. Look at me, not even a scratch." Philmore was obviously being sarcastic. This time he did deserve another smack to the mid back, and Gobaleski did nothing to stop the beating.

After Philmore was done cringing in pain, he continued. "They took me to stand in front of your boy Ty, who was dressed in some high powered suit of some sort. He was about to kill all of us, when he just stopped."

Philmore faked a cough and sputtered and spit blood. He depended on the man punching him in the back or something of the like. When the man went to pull on Philmore's hair, to grab his head back up, Philmore took his hands completely out of the ropes, and grabbed the gun. He shot the man behind him and the other two guards. He went to shoot Gobaleski, but his gun was knocked out of his hand by something metal that swished through the air. He saw it coming from the mysterious man.

Philmore had only seconds to react. He jumped out of his chair, and grabbed it and launched it at the light. Breaking the bulb, the whole room went dark. Philmore didn't waste any time, heading for the stairs. He heard a leather whip slash at his ear, and for some odd reason, he ducked in time. He was grateful for the quick reflex, for having just been beaten and counted it as good fortune. Philmore raced up the stairs, shot in the nearest direction of the front door, or any door for that matter leading to the outside.

Philmore took off running toward the door, and flung it open. He took off running down the front stairs. He heard shouting from behind him, something in Russian. It was Gobaleski's voice. Then he heard shouts on all sides. Philmore took off down the drive path, hoping to make it to the road. Suddenly he took a quick left through some bushes and out the other side of the neatly cut grass. He figured that would be easier than getting shot where cars might be able to travel. He came to a wall. Philmore didn't know what possessed him to make the jump, but he did grabbing at the top of the ten foot wall. He pulled himself up, and just in time; a silver metal flying object hit the wall where his legs were. He ran out to the road, and thank God a car was coming just at that moment.

The car stopped and the door flew open. "Get in," came the female's voice on the inside.

Philmore didn't need to be told twice. He turned to see the mystery man jump the wall without any problem and started running his way. Philmore got in the car and slammed the door.

It sped away.

Breathing a little easier, Philmore turned to thank his rescuer. His heart nearly jumped. "Ms. Darnell?"

Sumiko drank for longer than she wanted to which was longer than she even wanted to have started. She couldn't explain the impulse, but it helped sooth her body. She gulped down huge squirting amounts of blood before stopping. She refrained at last, sitting up. Blood dripped from her chin, onto her chest of her nurse's uniform. She looked down and sat back against the floor skirt of the couch. She breathed having felt the release of the pain from her body. She reached up and felt her teeth. Her fang teeth were a bit longer than usual. She felt them, with her fingers; retract back to their normal size. She also felt her fingernails retracting. She felt her face. Those seemed to be the only differences her body took on.

She looked at the still body of Ren. Sumiko nearly gasped at looking at what she just done. She felt for a pulse, but there was none. Sumiko remembered the convulsions stopping half way through the draining of Ren. She didn't know what to do.

A thought came to her head that she finally had her apartment back, but Sumiko pushed it aside. She sighed, the pain was finally gone.

Sumiko got up and found the bathroom. When she looked in the mirror, she saw her eyes were the normal shade of brown that they had been before all this happened. She grabbed a rag from under the sink and wetted it. Sumiko tried rubbing the blood off, but it only lightened it a bit. She had to change her clothing.

Sumiko moved to the bedrooms, looking for something to where. She found Ren's daughter's room, and found a nice darker sweater, and jeans that would fit her well. She looked down and saw a nice pair of knee high boots that would work perfectly. Luckily she was close to the same size as Ren daughter.

Close to the same size, Sumiko thought.

She rushed over to the girl's desk, and gasped. The girl in the picture with her arms around Ren looked exactly like Sumiko. She turned and ran out of the room to the still body of Ren.

Her deepest fears came true at that moment. It was Ren, her mother.

It took a little bit for Gobaleski and his men to catch up to the mystery man on the other side of the wall. He was out at the road, crouched down, rubbing something. He brought his fingers to his nose and took a long whiff.

"What are you doing? How did you let them get away, Julius?" Gobaleski asked, behind him. "We can't afford to—."

Julius held up a hand to calm Mr. Gobaleski. "Do not worry, I know where their headed."

"Then let's chase after them," Gobaleski said fervently.

"I'll go. Don't worry about anything. No one will know what happened here today."

"They had better not. I have invested a lot of money in this weapon. I need to find him."

"Where, their headed, you'll get a lot of answers," Julius nearly whispered.

"I'd better." Mr. Gobaleski said. "I'll send some guys—." Mr. Gobaleski was cut off.

"I work better alone." Julius stood up and turned toward Gobaleski, his leather trench coat blowing in the wind. "I'll find the boy."

He took off through the woods in the opposite direction in which the car went.

Gobaleski rubbed his forehead. "You'd better," was all that he could say, as he and his men walked back into his mansion.

Ty blinked a few times, before letting his gaze rest on Noel. "What are you talking about, never have seen a vampire until now?" Ty got out. "I know I'm not a vampire, so that only leaves you." His suit dissipated. The adamantine plates that made up his helmet folded back into nothing. His suit folded back, his weapons disappearing also into thin air.

"I'm sorry I didn't tell you earlier," Noel started.

"There are just so many questions that come to mind right now." Ty started pacing around the car. He stopped and turned toward Noel. "Like how long have you been a vampire, and why have you not sucked my blood."

Noel put her head down. "Listen Ty, I have never felt this way about a human before. I can't exactly explain it. The reason I was so weak was not because of the program, but because I haven't fed in over three weeks. When I held you close in the hospital, I felt your blood flowing through your neck, and even in my weakened state I would not bite you, unless you wanted me to turn you." She raised her eyes to meet Ty's. "I love you. I don't know why, but I do."

This put Ty back on his tracks. He had so much thrown at him in the last few hours, not to mention his whole life, that he had no idea what he was doing.

Ty shifted on his feet. "But you're a vampire?" he said at last.

"Yeah," Noel said shrugging. "I have been a vampire my whole life. I was born a vampire. I have never known another life."

"But what about day time; can you be out in the sun?" Ty asked.

"Don't believe everything you hear in the legends;" Noel began. "A vampire's skin is very resilient. We are sensitive to the sun. Think of it as a little worse than the most faired skin person you know. The whole silver and garlic idea, yeah, it doesn't work. Don't get me wrong, we have a little higher allergic reaction to it like, any person would, but it won't kill us. It'll just make us sick, if we touch it or eat it." Noel looked up to the night sky. "Think of it as your poison ivy," she said at last, thinking of the perfect illustration.

"So that goes along with crosses and that sort of thing?" Ty sincerely wondered.

"Yep, you guessed it. Crosses, holy water, and everything of the sort don't harm us at all. Heck my parents even had a crucifix hanging in their house for a while." Noel took a step toward Ty, and he backed up a step. "Ty I am still the same person. You just know a little more about me now."

"Yeah, you're a vampire now," came Ty's reply.

"Ty I am still the same. You don't understand, the love I have for you," she pleaded with him. "Yes, we need blood to survive. My body drank some of the blood of the man you killed near me. That's how we draw our strength, but I promise you, for as long as I live, I will not bite you, unless you want to be turned.

Ty rubbed his face, and walked back to the car to lean against it. "I just . . ." he started. "I just, don't know. I mean—." Ty remembered what Bones and Jonas told him. His face looked frantic.

"What's the matter, Ty?" Noel asked taking a step toward him.

"I'm supposed to be a weapon. I think I'm supposed to kill vampires," he bluntly said, really worried.

Noel put her shoulders down, as well as her head. She looked back into Ty's eyes. "Do you remember the Doctor on the screen?"

"Yeah."

"He is also a vampire."

"You mean I had a vampire looking over me in the coma state, and he didn't turn me."

Noel grew very impatient and was deeply offended by the comment. "You know," her voice became louder and more upset as she spoke. "We're not monsters. He was paid to make you into a vampire killer. He didn't turn you, because he wanted you to want that for yourself. He wanted you to see what we are all about; what we have to offer. He didn't turn you because he knows you have a bigger purpose in your life, and you need to learn a lot about life before you can take that step for yourself." Noel started to walk away.

Ty sincerely felt bad for what he said. He didn't know. He only knew what he heard about vampires. He ran after Noel. "Noel, wait."

She turned.

"I'm sorry. I didn't mean it. I… I just don't know. The only thing I ever knew about vampires was what I was told when I was a kid. Even that's a little hazy because I don't remember much about when I was a kid with the program making my thoughts all weird. "You're right," he called.

Noel's eyes lit up, and she cocked her head.

"I want to find out who did this. I want to find out why. I need to find Sumiko. I need to find out about my past and exactly what happened."

"Do you forgive me for not telling you sooner?" Noel asked puckering out her bottom lip.

Ty smiled. "I do."

"Can we hug?" Noel asked.

Ty was going to say no, but with the sincerity of her face, he couldn't. She was right. She could have bitten him many times, and even in her weakened state, she still refused. She might have died and probably was about to, and she still wouldn't bite him. Ty walked toward her. She met him half way and they embraced. Ty found himself smelling her hair; her long dark hair. It smelled so good. After a few long moments, they pushed apart gently.

"What?" Noel asked.

"You're really beautiful," Ty answered.

Noel went in for a kiss, but Ty pushed her back. "I am still confused about what I'm feeling though. I am falling in love with you too, and this has never happened before for me either." Ty paused. "I'm not ready to be turned yet. I will let you know when, but I'm not sure if I want to be, you know?"

"I understand. It's okay. Please, though, don't be frightened of me." It looked like Noel was about to cry.

"I won't."

They embraced again, tighter this time. Ty even kissed her neck once then again. They pulled apart to arms length then kissed passionately on the lips for a few very long minutes.

They separated, when they both heard something.

It sounded like a shriek. It wasn't human. It was coming from the sky. They both looked up, but saw nothing. Noel's eyes were more in tuned to darkness than Ty's so she saw it first.

"Night ravens," she whispered.

"Night ravens?" Ty asked. "What is that?"

"They're a form of vampires. I'll explain later. They're not part of any normal clan of vampires. They're not part of the Illuminati either. If you want to call anything a monster, they're it. Come on." Noel ran toward the car. Ty turn around and got in the passenger seat, since Noel seemed to know more about the enemy that Ty had not even seen yet.

"What are they?"

"They're nearer to a mutant than anything. They are the vampire's enemy." Noel pulled the driver, which had a sword wound going through his eye, out of the car. "They're the vampires that never evolved. They refuse. They say it's getting away from our roots." She started the car, and peeled out of the drive path weaving in and out of bodies and SUVs. She didn't miss all the bodies. The car sped out of the path and took to the main stretch of road.

"See vampires are a spiritual people," Noel continued her lesson while driving and looking in her rear view mirror. "The Illuminati were set in place years ago, to keep our people in place. Most vampires embraced this government, but not the night ravens. They live to feed off humans and vampires alike. They don't care the amount of blood they spill, they live by no rules. They are death of the sky and land."

Ty looked up and saw a darker flying object in the night sky, barely visible.

"Ty!" Noel yelled.

It snapped Ty out of his gazing trance.

"I need you to see if there are any guns in the back?"

Ty looked and saw a sawed off shot gun lying on the back seat of the car. He yanked it up front. "Yeah, but if silver can't hurt vampires, then what can regular bullets do?"

"Hurt them like a mother. I don't know. Every time I've seen one, I've always ran. They know you're alive and well. They're after both of us. Me for what I am and you for what you will be."

"A vampire?" Ty asked.

"No, a vampire hunter. Somehow they know you're bred to be a weapon. You were not created to just kill us, but them. The Good Doctor wants you to kill them I'm sure, while joining us."

Just then the car rocked back and forth. Noel looked straight up, and felt the ceiling of the inside of the car with her left hand. "They're on top of the car. Shoot them!"

Ty opened the gun up. The shot gun held eight shells. It was full. Ty cocked the gun. "Just shoot the roof?" he wanted to make sure.

"No shoot them on the other side of the roof. It's a shot gun. It'll go through metal cars at point blank range."

The night raven grabbed at the top of the car and Ty saw its nails carving through the roof just inches away from Noel's head.

Ty aimed the gun, and shot a rather large hole in the roof. He heard a loud shriek, as the night raven let go, hopefully in pain and flew higher.

Noel sped up. Good. That should keep 'em at bay.

She barely finished the sentence when something hit the car from her side. The car swerved off the road, but Noel got it back on and under control. Ty looked at the speedometer; she was nearing eighty kilometers per hour. On these windy roads, that was way too fast.

Noel looked at the damage to the side of the car. "Yeah, we're going to need a bigger gun."

CHAPTER 18

Sumiko stared at her mother crying. She sobbed for hours touching her mother's face, rubbing her hands over and over her face. Sumiko felt the two puncture wounds that her fangs had made on her mother's neck. She cried all the more. She cried until she had no more tears to cry. Then she just buried her face into her knees, sitting on the floor beside her still mother.

Sumiko almost fell asleep, due to all that she had been through, but a searing pain, pierced her back. She jerked up, and shook in pain. She ran to the bathroom, where she lifted up her shirt and faced away from the mirror, so she could take a look at her back. Horror filled her face as she saw two creasing lines running from her shoulder blade down about a foot and a half. The skin pulsated, as if giving birth to something. Something foreign.

Sumiko didn't know what to do; she pulled her sweater back down, and sat on the lid of the toilet. She buried her hands in her face and began to moan. She stood back up and looked in the mirror again. Her eyes were black as night. She had no idea what was going on, with her body now; what changes it might take on.

Sumiko finally decided to leave her apartment again, and go back to the hospital. She had to talk to Takeo about this. She picked up a pair of sunglasses, and put on a stylish hat, and left the apartment. No one looked at her suspiciously, with the sunglasses hiding her black eyes. Sumiko was glad she grabbed them anyways, because the sun seemed extra bright today. She looked down at her skin; it felt like it was sizzling. She walked briskly onward.

She finally made it to the hospital and took the stairs down to where she last seen, Takeo. Sumiko went to the same room that she was in, but Takeo was nowhere to be seen. Finally she stopped a nurse in the hallway. "Excuse me," Sumiko said.

The nurse looked at her curiously for a few moments, and then finally said, "Yes, what do you need?"

"I was wondering if Takeo was around and if I might speak with him."

The nurse's eyes lit up as if she just had an epiphany. "Yes, follow me."

She took Sumiko through mazes of underground hallways, around corners, and through double doors. Finally she ended at a room. "He will see you now," was all the nurse said before leaving Sumiko to stand in the door way.

Sumiko thought to knock on the door, but decided not to. She walked on in and saw an office, quite out of place, in a hospital. It was dimly lit all around. Gothic pictures hung on the wall throughout the entire room. Takeo sat behind a stone gothic desk, with, what looked like, fangs as desk legs.

"Aha, I see you've decided to come back. The prodigal daughter returns to the flock eh?"

Sumiko didn't say anything.

"So what shall we do for you today? I see you've been feeding."

"Yeah, I killed my mother," Sumiko spat with as much anger as she could muster.

"Yes, well pity. The first feeding, you hardly ever have any control over," Takeo spoke flatly.

"What is wrong with you?" Sumiko finally asked, throwing her hands in the air.

"What is wrong with me?" Takeo repeated the question. "I do not believe I fully understand what you are asking. Nothing is wrong with me."

"You act as if this is strictly business for you."

"It is," Takeo said shrugging his shoulders, and sitting back in his chair crossing his legs.

"My mother is dead," Sumiko said again, hoping to get some sort of human reaction from the man.

"You have already stated," Takeo pronounced. "It is better than your demise, is it not?"

Sumiko opened her mouth for a quick answer, but was cut short by the question. Something inside her breathed and lived. It wasn't human, but it was geared for survival. Sumiko's last bit of human conscience feared it would do anything to be the last one alive.

"You see Sumiko. I injected you with my blood, when you were about to die, so you could live."

"What am I then?" Sumiko asked.

"What are you?" Takeo repeated the question again. "I will tell you what you are not. You are not human anymore. You are not weak. You are barely a vampire either."

"What do you mean barely a vampire? Isn't that what you are?"

"Yes and no." Takeo answered. "I used to be a vampire, now I am better than a vampire."

Sumiko looked at him curiously. She cringed and shook as her back convulsed again, then glared at Takeo again.

"Aha, I see the final affect is taking place. You may feel a little bit of discomfort, but I assure you the end result will be quite worth it."

Sumiko dropped to her knees, nearing to passing out. "What are you?" she demanded.

Takeo got up from his desk and knelt down to Sumiko. "Child, I am a night raven. When your transformation is complete; you will be too.

Julius attacked the trail, as if his life deepened on it. In some ways, his legacy did depend on it. He heard a shriek off into the distance. He looked up in the night sky. His whip automatically appeared in his hand.

Julius took out his phone and dialed a number. "Yes, Archer. Tell Tommy to fire up the chopper. We're not far from Ty. I think he's in danger." He paused. "Alright, I'll send up a flair, don't worry. Meet me there soon. You'll see the bright lights."

Julius took off running in a quick, but untraceable run through the woods, following the shrieking. He made it to a clearing in the trees. He took a gun out from under his leather trench coat and let a flare fly high. He waited a minute or so; then let another fly. "Well," he said to himself, "Let's see who that brings first."

Noel nearly careened off the road, due to another hit in the side of the car. She was speeding along, around turns going up a mountain. The higher she went, the lower the edge of the road became, which meant the more dangerous things became.

"I don't think we got a bigger gun," Ty finally said, looking in the back seat of the car.

"Hmm…let me think." Noel leaned forward and looked up through her windshield. "I think there's about three of them, from what I've seen."

"How can you see them; I can't see a thing."

"Why don't you pull that suit out of yours again, and have a go at it?" Noel said, smiling a sly smile at Ty. She raised her eyebrows, and winked at him. "That door, that you so meticulously ripped off its hinges isn't going to suit us well either. I think we'll need your suit."

Ty looked back at the gaping hole behind his seat. He had forgot-

ten about ripping that off, to get to Jonas the quickest way he could.
"Right," Ty looked forward at the dashboard and focused. His body quivered, but he didn't feel it. His suit appeared around the back of his neck first, traveling up over his head to his face. The facial helmet sifted down through; the adamantine plates winding down his face in perfect unison. His suit traveled down, until it reached his feet, replacing his shoes with suited anti-gravity jump boots.

"Hmm … those are new," Ty said smiling.

His weapons appeared not long after and not a moment too late. Another crash in Noel's side of the car again, brought them both too attention. Noel nearly lost control of the car, and thanks to her quick reflexes, she got the sliding wheel back on the road.

"Phew," she breathed, "Nearly lost that one. This door won't take much more. It won't be long before the uglies, are picking us out of the car, like a cat and tuna style. You almost done?" Noel asked, not even looking at Ty; not wanting to take her eyes off the road, even for a split second.

"Gun's in place. Say hello to my little friends," Ty yelled out from under his suit.

Noel rolled her eyes. "Just shoot 'em," she yelled above the rev of the engine and the shrieking from the outside.

Ty reached for his Mac-10s, and wound down his window. He leaned out and didn't see anything. "Maybe they left us alone,"

"What?" Noel asked, because the extra wind blowing in the car caused her to not hear what Ty said.

Ty never heard the question, but his own comment was answered, because he went infrared. The night ravens didn't give off heat like humans, but they were still warmer than the icy air, which gave them a tint of yellow. Ty began to spray. The night raven peeled off, and dove disappearing behind some trees.

"How's it goin out there?" came the question from inside the car.

"I don't know. I don't think I got him."

"Be careful, there are two more somewhere. We're almost there?"

Ty leaned back in the car. "Where are we going?"

"You'll see. We have safe houses all over for just such a predicament," was the answer.

Just then a night raven attacked the top of the car again; sinking it's talons into the top of the car. Noel tried to careen around turns as fast as she could, to shake it, but it dug in all the more. It looked through the whole that, Ty shot. Ty jumped back toward the dash at the site of the ugly thing. It looked, like a stretch between a human, a vampire, and a bat, and its own twist of messed up features. Its skin looked dry, as a corpse would that wasn't completely decayed.

"Okay that is ugly," Ty made mention.

Just then the night raven reached in with one of its talon hands. Noel looked back and rounded a turn to throw it off. The night raven grabbed a hold of her shoulder, to not fall, causing her to yelp in pain. Ty took out his Mac 10s again, and began spraying without abandon. At first he thought it wasn't working, then finally, after a few hundred shots in the arm, the thing left go. The bullets nearly took out that whole section of car also.

Noel moaned in pain. She was losing a lot of blood. The raven still held onto the top of the car. Ty knowing their sensitivity to light, decided to grab one of his high powered, flash bang marbles. He twisted it together.

"Try not to look back here," Ty yelled in Noels ear, but the wound was making her groggy. Ty doubted she heard, but it was too late to go back. He threw the marble at precisely the right moment, causing an extra exceeded amount of light and smoke to hit half inside the car half out.

The night raven jerked back, and fell on the road bouncing and sliding as it went. Unfortunately the flash of light made Noel flinch and jerk the wheel. The car careened off the side of the road, toward the left. It hit the hill face, and bounced the other way. Ty grabbed the wheel and jerked it back before it could break the guard rail and fly off the side of the mountain. Noel was completely unconscious. Ty flicked the wheel to hard, the other way. The car flew up the side of the hill, and flipped onto its roof. Ty, who wasn't buckled in, immediately went upside down with the car. Noel was buckled in, but the jolt didn't do anything that she would have noticed. She was at least already unconscious and wouldn't tense up with the flip. The car slid on its roof for many feet before crashing through the guard rail, and teetering off the side of the mountain.

Ty barely knew where he was at, his eyes closed. Something got his attention. His eyes opened abruptly. He laid all jumbled up, in the car, his feet over his head, his back bent around his neck supporting his weight. He flipped himself around, and realized where he was real quick, because the vehicle started to teeter again. He didn't know how long he was out; he hoped it wasn't too long. He looked at Noel, who was still unconscious, dripping a good amount of blood onto the roof of the car, which was below them.

Ty tried to look out. He saw feet walking toward the back of the car; the only part of the car that was still on the side of the road. Ty looked down at his swords. His guns replaced back on his suit. Ty grabbed Noels seat belt, fast and clicked it free. The jolt made the car slide a little more over the edge. He regretted doing that, because she fell on her head. He hoped he didn't break her neck, but he had no time to think about that now.

Ty climbed out of the car, and pulled Noel free, and just in time. A night raven was walking toward him. The other two were still in the air. The one on the ground was tall. His skin was more that of a vampire or a human now, his wings retracted back into his body. The night raven said nothing, just kept walking toward Ty.

Ty pulled out his swords from his back scabbards. "So this is how it's going to be," Ty spoke to himself more than the monster before him. The night raven was a few steps from him. It lunged at Ty. Ty was about to swing, but something knocked him out of the way. It was Noel.

"Ty, you cannot defeat them. Come on, we must run," Noel yelled. She held onto her right shoulder with her left hand, crossed in front of her. She limped.

Ty looked at the raven walking toward Noel now. "Mmm ... vampire blood will be good." It sniffed the air.

This was the first time, Ty heard it speak, which was a mix of the shriek they heard earlier, and a deeper voice. The other two landed and their wings retracted. They joined their blood brother.

"Ty!" Noel yelled off to the side. This broke Ty out of his trance.

"Use the bright marbles you have. You have to have two more at least."

Ty looked down at his chest, right below his neck line. He pulled one free and twisted it together. "Get ready," he said.

He threw the marble in the air at the night ravens faces. It went off bright as the noon day sun, even brighter. Noel hid her face this time, and she took Ty by the hands beckoning him to follow her. The ravens grabbed at their faces, falling over themselves at the brightness of light. Ty knew if it blinded a human, it must do some serious retinal damage to one these guys.

Noel dragged Ty along a side path, through the woods. The sun was rising over the horizon. "These guys definitely don't like the sun. They may leave us alone for now. Let's hope."

Ty started to run beside Noel, helping her with her limp. His suit was constantly charging his body. They ran along that path, and then Noel darted to the right. They came to a tree that looked like every other tree in the woods. The sun was peaking a little more over the horizon causing more light to shine through the forest. Noel turned around, seeing nothing. She turned back toward the tree, and reached up to open a secret door, out of one of the low hanging branches. She pushed a button, and the tree opened up, into a rather large underground hide away. She closed the secret hatch, and dragged Ty inside.

What Ty saw, amazed him incredibly. The place was definitely nicer than some people's houses. Once the room detected movement, lights came on to give the place a nice cozy feel to it. It was all made of concrete, but the amenities definitely took that edge off. It had refrigerators lined up on the one wall, and couches and a nice rug in the center with side tables, near the couches. It had paintings of exotic art on the walls, and Persian rugs hung off to the side. The underground hideaway even had a side bar with stools and everything.

"A little touch of home," she smiled. "Excuse me," she said letting go of Ty's arm and limping over to the one of the refrigerators. She opened the door, and pulled out a pack of blood. She checked the date, and then winked at Ty. "Good year," she giggled.

Ty chucked too, although the thought of drinking blood repulsed him. He wondered over to the couch, and took a comfortable seat, propping his feet up.

"So they don't know we're here?" Ty asked.

"No," came Noel's answer, as she punctured two holes in the bag with her fangs and begin to drink. She pulled the bag away. "Like I said, they don't like the sun. I'm sure if they had it their way, their hiding too, until the darkness again."

"Does the sun and bright lights harm them?"

Noel took another swig from the blood bag. "Think of it, as a thousand watt bulb being shown in your face without you preparing to close your eyes. Take that times ten, and you have their eyes compared to the sun. I'm sure it would blind them, as it would blind anyone if they stared at it, but it's not just their eyes. Their skin is really sensitive to the sun, even more than regular vampire's. It is said, that you can actually hear a night raven's skin crackle and boil, if they are out in the sun too long. Whether it's true or not, I don't know." Noel finished the bag and threw it to the side of the counter.

"Aha," she sighed. "Much better," she wiped her mouth and walked over to the couch jumping on Ty's lap.

Ty jerked, and that made her laugh.

"How'd you find out about this place?"

Noel put her hands around his neck, and looked around. "This place? Well we vampires are very resilient. We have to be when fighting against the night ravens. They don't give up too easily, as you've noticed. They are faster, more powerful, and can heal more quickly, without consuming blood, than a vampire. We have to set up places like this so that we can be safe." She looked back at Ty. "These places are all over the world. I've known about them since I was a little girl."

She started to bend in to kiss Ty, when he interrupted. "How old are you anyways?"

Noel pulled back and smiled out of the side of her mouth. "Why, how old do you think I am?" she teased.

Ty chuckled a bit. "I don't know, twenty-five or twenty-six is what I would guess."

"Oh you're too kind," she giggled. Noel put her face real close to Ty's.

"Why?" Ty cut in. "You can't be much older than thirty then."

"Well, some of the legends are true. Grant it, vampires are not immortal per say, but we do age a lot slower than humans. I happen to be two hundred and fourteen years old."

Ty's eyes, widened.

"Think of it this way. For every ten to fifteen years in a human's life, that is about a year for a vampire. That is approximately how slow we age. Some vampires can live to be seven or eight hundred years old." She stared deeply into his eyes. "Why does my age scare you, because I am old enough to be your great-great-grandmother?" she giggled again.

"Oh stop," Ty made a face. He noticed her shoulder. Through the torn shirt, he could see a good part of the skin. It looked almost fully healed.

Noel noticed him looking at it. "Amazing huh? Like I said, very resilient, us vampires. But . . ." Noel paused for a few seconds. "I should get a shower to wash the outside of the blood off."

"They have showers, in here too?" Ty was amazed.

"Oh yeah, through that door." Noel pointed off to the side of the couch along the wall.

"Huh." Ty said. "I didn't even see that door."

Noel jumped up. "Yeah, you know the shower has room enough for two." She walked over to the door and opened it. "I don't think I have to spell that out for you any more than I already have." She let a sly smile slip through her lips. Noel pulled her sleeve shredded sleeve down past her arm exposing her slender shoulder. Ty gulped, getting a glimpse at the top of her breast, as she twisted her body away from him. She closed the door.

Ty was trying to fight her wiles; trying to focus on the mission at hand. He looked at the door then down at his own pants where Noel had sat. He shivered as a smile came to his face. Maybe it wouldn't be so bad being a vampire. He got up and walked toward the door.

CHAPTER 19

Julius listened for the shrieking in the air. It became louder as the moments went on. Julius readied his whip. The night raven came at him from behind. Julius ducked just in time; the claws tore at his coat. He didn't have enough time to return the attack, because the raven hit the air again. Julius followed it with his eyes, trying to decipher its movements. The sun was caressing the horizon. The night raven noticed it too; it made an effort for one more attack. Julius jumped out of the way, and swung his whip, grabbing hold of the raven's foot as it tried to pull away. Julius grabbed one of his razor throwing suns, a weapon that's rays were sharp enough to cut through any kind of skin. Once thrown, the rays would double causing more damage. Julius let one fly. It nailed the beast right in the back. It screamed out in pain, and hissed at Julius. It looked up to the sun, screeching. It wiggled its foot free from the whip, and flew off to hide from its wounds and the sun, taking Julius' weapon with him.

Julius stood there for a bit, basking in the sun. "Hmm," he sighed. "It's good to be human." He rolled up his whip and placed it around the hook on his belt loop. He folded his coat back over to conceal it.

Just then a chopper rose from the tree line. It landed in the clearing. It was Archer, and Tommy.

"So good of you guys to join me." Julius said saluting the two, with a tip of his hat, when the helicopter landed.

Archer got out first, while Tommy stayed behind the controls. "Yes well, we would have left quicker, but Tommy here was working on some kind of computer program. Something about the next level in killing vampires and night ravens." Archer looked at the young man still in the chopper. To his mentors, he was more a boy, considering him barely over a score of years, and the other two having seen six and seven decades.

Tommy left the chopper running. He knew they wouldn't be staying long.

"So almost caught another one have you?" Archer asked, noticing the blood lying on the forest floor. He had a knack for spotting the blood of baddies, with his old eagle eyes.

"Yeah, but the bugger got away. The sun scared it off."

"Perhaps that was a good thing considering." Archer took notice to the shredded coat.

Julius turned his head to look at his back. He saw where the night raven had dug in with his talons. "Didn't even break the skin, thanks to that new armor you two made for me."

"Yes, live to fight another day and all that." Archer having grown up in Scotland most his life had a most peculiar accent to most people.

Julius changed the subject. "The boy is safe for now."

"How safe?"

"Well, he's headed south, I can tell you that. I can smell his blood. It definitely is a match. He's got a companion, and that I'm not too sure of?"

"Why's that?"

"Because, the iron count in it smells too much like a vampire?"

"What? Tyson, made friends with a vampire? Has he yet been turned?" Archer was aghast.

"No. I'm just not sure. I may be wrong. This vampire smells familiar though. I think it's the same one, the two idiots were murmuring about in Gobaleski's mansion."

"Yes, how is that going?" Archer made mention to Julius and Gobaleski's work relationship.

"Gobaleski's research seemed to be going as planned. He sent that Jonas character up to pick him up, but I knew better. I knew the boy escaped once I smelled the blood."

"You paid him?"

"I did, the full amount and the bonus for finding the girl."

"Are you sure it's her?"

"I'm sure. It's too familiar a story, from the two wannabe's in the program, and this blood." Julius picked up a leaf to his nose and took a long whiff. "It's her."

"Well you 'vet been doing this a long time Julius, too long to be wrong. What now?" Archer put his hands in his pockets.

"Well, I think I know where they stopped. Let's take a ride, and I'll show you. We should be able to catch them on foot with this." Julius pointed at the chopper. "They're not far from here."

Julius and Archer climbed into the chopper; Archer in the co-pilot's seat. After they were all buckled in, Tommy pushed off, and the helicopter lifted ground.

"I can't believe it," Philmore started. "It's you. I tailed you for a while, and then. . ." Philmore didn't know what to say precisely.

"It's okay dear. Don't worry about it." Ms. Darnell was driving steadily away from the men and the house. The sun was rising steadily, in the sky lighting the beginning of the day up beautifully. "You are familiar with the fact that you are in the real world now aren't you?" Ms. Darnell asked.

"I'm beginning to grasp the idea, more and more. Not to forget the importance of whatever I went through, obviously." Philmore showed Darnell the cuts and bruises to his face from the earlier beating. "I know I was just dreaming, but the lengths some people go through to find out what I was dreaming about."

"What did you tell them?"

"The people that had me in their basement?" Philmore asked. "I . . . I told them the truth, why?"

"Oh. Hold on." Ms. Darnell made a phone call. "Okay, I have it. He lives at 341, Converse Drive." She paused. "Right, pick him up." She hung up the phone and regarded Philmore again. "Sorry about that. Where were we?"

Detective Miller was grateful for the rest. His migraine was practically gone. He realized that he slept most of the day away which was not his intention. He sat up, and headed toward the bathroom. He had to get into the precinct to debrief. Miller splashed some water in his face, then grabbed his keys and left his house. He was on his way to work, and got this uncanny feeling that he was being followed. He checked his rear view mirror many times, but nothing seemed out of the ordinary. People were bustling all around, walking the streets, nothing seemed different.

Miller pulled into the precinct and went inside. He marched to his captain's office and saw him through the window. When he knocked on the door, His captain bade him inside.

"I thought you dead. How is it that you are still alive?" his captain was first to speak.

"Excuse me sir?" I was only gone for a little while. I was here a few days ago, when we got the package, with the finger."

"I'm sorry; Miller, but I don't remember any finger. Are you sure you're feeling alright?"

"Yeah, I slept it off, I feel fine. I'm ready for work. I just wanted to debrief," Miller said. "How is it that you don't remember the finger?

Plus you came up to me, when I was questioning the old nurse; you wondered what my intentions were."

"Sorry, Miller, that didn't happen. Have you hit your head or something in the last few days you've been gone? "No, as I said, I feel fine." Detective Miller's voice got a bit louder.

"Look," the captain folded his hands in front of him. I think you need to take a few days off and regroup. Come back and debrief after you've done that."

"But…"

"That's an order. Go."

Detective Miller got up from his chair, and left the office. Miller thought to go back in and argue his case, but when he turned around, the captain was directly on the phone. He got in his car, and pulled out of the precinct parking lot.

When Miller pulled into his drive way; he noticed a curtain fold back down suddenly. He looked around at his neighbors houses, and nothing seemed out of the ordinary. Miller took his spare revolver out of his glove compartment, and made sure it was loaded. He didn't have to unlock his door, as he had presumed.

"I have a gun!" he yelled out into the stillness. "I'm a cop."

He rounded the corner and looked at the window in which the curtain was moved. There was no one there. When he turned around, someone grabbed his throat. He emptied all six shots into the gut of whatever it was that had him, but the thing just kept hold. Miller started hitting it over and over. Then Miller saw the fangs. His eyes became huge. He had never seen a vampire before, definitely not this close.

The vampire pinned him up against the wall, squeezing the life from him. Miller hit the thing over and over, but it just would not give up. Finally, due to the lack of oxygen getting to his brain; Miller's brain shut down. The vampire didn't give up. He held its hold, squeezing slowly. Miller awoke, gasping for air, but none came.

He could feel the bones in his neck, breaking. Just a little more pressure and he would be dead. He looked for a way out, a lamp, or anything to hit the vampire over the head with.

The vampire lifted him high into the air, snuffing the life from him again. As his eyes closed to give into the pressure; Miller heard one last thing. The sound of his neck bones caving in, before he fell limp and lifeless on the floor.

The vampire picked his phone out of his pocket and dialed a number. "It's done," was all he said.

"Oh thank you dear, so good of you to do that for me. Thank you for making sure he's okay." Ms. Darnell hung up the phone. "Good news." She turned to Philmore

Philmore looked at her curiously. "What is it?"

"Your friend, in the dream state, Detective Miller, I believe his name was."

"Yes,"

"You'll be joining him shortly."

"Oh is he in Russia,"

"Not exactly." The nurse pulled out a dagger that was strapped to her left thigh and in one motion stabbed it into Philmore's neck. He flew forward, the slack of the seatbelt letting him fall slowly toward the dash of the car. "And the name's Vadora, none of this Darnell anymore," she told the dead body of Philmore.

Vadora picked up her phone, and dialed a number.

"Yes Doctor, everything is finished. They all three been taking care of."

"Even Roanoke?" the Good Doctor questioned.

"My clan has said that he is already been taken care of. I have men on the inside, of Gobaleski's mansion."

"Yes, he definitely is a thorn in my side. How pleased will he be, once

I turn his weapon against him, and anyone who stands in my way?"

"Oh Doctor. One of my clan members said there's a wild card in the mix. Julius is working with Gobaleski."

There was silence on the phone for quite a while.

"Julius you say?"

"Yes."

"He has been an even bigger thorn in my side. I thought him dead?"

"Apparently not." Vadora looked in her rear view mirror to make sure she wasn't being followed.

"Yes, well funny how this all happens on the eve of the ritual," the Good Doctor grumbled. "Well, the three are taken care of, that is all that matters. You will be here tomorrow then for the ritual?"

"I'm on my way there already."

"Excellent, I will see you then,"

"Oh Doctor before I forget," Vadora quickly blurted.

"Yes, my sweet," The Doctor answered.

"I want the Illuminati to know that giving me, the elder of the Dominicus Clan, this great responsibility to serve, is greatly appreciated."

"We knew we could count on you, Vadora," the Doctor announced.

"I just want the Illuminati also to know that if ever you need the Dominicus Clan to serve, that we are here. We will not fail."

"I know you won't. Drive safe, my child." The Good Doctor hung up the phone.

Ty woke up pleasantly for once. His body fully aware fully re-charged. He remembered the night before, or this morning rather, for he slept most of it away to the afternoon. Ty remembered Noel easing his nerves, saying that if they used protection, he would not be turned. Vampires definitely were passionate lovers. He was a bit sore in the nether regions. Noel had to go easy on him, as to not bite him in the passionate moments. Ty looked up. Where was Noel?

"Noel?" he called.

"Relax lover boy; I'm right here." Ty turned and saw Noel, fully garbed in black Kevlar and leather combat gear. Her adamantine whips strapped to her side. She pulled the zipper on the side of her tight black suit, running it along her hips and waist. She placed each and every throwing knife in the right slot traveling down her thighs.

"Whoa," was Ty's first reaction. "Wow," was his second. "Where'd you get that outfit?" he asked.

"Do you like?" Noel asked teasingly, swaying her hips purposely, as she walked toward him.

Ty was nodding way before he answered, "Oh I like," he finally said.

She smiled and blew him a kiss. "Listen, I've been using the vampire's satellite system to try to locate Sumiko's particular blood DNA." Noel changed the subject.

"What did you say?" Ty asked getting off the couch.

"The vampires have satellites all over the world. We can zoom in on a particular person, or find them throughout the whole world, using the systems sensitive DNA finder."

"So, you are in the process of locating her?" Ty asked.

"Well, I know her DNA. I put in this machine, and when I run a search, it should be able to find her, but it can't."

"What do you mean it can't? What does that mean?" Ty questioned.

"Well, it either means, she's dead, or . . ." Noel stopped herself realizing the possibilities.

"Or what?"

"Nothing. Don't worry about it."

Ty walked closer to her, and shook her. "What?" he beckoned.

She pulled away. "It may mean that someone has gotten to her."

"What do you mean someone? What could they have done? What's worse than being dead?"

"It might mean that she has been turned."

"What into a vampire?"

"Not exactly. A vampire's blood isn't too far from humans. The machine is sensitive enough to catch the differences. If it doesn't find a human with the DNA match, it will go the next vampire with the closest DNA. The computer has always right on. I've never came across a mistake that it has made."

"So this means what, she's dead?" Ty grabbed Noel's arm, and pulled her body to face his.

"Ty, I know you care about her. I love you, you know that. I want you to be happy, and even if that means running to her, I will understand." Noel paused choosing her next words very carefully. "It's just that I'm not trying to be rude, by this next statement, but for her sake and yours, it would be better, if she was dead."

Ty back handed her across the face with his left hand. Noel turned with the slap accepting it.

"Don't you ever say that again," Ty nearly shouted, trying to hold back tears.

"Ty, if she's not dead, then she's one of them."

"One of who?" he questioned.

"A night raven. It's the only other option," Noel answered.

Ty nearly slapped her again, for her blasphemy, yet he knew in his heart that it could very easily be true. He trusted Noel more now than he ever had, and he didn't want to lose that bond. Her being a vampire took some time to get used to, but he wanted desperately to find Sumiko. If she was dead, then he would grieve, and move on. But if she was a night raven, the very thing, he was bred to kill, then that was a whole other story.

Ty paced around the room.

"Maybe the machines wrong," he emphatically said.

"Ty, I ran the search more than five times. It came up with the same answer every time," Noel said calmingly. "The only other option is we go to the Good Doctor, in Ireland. He is part of the Illuminati;

they will know what to do. They will be able to tell you a definite."

Ty all of sudden felt guilty for sharing his bed with Noel. He had never given his heart to Sumiko, and although he thought he loved her, he didn't really know what love was at that moment. He was falling in love with Noel to the point where he couldn't imagine himself with anyone else. Sumiko and he were still friends and friends search for each other.

Ty paced some more. Thinking.

"Alright," he finally said. "We'll go see this Illuminati. I need some answers anyways from this Doctor guy."

Noel gave a calming smile. "The Doctor punished me for my insolence, but he is a powerful vampire. He should be able to tell us what happened with Sumiko."

Ty grabbed a few things, and they headed out of the temporary hiding place, grim as they walked.

"We have about six hours of daylight yet. We need a car," Noel said as they hiked back to the road. They both shuddered, as they heard a screech of a night raven in the distance.

Bones awoke, automatically thinking. He took his lap top out, and started clicking right away. He wondered if he could hack, into the vampire satellites system, to see if he could find Ty. Bones did some pre-hacking, to try to find some answers when he was in the experimental program, but only touched on the answers, because he feared for his body being held in the comatose state, had he been found out.

Bones brought up a black screen. He typed commands, and passwords, his fingers working like lightning. He clicked for what seemed like a good hour. Finally a knock came to his door. He ignored it at first.

"House keeping," a female voice said from the other side.

"Not right now, can you come back?" Bones asked rhetorically.

"House keeping, right now," was the reply.

"Oh good grief, I'm so close." Bones stood up and looked out the peep hole. He didn't see any woman, or cart or anything in front of his door.

He figured they must have left, so he was walking back to the bed when he heard the knock again.

"House keeping, please. I clean room now."

Bones became very suspicious. He looked at the window. It was nailed shut. Bones looked for something hard and heavy. Bones reached for the TV and heaved it free of the wall. He took a running start and threw the television through the window. It hit the fire escape before bounding to the road below, stopping cars in their tracks.

"Did you hear that?" a voice came from the other side, but it didn't sound like the woman any more.

Bones quickly grabbed his bag and laptop and headed out the window. They banged on the door trying to open it. Bones was down the fire escape in a hurry. He figured he'd only have a few moments.

He hit the ground running, in a dead sprint. Onlookers stared at the running man who just came out the same window, the TV flew from. He heard voices behind him. "There he goes, I'll head him off."

The sun was cresting over the horizon casting the first few looks of morning. Bones didn't know who was chasing him, but he knew he needed to get away. Bones ran down an alley, and through an abandoned back parking lot. He jumped over dumpsters, almost dropping his laptop in the process.

Bones cut down another alley, and when he was about to get to the end of it, a vehicle pulled up blocking his exit. He flipped over the car dropping his bag and laptop. Money spilled out onto the road. Bones got up, but the men were on him, fast. They grabbed him and threw him in the car forgetting about the money. One man did grab his lap top, before he got in. The car sped off.

CHAPTER 20

The chopper touched down not far from the vampire hideaway, in a clearing. Julius, Archer, and Tommy all strapped themselves with weapons and gear, before heading out. Julius followed his nose, eastward. The three hiked for a couple of minutes, until Julius stopped.

"What is it?" Tommy asked?

"It's blood," Archer answered, noticing what Julius was looking at.

"Vampire blood," Julius finished. "She's been through here."

"And the boy?" Archer questioned.

"Him too," Julius spoke looking up gathering the direction of the wind. "There was a struggle, but not with each other. There are feelings of worry, but not about the other. They were being chased by something."

"Perhaps the night raven that practically had your number?"

Julius turned and rolled his eyes at his old friend. "This way," he said at last.

The threesome moved onward for a little while longer, until finally coming to a tree.

"There's something about this tree," Julius said searching the bark of the wooded pillar.

Julius reached on one of the lower branches and opened a little hatch. He saw the button and pushed it. The door opened up, below them. Julius looked at the other two and raised is eyebrow. He took out his whip from under his long coat, and took the lead inside.

Inside the hideaway, they saw what looked like an old war bunker, made to look like home. Grant it, it was better than anything they had ever lived in, having to be on the run, and still better than their current location, in an old abandoned warehouse.

"They were here," Julius noticed.

He moved around noticing the blood bag carelessly thrown to the side. He bent down and picked it up. When he smelled it, he realized the scent. "It's got to be her," he whispered to himself.

"Who?" Tommy asked.

"An old friend of Julius'" Archer picked up. "An old friend indeed."

Tommy walked over to the couch and grabbed a seat, while the other two looked around.

Julius walked over to the same couch, and smelled the air. Grief struck his face. He followed the smell all the way to the side door. When he opened it, he saw a shower, a sink, and a toilet, in a modest size bathroom. "Oh no," he spoke more to himself.

Archer put a hand on his shoulder. "I don't think he's turned yet. We can still stop it."

Julius didn't say a word; he just walked out of the bathroom. He walked over to the side computer on the desk. With a few clicks, he brought up the last page that was looked up. His eyes narrowed.

"What is it?" Archer asked walking up to the computer.

"They're looking for someone, a Sumiko Nakamura's DNA has been put into the vampire's satellite system, but no such girl was found." Julius looked at his friend. "We know what that means."

"They had to be here, just a few hours ago," Archer finally said.

"Right, maybe two or less." Julius looked at his watch. "We got four hours until dark. Let's keep moving. Grunt," Julius yelled over to

Tommy. "Grunt" was his nickname, because he did most of the "Grunt work", and until he became higher up in the tiny clan of slayers.

Tommy jumped up.

"We're moving. I know where their headed. They didn't find their friend. They're headed to Ireland, now."

Julius and the other members were about to walk out, when he stopped. He stared at the couch and bathroom door.

Archer, taking notice stopped. "He still may not be turned yet. We must keep the faith."

"That's not it. He has lain with a vampire. I would figure my own blood line to be more wise."

They left the hideaway and headed back to the chopper.

Sumiko woke gently. She was again lying on a soft bed. She felt a little pressure in her back, but all around she felt okay.

"Do you feel better now?" Takeo was looking over her while she rested.

"Yeah, I think. What happened?"

"You fainted. Sometimes the pain becomes too great, and your body simply gives in. You feel stronger now?" Takeo smiled and put his hand on her shoulder.

"Yeah, I think so. I feel different."

"You should; the transformation is complete. Welcome to the top of the food chain. Here let me help you up."

Takeo grabbed Sumiko's hand and helped her off the bed and onto her feet. She was wearing her gown again. "You seem to like this outfit on me, huh," she remarked.

"Merely procedure, so that everything can change with the least pain and discomfort as possible." Takeo walked over to a closet. "I do have some clothes for you. It's not your Kevlar suit that you wore in the program, but I think you will find it appeasing."

Sumiko walked over to the closet, and noticed her new attire. On the top shelf were sunglasses.

"Two hundred percent UV protection, trust me, you'll need it," he laughed.

She smiled. The second shelf down, she noticed a black long sleeve shirt neatly folded.

"The shirt is light as a feather. Think of it as a second skin. It will grow back, where it was torn. Really comes in handy." Takeo winked. "Perhaps for those wings."

Sumiko looked at her back, and raised her brow. She then looked down to the shelf below that. She noticed black leg tight pants. Looking below that, she saw a pair of black boots.

"The boots are made with the finest skin of past night ravens. It is crystallized so it will never wear out. It will last as long as you, which will be a lot longer than any human or vampire would hope to last."

Sumiko smiled as the words came out of Takeo's mouth. She didn't know why, but the last few days or months really were but a blur. She felt so alive; more alive than she ever remembered feeling. She felt no pain.

She looked back at Takeo. "If I may be able to get dressed?" she politely asked.

"Oh sure, my dear," was Takeo's answer. "Tell you what, let me know when you have finished, and I will be back in to discuss your first mission. I think you'll like it."

Sumiko smiled as he left. She didn't know why, but she felt for the first time in her life, like she belonged. She didn't really remember killing her mother, just killing a person for survival. Besides, she was only human.

"It was nice of that man to lend us his truck. Too bad for all the lumber, he lost in the process." Noel smirked.

Ty wasn't even paying attention. The last few moments, they spent walking on the road until a truck came by, gave Ty a lot of time to think of his life—what he could remember at least. He remembered his short period in the real earth; and the journey he took so far with Noel. He remembered this odd feeling for love that he felt for Noel. He regretted slapping her, and if he hadn't apologized three times already, he would have at that instant.

Ty looked over at Noel who was driving the truck. That curious smirk she wore, on her face that he was falling fast for. She certainly was beautiful. Yet beyond that, there was something so appealing about her. She represented everything, that Ty couldn't imagine living without. She was a vampire, yes, but beyond even that, there was a bond they shared, that couldn't be shaken.

Ty nearly laughed aloud, as he remembered Noel batting her eyes at the driver, a few minutes before. The driver promptly stopped. Ty imagined that he would too, had he seen her on the side of the road. Ty had hid off to the side behind a tree. When the man wound down his window to see what Noel needed, Ty went around the back of the vehicle, snuck up the driver's side, and cold cocked the guy knocking him clean out. Noel wanted to kill him and take some of his blood, but Ty got a compromise out of her. Finally, after a little coaxing, they just stole the truck and the let the poor guy on the side of the road where another vehicle was sure to pick him up before nightfall.

They drove in silence most the way. Ty couldn't believe what he had heard in the hideaway. Sumiko could be dead, or a night raven. He wasn't sure what was going through his thoughts. He didn't even know where he came from, if he even had parents or any family that cared about him. The only person he really had was Noel, and she was a vampire. The thought of becoming one sickened Ty. The morning before, in the midst of their love making, Ty almost screamed the words "bite me." He knew Noel would gladly and quickly oblige.

Yet, there was something inside him that kept the words from forming on his lips. He just couldn't say it.

Ty turned to regard Noel, driving the truck again. She was so gorgeous indeed; so delicately beautiful, yet independently able to take charge at a moment's notice. Oh the thoughts just swarmed around in his head. Did he love Sumiko, whom he just met, or did he love Noel, a vampire, who he also just met, but spent more time with.

Ty couldn't remember much from his past. The experiment made his real memories all a jumbled up. Ty didn't know if he would ever get them back.

Ty wound down his window a crack. He heard something. He cocked his head toward the window, and wound it down some more.

Noel looked at him. "What do you hear? It can't be the night ravens; we still got an hour and a half of full daylight left, before the sun starts to go down."

Ty listened harder.

"It's not night ravens. It sounds like an engine of some sort." Ty cocked his head even closer to the outside, but the wind of the moving vehicle took away his sense of hearing for anything outside. "Slow down a bit," he told Noel.

She left off the accelerator, and shifted down a gear.

"Wait, I do hear that," she noted. She stopped the vehicle and wound down her window.

The sound got louder and louder. Then they really heard it. Propellers.

"It's a chopper, drive, drive, drive, drive," Ty screamed out."

Noel punched the gas pedal, and shifted up as fast as she could.

The helicopter was on them in no time, right above their heads. Ty looked out of his window. His adamantine plated suit began his body.

Noel looked in her side mirrors, but she couldn't see the chopper overhead. She shifted up another gear. She was reaching speeds far too dangerous for traveling down a mountain.

The chopper backed off. Ty and Noel looked at each other. Ty drew his guns just in case. The chopper started firing. Wood chips flew everywhere, due to the stacks of lumber in the back.

Both Ty and Noel ducked.

Ty leaned out his window, with his MAC-10s in hand; he let fly a volley of bullets. The chopper stopped shooting and back off a bit again, but kept right on the truck. Ty didn't let up. He held his hands on the trigger; his suit making the bullets just as fast as he could shoot them. The chopper veered off, above the tree tops beside the truck, on Ty's side. Ty stopped shooting, but he saw the chopper.

"Gun it!" he yelled at Noel.

"I'm gunning it as fast as I can," she yelled back.

"Who do you think they are?" Ty leaned back in the window, keeping his eye on the chopper.

"I don't know. They're definitely not night ravens. I can't think . . ." Her voice trailed off.

"Can't think of what?" Ty demanded looking at Noel.

Noel bent over to his side to look at the chopper. "Couldn't be," she gasped. She bent back to the wheel. "Hold on."

Noel gunned it even faster, taking the truck to the limit. Suddenly the chopper was back. It swept back behind the truck fast. Ty barely had time to react. The chopper flew low, hooking one of its legs underneath the truck. It shot upward. The truck flipped in a total somersault. Again Ty was not buckled in, but his suit cushioned most of the flipping vehicle. Lumber flew out in all directions. The truck was moving so fast, it kept somersaulting end over end, over end. The road curved, but the truck wouldn't stop. It plowed through the guard rail, and hit the trees, crashing to the wooded valley below. Ty barely opened his eyes.

"Why do we always get in accidents? Twice now, with two vehicles. Why can't people just leave us alone," Ty chuckled, although this was not a chuckling matter.

Noel and Ty realized the truck was hanging upside down in a big oak tree. Ty was lying on the ceiling of the cab, right below Noel's head.

She groaned. "I think I threw my arm out."

All of a sudden the truck shifted, and waivered.

"Hold on!" Ty yelled.

The tree let go of the truck, and it crashed to the forest bottom, a good sixty feet, back onto its wheels. Whatever window wasn't broken if any were broken now.

"You know," Ty laughed again. "I really should have buckled up when we were hanging."

Noel laughed, then groaned and held her arm.

"We really shouldn't be laughing," Ty noted. "Good thing for this suit bracing for the impact. Who was that guy?"

Noel sighed and shrugged, grimacing in pain.

"Is there something you're not telling me?"

"I think it might be Julius."

"Who's Julius?" Ty asked bluntly.

"Julius is a vampire hunter. He hunts night ravens too." Noel cracked her arm back into socket. "I need some blood again, to help repair myself." She looked at Ty.

Ty let his armored sleeve dissipate. He took a knife from his chest, and sliced a bit of his own wrist.

"Here," he held his arm up. "Let the blood pour into your mouth."

Noel smiled at Ty, like he never saw her smile before. Her eyes said thank you. In case Ty didn't see it, she mouthed the words. She opened up, and Ty let his blood drip onto her lips.

Suddenly she stopped pulling herself to eye level with Ty.

"What, what is it?" he asked.

Her eyes grew in size, her mouth dropped. "I see you." Her fangs started to extract from her mouth.

Ty stared at her curiously. "What?"

"You killed vampires."

"I sure wish you would tell me where you're taking me," Bones said flatly.

"Shut up," came the voice of the driver.

There were two guys beside Bones in the middle of the back seat, and the driver and a passenger in front.

"Does it really take this many guys to capture me?"

"We had to be sure, you didn't escape," one of the men beside Bones exclaimed.

"Shut up Jax!" the driver yelled. "We don't have to tell him nothing."

"Why don't we bleed him out and suck him dry," the one on Bones' other side said.

"Because the Good Doctor wants him to witness the ritual," the driver said.

Bones didn't like the sound of that at all. He had a feeling these were vampires, although he had never seen one before. They were out in plain daylight which Bones thought was unusual.

"Excuse me, but are you vampires?" he asked as politely as he could, as to not upset the men in the car.

They all laughed at him.

The car pulled up to the gate at the airport. The gate opened promptly bidding them entrance inside. They drove across the runway parking lot to the private jets section. There were men waiting at one particular jet, as if waiting for the vehicle.

When they drove up, the men in the back got out and forced Bones out of the car. They were rough with him, pushing him and shoving him along toward the private jet awaiting them. Bones practically fell down a few times. He decided to see how this would play out before making his move. He purposely acted weak.

The men forced him inside the seven seated plane.

Once they were all inside and buckled up, the private jet started up and pulled onto the runway getting ready for takeoff.

Bones noted one of the men, holding his laptop under his arm. He made sure he knew where that thing was at all times. Yes he would play weak for now. Find out his odds, before striking. Perhaps he would see the Doctor and find out who was behind all of this.

"What do you mean, I killed vampires?" Ty asked quickly. "What are you talking about?"

"You are his bloodline?" Noel hissed.

"Noel, whose bloodline?"

"Julius,"

"What?" Ty blurted out. "How do you know? Who is Julius to me?"

"Julius was in that chopper." Noel chose her words carefully, because although a vampire, Ty was tougher than most humans, especially with the suit equipped. Definitely so if he was part of the bloodline of the slayers. They were a line of family, born with extraordinary gifts for hunting and killing vampires. "Ty, Julius is your uncle." Noel paused for a moment before saying the next part. Ty looked at her earnestly. "Ty, I killed your father when you were just a baby. I'm sorry."

Ty eyes scowled in anger, his armored sleeve grew back around his exposed weapon. He reached for one of his guns.

CHAPTER 21

The dawn of the day before the ritual was fast approaching. The blood moon would be at its highest on the morrow. Magnus came rushing into the Good Doctor's inner sanctum. The Doctor was playing a melodious tune on an ancient violin. He swayed with the music, his eyes closed, letting it take him to a different place. Magnus cleared his throat to interrupt, stopping the Doctor's playing and gathering a disturbed look his way.

"What is it Magnus?" the Doctor snarled.

"It is about the ritual. Are you sure that everything is going to plan?" Magnus asked cautiously.

"Everything will be ready, come midnight tomorrow. The weapon will be here and ready. He is in good hands," the Good Doctor replied.

"You think this will seal the deal for the ritual, allowing the vampires to rule out over the humans and night ravens."

"It is written in the ancient manuscripts is it not?" The doctor's perturbed voice let Magnus know that he was overstretching his bounds.

"It is. Are you sure the weapon is to be human? I thought with my interpretations of the manuscripts, he was to be a vampire."

"Magnus," the Doctor spoke, as if settling a child's nerves. "There is no need to fear. Everything will go as planned tomorrow. Gather the others for the preparations of the coming blood moon. Everything will go as planned," the Doctor reiterated.

With that, Magnus left the room and headed away. Something just didn't seem right about the Good Doctor. He had to see those manuscripts again.

Ty held his Mac-10 up against Noel's forehead. Still seated in the truck neither one moved for many minutes. The anger wasn't in her eyes any more. The resentment and bitterness was replaced with confusion and love. Ty noticed her eyes changing from black to their normal green hue. Her fangs retracted. He still pressed the gun to her head. His hands through his suit started to shake. His suit help to stabilize his nerves, but he could tell the anxiety was becoming too much to bare.

"That will be all boy; you've done well." Ty heard a voice from the outside. He turned for a second realizing; it must have been this man Julius. The man walked a little closer to the torn truck. From the outside he said, "I underestimated you; I shouldn't have. You are worthy to be of the slayer bloodline."

Ty blinked for a few seconds; his mouth agape. What was he doing? So many emotions screamed at him, wanting a release, but yet he couldn't find any. His heart thumped hard for a few seconds. His suit helped to stabilize that too.

Ty saw the other two companions coming up behind Julius. "It's okay boy. You can put the gun away. They have poison crossbows trained on her, if she moves an inch. We have much to discuss." Julius spoke with compassion in his voice, as if he knew what Ty was going through. The gentle flow his voice made Ty feel even more relaxed.

Ty looked at Noel. Her eyes had turned black again. It wasn't at Ty though, but at Julius. She deeply hated the man. As much as her hate, her love for Ty grew stronger. Even if he was to kill her; she would love him to the end. He was human, but there was something different about him. She made up her mind.

"Do it if you must; I am ready." The words stung Ty. His face grew hot under his suit, the blood rushing to the surface. He stopped pressing the gun to her head, even lowered it.

He turned to Julius. "Do not harm her in the least, I warn you," he demanded.

"I wouldn't dream of it," Julius answered. "Although I do have some questions for her, if you don't mind. We can make the short hike back to the chopper, then to see what we have here." Julius looked at Ty then Noel, not backing down an inch. "If you please sir, and malady, come with me."

Ty looked at Noel, then at the other two of Julius' companions. He got out of the truck.

"You too, my dear," Julius said, taking out his own cross bow.

Her whips were still at her side. The thought of taking off Julius' head crossed her mind, but then she would probably never gain Ty's trust again. She couldn't kill another one of his relatives even if it meant letting a vampire slayer live.

She got out of the truck slowly, non-violently.

"Give me the whips love," Julius commanded. "Just toss them over here by my feet, easy now."

Noel made no sudden moves. She kept her eyes on Ty the whole time, burning holes in his soul for his betrayal. He was crying inside, for what he had done. Vampire or not, she was the only one who truly understood him, and deep down he understood her too.

The hike back to the chopper proved not so far indeed. Julius held the back of Noel's bound hands and arms with a special garlic dipped wire. They all climbed in and Tommy "Grunt" climbed in the pilot's seat and fired up the engine. The chopper lifted ground and flew the few miles back to a small nearby town to an abandoned warehouse. Tommy took it down on the roof of the building.

They got out, and Julius showed them all inside. Ty's suit dissipated from his body. Julius and Archer tied Noel to the wall, with specially made handcuffs that were meant strictly for vampires. She bore through it, her eyes falling to her feet. She felt; she truly deserved her impending punishment for what she had done in the past, although that was her livelihood. She also deserved it for falling in love with a human. Perhaps the Doctor was right. Perhaps her love for this human man was not meant to be. Humans would never understand vampires. Her eyes closed, and the tears came in the dimness of the warehouse.

"Come my boy. We have much to discuss." Julius motioned for Ty to join him off to a room on the side.

Ty followed apprehensively.

Julius led the way in and closed the door behind Ty. The room was dark, very dimly lit. It smelled musty. Julius turned on a few battery operated lamps he had around the room.

"Don't worry; your little friend will be fine. As long as she doesn't do anything to bring her untimely death, she will not die without your say so," Julius spoke as if giving a speech that he gave to everyone he brought in this office. "I must admit," he continued. "You had me scared there for a bit. I thought you joined them."

"Joined whom?" Ty questioned.

"The vampires," Julius spoke as if the answer was obvious. "They are crafty, and able to defeat most a weaker man with their wits, if not their looks, I warn you. Yet, she had not defeated you with her wiles. The charming spell they cast over men is uncanny to be sure, dear boy."

Ty stared at Julius completely dumfounded.

"My name's Julius by the way. The old man, about my age is Archer. The boy is Tommy, but he get's called "Grunt" from time to time. The most trustworthy friends I've ever come to know." Julius face went low, as he sat on the corner of the abandoned old desk. "That was not to say about your father of course."

"Who are you to my father?" Ty asked.

"I was his brother. I am your uncle." His voice became very solemn. "Son, the blood of the slayer is in your veins. It's meant to be there. You come from a long line of slayers since the beginning of the vamps. Your father served that to his dying breath. The girl, that you so casually shared your bed with, killed him."

Ty acted more surprised at the fact, that Julius knew of his relations with Noel than the fact that she killed his father who he never really known.

"I know," Julius continued. "It's hard to all take in."

"She already told me about the death of my father."

"She told you a lie no doubt," was Julius' rebuttal.

"No, she told me that she killed him," Ty continued.

"Then why hadn't you . . ." Julius paused finishing his own thought. "That is why you held the gun on her at that moment. She knew we were closing in on her."

Ty smiled a sideways smile to let Julius know he hit the nail on the head, but the graveness he felt in his heart, meant he didn't smile because he was happy of the situation.

"Well, it all get's washed out in the end. Forgive, and let bygones be bygones, I always say," Julius muttered to himself. "It was an awful night for our blood line, you and I. I remember it as if it just happened. You were just a baby. Your father and I were gathered around the kitchen table planning our next attack on a night club that housed the blood suckers when all of a sudden the door burst open. We immediately jumped up grabbing the nearest weapons. In walked this gang of vamps all dressed in black. The leader of them was this tall guy I remember. I think they were all family."

"Like a clan of vampires?

"That, and an actual family. They were all related. Your father and I fought with grace and style, son. We killed three of the blood suckers, before we were too wounded to fight."

Julius stopped for a moment as if choking back tears. "I remember the girl standing above your father. She said this was for my father, and then she slit is throat, soaking her hands in his blood. She took her whips out from her side under her long coat, and began swinging them back and forth. Her vampire brothers held me, and she swiped a few times at my face giving me these scars."

Julius turned his head toward the light so Ty could better see.

"Then lights had shown through the windows. They ran out of the house." Julius wiped his wet eyes. "I tracked all the suckers down. It took me three years to find them, except that one. Except the very girl that killed your father. I never would forgive myself, if my soul was cast into the fire, and I hadn't smote that very girl."

Ty looked at him curiously. "What about their family? Noel said something about her father, as if her attacking the house was payment or something."

"Yeah, we attacked her families cover business a few weeks before. We took seven of her brothers and three of her sisters, and killed them all in front of her. Then we took her father and cut off his limbs one by one. He couldn't regenerate that fast. We pushed garlic into his wounds, and his reaction to it was priceless in itself." Julius found solace in the brutal murders.

Ty acted disgusted by the act. "I have so many questions. Why would you do that to her family, and where was I when the house was being attacked? Do I even have a mother?"

Julius stared at Ty curiously for a moment or two wondering where these questions were coming from before answering. "We did that to her family, because they are vampires. Boy they suck the blood of humans. They treat us like cattle. I and our family kill them because we were born to do just that!" Julius' voice was near the yelling point by the end of the sentence. He continued, "You were in the house. I remember praying to God for your safety. The girl, "Noel" as you call her, took off running like a scared cat when she saw the lights. You were in a basinet in the kitchen with your father and me. She passed by and looked at your face, even had the nerve to touch you. She stroked your cheek, and smiled then ran out. Needless to say; I wiped the bloody smear from your father off your face after I tended to my own wounds."

"And what of my mother?" Ty questioned, staring dead on into Julius' eyes.

"Your mother," Julius paused. "Your mother is dead. She died giving you life."

Even without his suit fully equipped, Ty could tell that the man was lying. His mother didn't die in child birth, if she was dead at all. Ty figured, if a vampire had done it, he would have definitely said so. Ty put that thought in the back of his mind for now. So much was told to him in the last few minutes, but Ty knew exactly what his pact in life was from then on.

"Son, when you ran away from me, when you were seventeen, my heart was broken. Then I saw you on the news, killing. At first I was grieved, until after a little investigation, I found out you were killing vampires all along. The store clerk, the person in the car you stole. They were all vampires." Julius put his hand on Ty's shoulder. "The blood of the slayer runs through your veins. You were meant to kill vampires. You were just taking back what rightfully belonged to you in the first place. I just didn't see that when you ran away. I thought you wanted to take the easy road, but you wanted to find out what it was like on your own. I can appreciate that now. Now I want you to join with me again, and destroy all these vampires that walk the earth. The training you encountered was meant to do just that."

The words shocked Ty. "What training?" Ty asked, wondering if it was the program.

"The experiment training you went through for a few years. It was meant to better equip you for destroying vamps, son."

Ty turned away. “What of Noel?”

“That choice is yours. You baited her.” Julius words stung at Ty’s heart. “You decided on what we should do with her. I will tell you again, that she killed your father, and that she should be put to death.”

Ty thought it odd, that Julius knew about the experiment. He knew the Doctor was the one that performed it, but according to Noel, he was a vampire. Then there was Jonas, who said that a Mr. Gobaleski funded the experiment, wanting to turn him into a full fledged vampire slayer. It all came together now. Julius was obviously working with Gobaleski. He had no idea about the Doctor. Jonas was the middle man, taking care of the small daily operations. They were all working together, yet to bring about their own wills separately. Ty was the product. He was the “jug of milk” going through the conveyor belt. Well no more.

Ty simply nodded, and the duel walked out of the office. “Don’t worry fellas, I set him straight,” Julius said to the two waiting nearby, keeping trained eyes on the cuffed Noel. The garlic was wearing her down, causing her skin to have allergic reactions.

Archer walked over to Ty and said, “Good to have you aboard, dear sir. You don’t know how long we searched for you either. It has been a long time, and now we are a complete family again. You were born a slayer and you will die a slayer, thank the merciful God.”

Tommy nodded sitting on a nearby table, playing with his short dagger in his hand.

“Good to be aboard,” Ty emphatically said as much as he could.

“Now,” Julius cut in. “What shall we do with the girl, now that I set you straight, and you had time to think?”

Ty looked at the suffering Noel. It pained him to see his beloved in such a state. “Kill her,” he said bluntly.

She raised her eyes to meet his, and they nearly fell out of their sockets.

Ty made sure she was looking right at him. He winked and

smiled so none of the others would take notice. She put her head back down.

Ty turned to Julius. "Where's her whips?" he asked.

"Why?" Julius was suspicious.

"Because, it seems only fitting that before her death she become wounded the same way she wounded you. It seems only fitting that the next generation of slayer, does the deed; especially for revenge, for killing my father." Ty made sure his voice was well heard on that last part.

Noel kept her head down, and her eyes closed.

"I like your style, boy." Julius smiled and grabbed her adamantine whips off the nearby table.

"Please call me, Tyson," Ty exclaimed. Ty left his suit cover his body.

"I've been meaning to ask you about that suit—."

Ty put his finger up to his mouth right before it was fully covered by the shifting adamantine plates folding down over his face.

"Oh right, right." Julius nodded, and slapped Archer in the arm. "I like his style," he said pointing to the armored clad Ty.

His weapons started to appear, more and more on his suit. Ty wrapped the whips around each of his shoulders and made sure they were snug. He bent low to make sure Noel's eyes were closed. If there was a time he wanted her to read his thoughts it was now.

Ty grabbed a sword from his back scabbard.

"What do you got planned boy?"

Ty turned around and put his finger up to where his mouth would be under his helmet mask.

Julius put his hands up in surrender to the issue and stepped backwards a step.

Ty turned back to Noel with his back toward the other three. He secretly pulled one of his flash bang marbles from his chest pocket of his powered suit, and twisted it together with one hand. He waited a few seconds; he had this down perfectly by now, and flicked it behind him. The marble bounced twice before rolling to the feet of Julius. All eyes went for the bait, except Ty and Noel's who kept hers completely closed tight.

Just like the brightest of suns, the flash went off causing an incredible amount of light and smoke. Ty took two swipes, and cut both Noel's chains. He had no time to get her cuffs off of her, but she was free. Ty took her, and led her up the same stairs they entered the building. The disoriented bunch, knew they had been tricked, and ran in all directions. They were completely blinded for a little over twenty seconds. The pulse, the marbles gave off, would disorient them for a little while. Ty needed that much time and probably more.

Ty ran up the stairs, grabbing at Noel's hand pulling her along. They made it to the top. The men realized where they had gone. Ty closed the metal door behind him, and used his suited powered arms to crush it in place jamming it. They took off toward the chopper.

Ty opened the hatch and helped Noel inside. "Come on. If ever I need help piloting one of these it would be now," Ty made mention.

He got in and kind of remembered what Tommy did. He pushed the start button, and pulled the throttle, and let her rip. The suit seeming to know his confusion, gave him the right steps to fill in the blanks. Ty immediately started pushing all the right buttons and turning all the right levers to get the thing slowly but surely off the ground. "This suit is awesome!" he yelled above the propeller.

Noel looked sick, but offered a reassuring smile. It must have been the garlic. Ty had to get her to some blood fast.

The door burst open in the warehouse roof. An arrow flew breaking the glass, and barely missed their heads. They were over ten feet off the ground, but they quickly took a dive. This gave Julius enough time to grab a hold to one of the legs. He hoisted himself up, causing the equilibrium of the machine to teeter due to the extra weight on one side. Ty tried to compensate, but realized that he didn't rightly know how. He just had to get him off. He waved the handle back and forth, shaking the bird in mid air, but Julius held firm.

Noel laid her head back, against the seat. She looked like she was about to throw up. Her wrists were pulsing, and bleeding. The garlic cuffs were trying to eat their way through to her bone.

"Hold on Noel. I need some help here!" he yelled above the noise. He pulled up, and the chopper took flight. They were over thirty feet in the air now, but Julius was still attached, and pulling himself upward. He grabbed from under his coat, and pulled his crossbow out. He aimed it at Ty's head. Ty twirled the chopper around and around. Julius shot but thanks to the momentum of the circular motion, the rightfully aimed dart, shot off course going through the glass, but hitting the back of Ty's seat.

Ty looked at Noel. She was sweating profusely. He looked at Julius who was somehow setting another dart in his crossbow, and still holding on. Ty made a decision right there. He pulled one of his Mac-10s free from their holstered position, and let a burst of bullets rip through the glass at Julius. One or more hit their mark, because he fell the thirty feet to the ground. Ty was able to level off, and get the chopper in motion. He flew far higher, than any dart could reach, and over the tree tops. He might make it to the Castle after all.

Magnus gave the silent language of the vampire to the other Illuminati to meet him in the manuscript room. Seeing the alarm on his face, they quickly moved silently through the halls of the church as to not distress the Doctor in any of their plans.

When they descended the steps to the room, Magnus whispered so that only the ones in the circle could hear. He was sure of the Good Doctor's treachery and told them why.

They all quickly started reading the manuscripts trying to find out what they could see. They all came up with the same conclusion that the "weapon" had to be of vampire descent. He had to be born a pure vampire, to be the perfect weapon against the night ravens. They looked at each other with great worry. Magnus brought out the ancient book of the night ravens. They all searched through it, and their alarm was put to great respect. On the three hundredth page of the night raven's text, it stated:

The perfect weapon, to overcome both vampire and human will be a man of human descent. His greatest love will be a raven of the night, and his greatest friend a vampire in love. With these three; he will bathe in their blood becoming both one and greater than both before. For in his veins runs the blood of the slayer whom he will also be greater than. He will be one weapon to rule, one weapon to gain power through the acts committed. He will be one weapon to bring all sects and clans together. His advisor will be of great power, and be born of raven descent. He will be his greatest alley, and be subject to his rule, and feed him his power through the mind.

CHAPTER 22

Sumiko, fully dressed in her new tight fitting clothing, was ready to go. Takeo walked in right on cue, and admired his handy work. Sumiko looked older, more mature. She looked as if she had years of experience beyond the beauty of her youth. Her face glowed with a brightness that was unable to be contained.

Sumiko cocked her head to crack her neck, then to the other side.

Takeo smiled. "Let's go, we have a plane to catch."

They marched out into the night air, and got into a waiting car. The vehicle drove off toward the airport where their jet was waiting.

Once all boarded on the jet, Takeo began briefing Sumiko on her mission. "See this girl." Takeo said, pulling a picture of Noel out of a file to hand Sumiko on the private jet.

She narrowed her eyes. "I remember her."

"You should. She was the one who attempted to kill you, and would very much have succeeded had I not injected you with my blood." Takeo smiled. "Now you will see the glories of the night ravens in their fullness thereof."

"What of the girl?" Sumiko kept her mind on track.

Takeo took out another picture. "See him?" Takeo showed her a picture of Ty. "She is using her vampire's wiles to win him over. You loved him didn't you?"

Sumiko's eyes lit up when she saw the photo. It was Ty her beloved. She did love him.

"He will be one of us soon, but not before you destroy the girl," Takeo coaxed.

Sumiko remembered, spending a beautiful day with Ty walking in a rain forest. At least it seemed like a rainforest. She looked back at Takeo. "Do not worry, the girl will die."

"Excellent. We are going to the vampire castle for a party."

Sumiko looked at him curiously. "A party at the vampire castle?" she asked.

"We have a VIP invitation," Takeo stated. "We are part of the guest of honor crew. Ty will be there, and the girl." Takeo continued, "We will enjoy drink, and milling about, then when the right moment exercises itself, you will know when to strike at the girl."

Sumiko smiled, at the thought of killing her adversary; the one who shot her and left her for dead. She laid her head back against the seat, and dreamed of spending the rest of her life with Ty. She dreamt of being a night raven, powerful enough to crush any, who would be so unfortunate, to find themselves in their way. She dreamed of living forever."

Bones arrived with his brigade of guardian vampires, by helicopter to the castle. The sun was setting rapidly. After a short stop at the nearby airport, he then was forced to board the chopper that led him to this destination.

Bones noticed the detail that went into the architect of the building. This masterpiece had an elegant beauty that could not be rivaled. He was pushed inside, nearly falling on purpose a few times to make his weakness look obvious. Bones was pushed and shoved through long corridors, watching as the vampires of the house, gazed at the spectacle passing by. He was pushed down one more corridor and into a rather large room. The floors and pillars were made of marble, the ceiling and trim was pure—inlayed gold.

A man stood on top of a small three step stage. "My how nice to meet you face to face again. They call me—."

"The Good Doctor," Bones finished the Doctor's sentence for him.

"Aha, I see you remember. I invited you here today to witness a phenomenon that will greatly impress the world. Besides," the Doctor, wagged his head, and gave a sly smile, "you have had a hand in making the boy what he is." The Good Doctor quickly changed the subject. "I presume your money paid was well sufficient for your services rendered?"

"Well, I only got a million out, and only got to keep it for a few hours, until your boys as nice as they are, showed me the way to this most, inequitable estate."

"Yes my apologies for the run-around I assure you." The Doctor bowed low. "Perhaps after tonight, I will find need of you again, and compensate you handsomely for it."

"Yes, well spending the first billion would definitely suffice enough for me, if I ever got a chance to do that." Bones changed the subject back, "What about the boy, Ty? Where is he?"

"Oh I would trust he is on his way, no doubt. He should be here within the hour, with an alignment of many guests, human and vampires alike."The Doctor took the few steps to the floor bottom and looked Bones in the eye. "Did I ever tell you the full version of your story?"

"What story?" Bones questioned.

"The bedtime story you told all your students. The story of Omar Has'sir. The story that is stated in the old manuscripts, that humans and vampires took on the sect together. They ruled together for many years."

"I suppose; I would have remembered the vampire part of the story either way, if you had told me," Bones stated.

"Yes, I suppose you are correct in that assumption," the Good Doctor noted. "Well perhaps another time then; perhaps after the party tonight." The Doctor looked to the vampire guards. "Gentleman, please takes Mr. Bones to his room, and make sure he is comfortable. Get him a fresh tuxedo for the party tonight, and see that he is groomed accordingly. Do not harm him when completing any of these tasks or I will have all your heads and drink from your hollowed out skulls." The Good Doctor smiled as if he just spoke a pleasant poetic masterpiece. It was unsettling.

The men grabbed Bones and took him to the upper floors of the castle to show him his room, and make sure he was "comfortable". Bones didn't have to see them lock the door, to know that they did. It was obvious the Doctor didn't want him going anywhere. He turned around to gorgeous tapestries, and fine décor. It was all very gothic in appearance, yet beautiful to behold. The bed sat very high off the ground, and the closet was filled with clothing from every era of life. Bones looked back to the closed door. Alone in his room, he knew he only had a few hours to devise his plan, before Ty arrived.

Julius got up quickly, heavily wounded; more from the fall then the two bullets that pierced his rib cage and arm. The tough veteran slayer, took his knife from under his coat, and dug the bullets out right there on the spot, grunting away the pain. Archer and Tommy came rushing to his aid.

"Are you alright, Julius?" Archer asked, helping the man to his feet. "The fall was nearly thirty feet."

"I'm fine," was Julius' answer.

"They have escaped."

"I know where they're going," Julius replied, he looked at Tommy. "Grunt, get the jet glider."

"But it hasn't been fully tested on an actual run, yet."

"I don't care. You built it; it will work."

Tommy ran off with a smile on his face. He didn't get complimented very often.

"Julius, are you sure you're up to this?" Archer sincerely asked.

"That little lover of vampires crossed me in my own home. I've given life and limb to find him and that girl, and this is how he repays me. He takes on a vampire more than his own bloodline? No. That's not how it's going to end. They're headed to Dublin. They're headed to the vampire castle, so that is where we're going."

"How do you propose we get in?" Archer questioned. "The place is heavily fortified."

"If they are going to let the human that crossed me in; then we can get in. We'll just have to be disguised so they don't think we're human."

"Yeah, but Ty has the girl, a vampire. They may let him in, if he shows that he rescued her."

Julius looked right at Archer, and scowled. "Well get in, because I said we'll get in." He turned to walk away. "Tommy, is the jet glider ready yet?"

Ty had the, piloting the chopper, thing down pretty well by now. His suit was feeding him the knowledge that he needed to run the bird effectively. He looked over at Noel. She was suffering, he knew. He had to get the chopper on some kind of automatic pilot, so that he could get the cuffs off of her. He found a button, marked auto, and assumed its usage. He held the throttle steady, and then pushed the button. The chopper stayed straight and level. Ty was grateful for that. He turned toward Noel who was breathing very heavily. He took his strong armor clad hands and grabbed the cuffs, ripping them both off of her. She breathed out suddenly and opened her eyes.

"You ... saved my life again," she stuttered.

"Yeah, well you would probably have done the same for me?" Ty smiled and grabbed her hands, looking down at the wounds on her wrists. He brought them up to his lips and kissed them gently.

She returned that smile. "I'm sorry about your father," she finally said, in the awkward silence.

Ty put his head down, but kept a hold of her hands. "Yeah well, if he was anything like my uncle, it was only best that I never knew him."

"I saw you when you were a baby. You were so beautiful."

Ty chuckled.

"Why didn't you kill me then? Certainly you would have known that I would have grown up to be a slayer like my uncle."

"To be honest, I was about to, for vengeful purposes." Noel looked away from Ty when she remembered her past. "There was something about your eyes that drew me to you. I knew we would meet again under different circumstances. When I first came to your door in the program, I was excited because you bore those same eyes. After all these years, I never forgot those gorgeous eyes." Noel laughed to herself. "I practically fell in love with you right then."

"Why did you react so coldly toward me, in the truck when you drank my blood?"

"Because hidden deep in everyone's blood is DNA. It is the chemicals that make up you and I. The thing a lot of people do not know about DNA is that it holds the memories of your relatives past and present in it even without you knowing it. We are fearfully and wonderfully made, so it is said." Noel looked away. "Unfortunately, I also had the memories of every vampire you ever killed, some my family, and my clan; some trying to live out their lives in peace."

Ty patted her hand with his other, and put his head back against his own seat. "I see what you mean. I am sorry for that also. It was inherently, built into me, and I never knew it. So you got the memories of what my uncle had done to your family even without me knowing it was even in there either."

Noel shook her head.

"Wow. That is crazy in itself." He reached up and put his hand behind her head. "Truce?" he offered, pulling her toward him.

She leaned forward and they kissed, a beautiful passionate kiss, tongues swaying in and amongst each other.

When they parted, Noel said, "I think you have your answer." She looked out the window. "How long do we have yet?"

"It shouldn't be long now. From what you told me the coordinates were, we should be there a little before midnight."

Noel leaned back against her seat again and sighed. "Oh good. I need some blood to help get my strength back," she said closing her eyes.

Magnus spoke in quiet tones and gave the ancient hand gesture of the vampires, to mostly communicate with his brothers and sisters of the Illuminati. "In a few short hours, the most powerful elders of each clan will be her to celebrate the ritual of the Blood Moon. We need to act fast to warn them, upon their arrival, because the Good Doctor has turned against us. He is following the ancient text of the night ravens, which can only mean one thing. He is a night raven."

The other's gasped at the thought. They had to tell the elders when they arrived. They all heard footsteps coming down the stairs to the manuscript vault. The twelve Illuminati turned to see who it was. It was the Good Doctor, and about three dark creatures behind him. They appeared as vampires.

"Gentleman and ladies, I received some disturbing news?" The Good Doctor paced around the room, his small brigade following. "I hear there is treachery amongst the Illuminati."

The Illuminati of Vampires looked at each other nervously.

The Good Doctor continued, "I hear that there is rumor of a mutiny." The Doctor chuckled at the thought. He turned to face the twelve, "We just cannot have that, now can we?" He walked on. "Especially this close to the Blood Moon Ritual, I'm afraid. I'm going to have to contain you until full preparations for the ritual are complete. The men behind the Doctor spread their wings wide. Their faces turned to a shriveled scary, practically demonic site. More night ravens came out of the wood work; they were there the whole time completely invisible. They grabbed the Illuminati, and pulled them up stairs. The Good Doctor completely in human/vampire form led the way down a hallway, into a large room. In that room was a huge circle platform with small miniature square stages, set up all around to reach twelve spots. The There were two stages in the center; one for Ty and one, most undoubtedly, for the Good Doctor.

"Align them accordingly to their symbol in which represents them on each platform. Hold them there. I'll be back." The Good Doctor left the room.

He arrived down stairs and passed the main lobby to see his vampires talking, in their finest clothing, ready for the party. A knock came to the huge castle door, just as the Doctor got to it. It was Vadora (Nurse Darnell).

"Aha, Vadora, my sweet. So glad you could make it. The party will not begin for a few hours, but my vampires will see you to your room, where you can freshen your already beautiful face."

Vadora bowed allowing the Good Doctor to kiss her hand. She moved with grace, with a small bag of luggage. The Doctor snapped his finger, and two butler vampires came out from behind the door. The one took her coat, and suitcase, the other her arm and led her to her room. Once they made it to her room, she was astonished by the beautiful decorations that permeated the whole area.

"Will there be anything else malady?" the butler who led her inside asked?

"No that shall be all. Thank you."

He quietly closed the door.

She turned around, and sighed. "I think I'm going to like this place," she said to herself.

The Doctor was down stairs getting the orchestra ready to enlighten the guests with music closer to their arrival. The chefs were preparing the finest of drinks for all the races. Everything had to be perfect for this to work.

Sumiko and Takeo touched down at the airport, and took a car to the castle. Takeo assured Sumiko that it wouldn't be a long drive, and they should beat her rival for Ty's love, to the party. She followed the passing green fields of Ireland in the dimness of the evening. Her dream would soon come true.

"Grunt, is that jet glider ready yet!?" Julius screamed tying a homemade wrap around his wounds. So much for that cursed armor. The bullet got past it, he thought.

"It's ready," Tommy said, rushing to the room. "It's loaded up with the latest weapons. I couldn't fit all of them on, because of its light weight. You, me, and Archer will, pretty much, top out the capacity."

Julius finished wrapping his arm and walked over to Tommy and put his hand on his shoulder. "Son," he started, "you are about to embark on a battle that you have never seen. I hope that you are ready for it."

Tommy's eyes lit up. This was the first time Julius had ever called him son. He was an orphan his whole life, so when Julius and Archer found him in a cold alley one night nearly scratched and bitten by a vampire, they took him back with them, sucking out the venom before it was too late. He was grateful but all this talk on finding Ty, made Tommy regret the fact that they ever started this mission. It made him feel way down on the list, as if he could gain no respect for his lacking in the bloodline. Yet, since Ty rejected the cause,

Julius looked at him to be his son. Maybe even Tommy would take over the slayers after Julius was gone. He no longer would be called "Grunt." He smiled inside, and it burst force all over his face.

"That's my boy." Julius said, tussling his hair. "Let's get ready to pull out. It's going to be the adventure of a life time. It will be the blood bath of the century."

With that being said, the three travelers traveled out to the small parking lot and got into the jet glider. "Can this thing make it there before midnight?" Julius asked Tommy.

"It will if we don't have any problems. Hang on though. The G-force may take you for a ride of its own." Tommy smiled at himself for coming up with such a clever reply. Tommy shut the cock bit sliding window above all their heads, and started the engine, and turned the small bird in the right direction. Hitting the parking lot diagonal should give them enough room for takeoff.

The bird started to move on its tiny wheels. Faster and faster was the momentum. Tommy needed enough speed to clear the tree line. The jet glider was nearing the end of the makeshift runway, and Tommy pulled up on the throttle. The bird lifted into the air, and not a moment too late, or it would have surely scraped the trees. He banked it in the right direction, and set it to full speed. Needless to say, they all could already feel the G-forces taking their bodies on its own ride.

CHAPTER 23

Bones grew up a fighter. Having been in the program for the fifteen years, didn't mean he wasn't ready mentally for what he was to overcome. His body was a bit thinner, from when he first went in, but he was ready and just as quick; besides fighting is more mental than anything else. He moved throughout the room, noticing the huge metal rods that held the curtain tapestries in place. He cocked his head and stared at them for a bit. Those would do nicely. He grabbed a sitting chair off to the side and moved it into position. He climbed atop it and took a few good pulls to finally bring it down, curtain and all. The dust was most nauseating. Bones looked at the floor; it was made of granite. He took the rods which stretched about four and a half feet in distance then looked at the floor. Bones began grinding the tip of the rods on the hard floor sideways. He was making two very sharp swords.

Takeo and Sumiko just pulled up in front of the house, when the Good Doctor came out to meet them both. He helped Sumiko delicately out of the car. Her black clothes simply would not do.

"My dear," he said kissing her hand. "The vampires will show you to your room, and there is some fine clothing in there for you to enjoy. Please try them on, and do not worry about anything."

Sumiko cringed and made a face at the words "vampire" that sprung out of the Doctor's mouth. She looked at Takeo. He gave her a reassuring nod, and she went with them to her room.

After she was gone, the Good Doctor asked Takeo, "How was everything with the transformation?"

"As to be expected," Takeo said watching the door clothes behind them as Sumiko and the vampires entered the castle.

"She took it well?" the Doctor questioned.

"Well not at first, but once it was all finished; she was more than ready to kill a vampire or two. She should take care of the girl."

The Good Doctor's face furrowed. "You leave that one to me; I will chastise her. She is too valuable to harm. She already is doing her job; I can feel her energy from here. She and the "weapon" are on their way now."

Takeo nodded. "We'll see what happens," he simply told the Doctor.

The Doctor looked him straight in the eyes. "No you'll listen to me Takeo. Nothing is going to turn this to disarray. Everything will go as planned. We will rule with an iron fist, but not if you let your little-new pet get in the way. Do you understand what I am saying to you?" The Good Doctor nearly spit at him when he spoke.

"Crystal," the younger man said.

The Good Doctor heard a chopper coming in. He closed his eyes and looked up sniffing the air. A crude smile came to his face. "This would be the guest of honor right now," he grinned.

The chopper circled around a few times before finding a landing place in the court yard of the castle. Many vampires gathered outside to see who this newcomer was. Rumors were gathering amongst them.

Ty slid the broken glass door up, and climbed out. He looked at the spectators, as he walked around to Noel's side and helped her out. Ty grabbed her hand, and they walked toward the group of vampires. Ty was ready to equip his suit if he had to.

"My children have returned," the Good Doctor exclaimed. The largest grin appeared on his face as he walked toward the duet, his hands stretched out wide. He met them half way and gave both of them a great embrace pulling them close and tight.

Ty was a little unsettled, but figured with Noel's state that they would be better off not fighting for now, so he was grateful for the embrace.

The Good Doctor turned toward the crowd. "The guests of honor have arrived!" he shouted so all could hear. He turned back toward Ty and Noel. "Come children, we must get you cleaned up. The party has just begun. The rest of the guests are on their way."

Ty looked at the Doctor square in the face. "We need blood for Noel. We had a run in with Julius, and she's weak from garlic saturated cuffs."

The Doctor looked at him most curiously, then at Noel. "You haven't… no you didn't." The Doctor answered his own question. A smile slid its way back onto his face. "Yes, do follow me," he said.

They walked pass the staring crowd and into the house. Two vampire butlers came again from behind the door. "Gentleman, take Noel to the fridge down stairs, and get her some of our finest blood. She has been through a lot."

Ty started to follow, but the Good Doctor stopped him. "Come my boy," he said. "We have much to discuss."

Ty started to fight against the Good Doctors good arm. "I go where she goes."

"I admire your loyalty, especially for one who is not a vampire yourself; yet I assure you, no harm will come to her head as long as she is in this house. Please follow me. When you will see her again, she will be the most beautiful thing you ever would lay your eyes upon."

Ty reluctantly followed the Good Doctor away from his love.

They walked down corridors that held huge stone pillars. Ty's eyes were flipping every which way to look at the faces carved into the walls.

"So you had a run in with Julius. I am curious as to what happened there. You saved Noel from him; I see."

Ty nodded, although the Doctor was walking a tad in front of him and didn't notice. "Yeah, he told me about my bloodline."

This time, the Good Doctor did turn to regard Ty while they were walking.

"He told me what Noel, did to my family, and he told me what he did to hers."

"Hmm . . ." was all the Doctor said.

"I made a choice. The brutality, of what he represents, is not me. He is a monster. Vampires, well Noel, have been so nice to me. I spent my time out of the program trying to find Sumiko and my family, and you, that when I found my own blood line, I wanted nothing to do with them."

A sly smile came to the Doctor's face. "I am glad to hear that Ty. So glad in fact."

"Yeah, well this feels more like home to me anyways."

The Doctor's smile grew even bigger. "So tell me dear boy, did you kill Julius."

"I'm not sure. He fell a good many feet to the ground. I put a few bullets in him. By the way, thanks for that suit."

"Do you like it?"

"Oh yeah I do. I don't know what you did to me, but that suit definitely came at a time that I most needed it."

"Simple codes and commands. You have a chip that I attached to your cerebellum. It actually pulls the command to cover you in the armored suit whenever you think the thought. That is the beauty of it. When you were in the program; I saw an opening to do this experiment. Your brain pulls the suit from the program, into this world. I've simply made a door, so you can grab something from a different world into ours." They kept walking. "You see my dear boy; the chip has physically attached itself to your cerebellum. There is not prying it free. You will always be able to do just that. You are practically invincible."

Ty thought of the power that he had at that moment. He did pretty much have an unstoppable force backing him up.

"There is one other thing," the Good Doctor continued.

"What is that?" Ty asked incredulously.

"I mentioned you are practically invincible. No doubt you have had run-ins with the night ravens on your journey to this place?"

"Yes, it's been quite the trip," Ty answered.

"Yes, well I have something that may help with those particular situations if they ever rose again.

"What is that?"

"Tonight in a few hours, all the elders of the vampire kingdom will be here to celebrate The Ritual of the Blood Moon. It happens every five hundred years, so this is a rather rare, yet joyous occasion."

"Okay, how do I fit in?"

"You see my dear boy; in the ancient manuscripts it is said, that a human will rise up and be as one over the rest. You will be greater than the night ravens, and vampires alike, if you partake in the ritual."

"Where does this leave Noel? Ty bluntly asked.

"Aha, the girl you most undoubtedly fell in love with. I must admit, after I found out, what she did to your beloved Sumiko, I was worried you would have disposed of her. I am happy to see you kids getting along."

Ty stopped. "Yes well, she told me that you messed with her head, and made her do it, just like you did with me in the program. Face it; in that comatose state you had all the power," Ty snarled.

"Yes, I suppose I did. She told you that? Clever girl. Clever girl indeed. Perhaps I will have use for her in the future," the Doctor told himself under his breath. He turned to Ty. "Do not worry about Noel. I was merely seeing if she was worthy to serve beside you, in the new kingdom."

Ty looked at him curiously. "What new kingdom?"

"The new kingdom where you rule," the Doctor spoke as if it must happen.

"Why should I trust you?" Ty questioned.

"Let me show you something,"

The duet happened to stop right at the door where Sumiko was residing. The Doctor opened the door leading Ty inside. When Ty entered the room, he saw a woman looking out the window into the night. She turned abruptly to see who disturbed her room. Ty couldn't believe his eyes.

"You see my dear boy, there was never any real harm done to the girl in the program, that couldn't be fixed in the natural realm."

Ty ran to her, throwing his arms around her neck. She slowly returned the embrace.

Ty pushed away at arm's length keeping his hands around her upper arms. "Sumiko, I thought you dead. What happened?"

She looked at the Doctor.

"I can leave you alone for a few minutes," the Doctor closed the door slowly.

"Well, Noel shot me, and a man named Takeo brought me back. Now I feel more alive than I ever had." She gave him the quick sugar coated version.

"How... who is Takeo?"

"Takeo is a very wise man, and very powerful. Whatever the Doctor told you; I would listen to. These people have our best intentions in mind."

Ty pulled away completely.

"I don't know. Something doesn't seem right. I know Noel —."

"Noel!?" Sumiko repeated the name loudly. "You've seen her?"

Ty looked at Sumiko. He knew she would probably be angry, but Noel was manipulated. "Sumiko, she didn't mean to kill you, or shoot you rather."

"Well that's not what I heard come out of her mouth. She had every intention on killing me because she wanted you," Sumiko shot back.

Ty moved even further away, and his eyes lowered. "You don't know her at all. You don't know, what was done to me." He turned toward the door, as if hit by an epiphany. What was the Doctor trying to prove?

"Look at me, Ty!" Sumiko yelled. "Noel was not manipulated; she shot me deliberately."

Ty turned to see Sumiko staring into him. He looked again at the door. There was something wrong about this place. He looked at Sumiko and cocked his head to the side.

"What?" she demanded, what is wrong with you. Why can you not see things the way we do?"

"Whom?"

"Us, the . . ."

The door opened abruptly cutting her off.

"The rest of the guests are arriving. This will be a party to rival all others," the Good Doctor spoke quickly. "Come dear boy, I will show you to your room. We need to get you dressed and presentable."

Ty walked out of the room with the Doctor. When he made it to the door way, he stopped and turned back to Sumiko. Her eyes were different. They weren't like what they used to be.

Ty left the room.

The Doctor led him to his room a few rooms down and showed him inside. "Here is your room for the time being. Your clothing is in the closets, a tuxedo, shoes, the works. In about ten minutes," the Doctor instructed, looking at his watch. "Come on down to the main lobby area, and the party will begin." The Good Doctor patted him on the back and left the room.

Ty was left with his thoughts. He thought he would be ecstatic to see Sumiko alive, and he was at first, but he knew the truth in the matter. She was one of them. He could presume that the Doctor was too. The Good Doctor was way too powerful to miss such a rather large detail. No true vampire would let night ravens into his castle. Ty remembered Noel saying about the thirteen Illuminati, but where were the rest of them? They all might be in on it, so Ty may have to be careful.

Ty walked over to his closet. It was rather large in itself. It was filled with many different styles of clothing. Ty pulled out a dark tuxedo, with a dark silken overcoat. He looked at the door, then back at his clothing. He went over to the large dresser against the wall next to the closet. On the top were leather gloves. He began to get an idea.

The Good Doctor was busy greeting all the guests as they arrived. The small symphony of players were playing classical's favorites in the corner of the lobby. More and more people gathered in, and the place became crowded fast. The servers all worked for the Doctor, and spent many days memorizing who was a vampire, human, or night raven. They brought drinks to suit everyone's needs.

Ty left his room about twenty minutes before midnight, and came to the top of the stairs. He saw the Doctor at the top of the balcony a few feet from him overlooking the balcony.

"Ladies and gentleman," the Good Doctor spoke loudly so all could hear below. "Our guest of honor as now arrived to the party." He motioned for Ty to join him, by his side. Ty looked behind his back to make sure his sword wasn't showing through his overcoat. He looked down to make sure everything was buttoned correctly to hide his weapons. He kept his helmet-mask at bay. He walked to the side of the Doctor.

"Ladies and gentleman, this one is the reason we are here. He is the answer to the prophecy."

All the races down below held their glasses in salute. They had different versions of the prophecy of The Blood Moon.

The Good Doctor continued, "Now follow me to the adjacent room. There The Blood Moon prophecy will come to pass for the first time ever.

Ty put his face right up against the Good Doctors and spoke in lower tones. "I want to see Noel."

The Doctor turned and smiled. He looked pass Ty and motioned for her to come out of the shadows.

Ty turned and saw Noel dressed in the most elegant looking black dress he had ever seen on any woman. She was beautiful, with a thigh high slit, and black knee high boots. Her hair lay delicately on her shoulders as black as night. She smiled softly when she and Ty's eyes met. Ty held out her hand and she took it; he then turned toward the Doctor and nodded. "Now I'm ready to go," he said.

The Doctor smiled again, "Follow me all. He moved off down the hallway. People from all over began climbing the stairs to follow.

Ty was right behind him. He quickly whispered to Noel. "Be careful, Sumiko is here, and she wants vengeance."

Noel looked at him as they walked. "What?" she whispered.

"She's not who she once was, and neither is the Doctor."

Noel's eyes grew wide. "No, Ty he can read . . ."

The Good Doctor turned and clicked his fingers. Night ravens came out from everywhere, the walls, the skulls in the wall, everywhere. Ty jerked suddenly but before he knew it; he and Noel were separated, grabbed by three night ravens each. They dragged the both of them to the room, where the rest of the Illuminati were being held on the platforms. Vampires and humans screamed. The night ravens in the crowd grabbed all of them, holding them fast.

The night ravens were each given a vampire and human to grab and hold making sure they stood right beside them.

The three that held each of Ty's arms and one held his neck, dragged him to the center of the circle platform. The vampires gasped. Bones was waiting in side, with a night raven on each side of him holding him in place. He made no attempt to escape, yet. Ty saw him as they dragged him and set him in place. Also around the top platforms, Ty noticed a familiar face. It was Nurse Darnell from the program.

Vadora saw Ty being dragged in and yelled at the Good Doctor, "Why is he being treated this way?"

The Doctor snapped his fingers, and two night ravens came out of the walls beside Vadora grabbing her arms.

The Doctor climbed the few steps to the bottom of Ty taking his place beside him. Huge foot clamps came out of the floor grabbing Ty's feet and holding them in place.

The Doctor leaned closer to Ty and whispered, "Those are enhanced with a neuro-toxin to keep you from changing into your suit for the time being. They block that part of your brain from working. All I need is your body, not your mind right now." The three night ravens made sure he was bound properly, and then left the platform area.

Ty got the gist as to what the Doctor was saying and quickly stopped fighting the night ravens and acted as if he had no thoughts of his own; he acted as if he was paralyzed standing up.

A podium was brought in front of the Doctor and a large book was set a top it. Magnus face turned to pure resentment. It was The Book of the Night Ravens.

All the vampires and humans in the crowd was brought in and bound to watch what was about to take place. When all was settled, the Doctor put his hands in the air for total silence. The shuffling stopped abruptly.

"Mine` Fonghishu Sangiea," the Doctor spoke the ancient language of the night ravens. He spoke the very words that would cause the prophecy to come to pass.

Ty shifted slowly, looking down at his feet as to not be detected by the ranting Doctor. He shifted his suited feet backwards, and saw the screws coming out of the clamps. He looked up at the Doctor to make sure he wasn't being noticed. He caught Bones' eye. Bones winked at him, and slid his make shift swords from the back of his trench coat. He then looked at Nurse Darnell (Vadora), and she smiled at Ty. She took two daggers out of each sleeve with the other hand. His eyes caught Noel's. She smiled sincerely and looked to her sides. The two night ravens had their eyes glued on the Good Doctor and his mumblings; his eyes completely closed. She took out her classic adamantine whips from under the back of her dress, and nodded.

Ty smiled at her, and winked four times, to let her know to wait until he was fully ready. He had learned a little on their journey about the vampire's silent language. He broke free from the clamps completely, totally undetected. His facial mask covered his head, instantly. He was fully suited up. He took out his sword.

Bones took his two makeshift weapons and stabbed the two night ravens in the gut catching them both off guard. Vadora broke free from her night ravens and stabbed them in the temple in one solid motion. Noel had the handles of her whips in her hand and broke free flipping the two night ravens onto their back. Before they even could react she took the guns from their hands with two swipes then back lashed her whips to slice their throats.

The Doctors eyes were opened wide; he stopped his chanting. Each Illuminati member, broke free of the night ravens holding them, in the mayhem, and began fighting back. The vampire guests being held also began to fight as well as the humans.

The Doctor turned toward Ty and nearly missed blocking a thrashing sword, clasping it within the palms of his hands. He moved faster than Ty realized, for as old as he looked. The place was in disarray. The Doctor whistled.

Sumiko came from around the corner and spotted Noel. She began walking toward her, and took out two hooked sabers from under her formal dress. Noel practically missed the swipes of the swords, and it had to be luck that she was still standing. One missed her completely, but the other nipped her side slicing a good size slit in the top of her dress, causing it to expose some skin, as well as some blood.

Takeo came from around another corner, and spread his wings. His face immediately changed into a full night raven. He flew at Ty. Ty blocked the clawed hand with his sword. The force nearly flipped him backwards, even with his suit holding him up. Ty staggered backwards. He took out his second sword. Slicing, double the speed, double were the swipes at the next go round. Takeo landed, his spiked wings blocking the attacks of Ty's swords. Ty flipped out of the way, blocking an attacking claw.

Ty put his swords back in their place and took out his Mach-10s. He let loose a volley of bullets, and Takeo ducked down and spread his wings in front of himself cupping his whole body. They blocked each bullet, simply bouncing off. Ty quickly turned to see a clawed hand coming right at his face from another night raven. He moved his left hand to the side and shot six bursts of the weapon into the forehead of the beast. He fell instantly bleeding profusely. By the time he turned back, Takeo was gone. Ty looked to the side, where the Doctor had stood, and he too was gone.

Ty looked back at Noel. She was fending off Sumiko's attacks with her whips, but Sumiko was definitely on the offensive. She would not let up and pushed Noel back against the wall. All four arms of the two girls moved at lightning speed. Ty thought for a moment, while shooting another night raven in the head many times over. He stared hard at the dueling girls. Ty looked down at his two Mac-10s, held out in front of him. He held them up, aimed right at Sumiko. Sweat poured down his face inside his suit, but it internally dried it for him and calmed his nerves. Ty realized; he thought enough about it. He let fly a large volley of bullets at Sumiko. She quickly turned and blocked all of them with her two swords. Ty couldn't believe it. She hissed and shown her night raven fangs at him.

Ty's anger grew at Sumiko. He felt nothing for her at this moment. The pause in the offensive let Noel take it over, so she pushed Sumiko back a few steps with her whips lashing out in all directions. She nipped Sumiko's arm drawing blood and causing a hiss and snarl.

Ty looked at Bones who was fighting two night ravens with his curtain rod swords. He was actually coming out on top, keeping them on the defensive, his arms moving faster than Ty had ever seen a human's move before. He wondered for a second if he was still human or not.

Ty looked at Nurse Darnell, although she looked older; she moved with the grace of a vampire fending off her enemies with grace and ease. The whole place was in an uproar.

He looked back at Noel. He had to finish this, at least this part. Ty pulled both of his razor boomerangs out, and one of his flash bang marbles. He watched, out of the corner of his eye, an attack from his back and nearly missed the quick block, had his suit not told him the night raven was there. He turned and sliced four times with his boomerangs, holding them firmly in his hand. The night raven looked down as his blood and gore hit the floor. He fell too, very still.

Ty turned back toward the fighting girls. He wouldn't let Noel die, not by the hand of Sumiko. He hoped this would work. He threw both of his boomerangs right at Sumiko. He banked on her blocking both of them with her swords. He just hoped Noel would look at him as he threw the marble. He twisted it, and let it fly. Noel looked for a split second at the flying marble, and closed her eyes and turned her head. Sumiko saw the short opening and took her sword down in a swipe toward Noel. Everything seemed to move in slow motion. The sword was coming down on Noel as the flash bang marble went off. Everyone even the humans cringed at the bright light, but it really affected the vampires and night ravens in the room. The sword jerked, and sliced at Noel's face causing her to let out a blood curdling scream. It hurt Ty's ears, but he had to make his move. He jumped through the air, taking out two of his throwing knives out of his sprung-cupped legs. He let them fly in mid jump. They hit their mark right in Sumiko's neck. Her swords fell out of her hands, as her cringing body from the bright light, now jerked backwards. She flew against the wall, falling.

Noel got back up; the one side of her face shredded from the slicing sword. She swung her whips hard, wrapping them both around Sumiko's neck. Noel pulled hard with each hand, squeezing Sumiko's bleeding neck, squeezing the life from her. Sumiko fell the rest of the way to the ground.

Noel put her one hand up to her face, nearly crying when she felt the exposed insides. She looked at Ty. Ty was crying inside at what just occurred, more for Noel's expense than for Sumiko's. Ty had to chase after, Takeo and the Good Doctor.

Ty rushed out of the room, for the hunt. He looked down the darkened hallways, turning on his night vision as he went. It lit up everything, but he remembered seeing the night ravens coming out of the walls. They could be completely invisible. He thought to where he could be. He had no idea where they might have run off to.

Noel ran out of the mayhem into the quiet hallway. "Ty!" she yelled.

Ty turned. "Go somewhere safe, I'll finish this," he shouted back to her, so she could hear.

"No, we're in this together. I'm coming with you." The determination in her voice made Ty think twice before arguing.

"Come on," he said.

She ran after him. He started to creep down the hall way.

"Wait," Noel said, catching up to Ty. "The Doctor had a chopper on a flat part of the roof, of the castle, all the Illuminati did. I know he would have planned his escape, if everything went how it did. How did you know?" she asked referring to the fact that The Doctor was a night raven.

"Call it a hunch," he spoke in hush tones. He looked at her face, and took her chin gently in his hands. She pulled away.

"I'll be fine. We heal faster than humans," she said reassuringly.

Ty nodded, hoping she was telling the truth, and not just trying to make him feel better, for indirectly causing the accident.

"Let's move," he said. "Which way to the roof?"

"This way," Noel said, leading the way.

The two went through a maze of corridors that Ty definitely wouldn't have figured out. Definitely not in the time it took them at least. Noel finally led him to a stair that led up and out to the roof. Ty ran to it, but the door was jammed. You got to be kidding me. He thought. He stood back a step or two then flung up his armored foot, kicking the door free knocking it off its hinges. He walked outside and didn't see anything. Noel followed looking all around. Ty wondered around a small tower corner and saw the Doctor and Takeo in a brutal battle with Julius, Archer and Tommy.

Noel came running up, and Ty stopped her. "They're both our enemy, let's see how this plays out, and kill the survivor."

Noel thought that Ty was speaking more like a vampire would, and laid her head on his shoulder at the thought, but truly wondered what the chance would be him killing the victor if it happened to be the Good Doctor.

The fight was brutal indeed. Punch traded for punch, forget Bones' fighting, Julius was one of fastest human fighters Ty had ever seen, considering he knew at least three bullets or more hit their mark and the fall. Takeo and the Good Doctor in full night raven garb, fought taking off and attacking from the air. Ty and Noel watched at

Tommy shot dart after dart into the back of Takeo, but he wouldn't go down. Takeo turned and back handed Tommy, letting him fly a few feet before he hit the side of the chopper.

Ty watched as Archer pulled out a huge bow from his back quiver and let fly a volley of metal missiles into Takeo's arms and skull. The night raven plucked them each free.

"This is serious. They aren't going down," Ty whispered to Noel who was crouched tightly beside him.

She held onto his arm, her two whips strapped beside her. Her slit dress blew up to the coldness of the night air outside. She left out a short shiver.

Archer was knocked to the ground by Takeo, and the distraction was what Julius needed to move in. He ducked the Doctor's swing of his claw, and side stepped, flinging the Doctor to the ground. Then Julius moved in on Takeo right after the switch up and the turn; he jammed a poisoned dagger into the upper-inner thigh of Takeo. Takeo fell to the ground in an instant. The Good Doctor wouldn't let that go. He jumped on the back of Julius, and clawed at the back of his neck, but Julius was ready. He flung the night raven off, over his shoulder; he landed too close to Ty and Noel. They were seen by all.

Ty stepped out from his cover and walked steadily toward the Doctor. As the night raven began to rise, Ty took out his sword, and took three direct swipes at the Good Doctors stomach. The Doctor fell to one knee, holding himself balanced with his other foot.

"We were supposed to rule together, Ty. You changed everything. You know how long I've waited for that moment? Do you know boy?" The Doctor gurgled, but his voice was growing weaker.

A dart flew past Ty to hit Noel in the neck. She fell instantly to the ground as the poison sifted through her veins. Ty looked up at Julius, who wore a sly smile. "I told you I was going to kill that girl Ty, didn't I?"

The other vampires and humans that were left began climbing the stairs to stand behind Ty outside of the roof. Magnus walked up behind Ty and said, "Let me take care of this one, Ty. Let all of us take care of him." He was glaring at Julius as he spoke.

Ty held up a hand to stop Magnus from moving forward. "No. This one is mine. You tend to Noel." Ty looked Magnus in the face and pulled him close. "Make sure she lives," he sternly said. Magnus nodded, and rushed to Noel's aid. Many vampires had gathered around her to bring her back to the castle's infirmaries.

Other vampires rushed to the Good Doctor, but for a different reason. They held him firm in place making sure, he couldn't move. They would deal with his treachery later.

Ty took out both of his swords, from his back. His long silk coat was blowing in the wind.

"It's go time boy," Julius smirked. "Do you honestly think you can beat a veteran like me?" You're no better than your mother."

"Don't you say anything about her; this is between you and me," Ty shot back.

Julius took out both of his swords. "Why, did I hit a baby nerve?" His face took on a huge grin.

Ty swung first, swords clashed as Julius blocked. Sparks flew. Ty held the offensive, striking without abandon. The veteran slayer blocked each and every thrash. More sparks flew. On and on this went, each man an equal of the other. Ty couldn't imagine fighting this man without the benefit of his suit. Suddenly a side of the sword aimed high, and the flat side of it hit the side of Ty's face. Ty hit the ground hard. His eyes began to fade. Ty feared he was blacking out again. He couldn't focus.

His suit dissipated. Ty focused, but it wouldn't come back. His suit just wouldn't reappear. He rolled out of the way; a blade hit the ground where Ty was. He stood to his feet real quick and blocked another swing.

Ty's swords flickered, and then disappeared into thin air. Ty was left holding nothing.

Ty tried hard to bring it back but he couldn't. He backed away from the attacks and looked around real quick. He saw Noel being carried in, and the Good Doctor being held firmly by four different vampires.

He looked back at Julius. "What's the matter boy; your girlfriend and your little baby suit go by byes?"

Ty narrowed his eyes. He focused, closing his eyes. The oddest thing happened. Ty saw inside himself. He was looking into his chest. His internal eyes went upward toward his cerebellum. Julius waited, deciding to give the boy this. He was only human so what could he possibly do.

Ty focused hard, and brought the chip to life, causing his brain to recharge it. He opened his eyes. The suit didn't come; it didn't surround his body with the armor. Ty thought he had failed, but just for a moment. His body began to recharge. His mind was alert. He couldn't see the suit, but he felt its power. His body was not covered by the armor, but he knew it was there, inside him. He held out his hands as if holding an imaginary sword, and crouched down in a defensive stance.

Julius laughed. "What you got, play weapons? You're going to use baby swords on me?" Right after he finished the last few words; Julius couldn't believe his eyes. He saw two swords forming into Ty's hands. His eyes bulged out of their sockets, and before he could react, Ty swiped four, than five, than six times, hitting every vital vein and artery he could, with his two very real sabers.

Julius fell to his knees. "You still are weaker than me, boy. I still killed your little blood sucker girlfriend."

Ty was about to swing both of his swords in a criss-cross motion to cut off Julius head, to stop his ranting for good, but he didn't have to. Julius fell the rest of the way to the ground, very still and very dead.

Ty looked at Archer, and Tommy who lay propped up on the chopper he was thrown against; both their mouths agape. Archer dropped his bow, and bowed low. "We will follow you now," he said. "Your wish is my command.

Ty didn't have to look at Tommy; he already knew the boy's answer.

He turned around, and saw Takeo's dead body being carried away. The poison was already making Takeo disintegrate in the vampire's hands. He looked at the vampires and humans alike. They bowed low to the ground. Ty was a bit confused.

He rushed to the door. "Please," he spoke urgently to a nearby vampire. "Show me the way to Noel."

The vampire picked his head up and led Ty back inside the castle. He led him down the stair, and past two adjacent hallways, and into a large room. This room was the medical room for the vampires of the house. Noel was hooked up to what looked like dialysis machines. Ty pushed past the vampires, rushing to her bedside. The remaining seven Illuminati were in the room, not all of them lived through the fight with the night ravens.

Ty grabbed her hand. A hand lay on his shoulder from behind. It was Magnus. Ty turned.

"She is still alive. We got the poison out of her system before it took effect, but she may not be conscience for a few hours."

Ty let a breath out slowly, surely relieved at the news.

"You have done our people a great deal," Magnus continued. "We have never been treated quite this way from a human before. You killed your own bloodline, the slayers of the vampire and night raven alike. This speaks volumes amongst these halls, and to the remaining Illuminati." Ty didn't look at the vampire, but kept his eyes on Noel. "You had a chance of unimaginable power, yet you turned it down to be with this one." Magnus held a hand to Noel's face, and rubbed it as a father would rub a daughter who lay, with shallowed breaths.

"Ty you know she is a direct descendant of Omar Has'sir?"

This time Ty did look at the vampire. He didn't know and looked confused. He didn't hear the vampire part of the story.

Magnus continued, "Long ago, vampires and humans walked the earth in peace. Omar was afraid of his new found power, and we still do not have any idea what has caused it. He adopted humans and vampires alike into his assassin's clan although he was a vampire himself." Magnus stared at Ty in the eyes directly when he said this next part. He wrote the ancient manuscripts and in them, it is said. Omar took on a wife; she was human. They had a son. He too took on a human bride, and so the line was passed down, until you get to Noel."

Ty's eyes grew in size, his mouth dropped.

"Ty we know that you are of the slayer's bloodline, and we find it very ironic. Know that you have a place in these walls, and in our hearts all. Yet there is something we must tell you."

Ty was looking directly at Magnus, his brows raised.

"Ty, she is with child."